Y0-CKG-339

BY WILLIAM T. HORNADAY

WILD ANIMAL INTERVIEWS

TALES FROM NATURE'S WONDERLANDS

A WILD-ANIMAL ROUND-UP
   Stories and Pictures from the Passing Show

THE MINDS AND MANNERS OF WILD ANIMALS

CAMP FIRES ON DESERT AND LAVA

CAMP FIRES IN THE CANADIAN ROCKIES

TWO YEARS IN THE JUNGLE
   The Experiences of a Hunter and Naturalist in India, Ceylon, the Malay Peninsula, and Borneo. Illustrated. 8vo.

THE AMERICAN NATURAL HISTORY
   A Foundation of Useful Knowledge of the Higher Animals of North America. Four Crown Octavo Volumes Illustrated in colors and half-tones.

THE SAME
   Royal 8vo. Complete in one volume.

TAXIDERMY AND ZOOLOGICAL COLLECTING

CHARLES SCRIBNER'S SONS

WILD ANIMAL INTERVIEWS

WILD ANIMAL INTERVIEWS

AND WILD OPINIONS OF US

BY

WILLIAM T. HORNADAY

FORMERLY DIRECTOR
OF THE NEW YORK ZOOLOGICAL PARK

WITH ILLUSTRATIONS BY
LANG CAMPBELL

CHARLES SCRIBNER'S SONS
NEW YORK · LONDON
1928

COPYRIGHT, 1928, BY
CHARLES SCRIBNER'S SONS

COPYRIGHT, 1926, 1927, AND 1928, BY WILLIAM T. HORNADAY

Printed in the United States of America

TO
MY ESTEEMED FRIEND
CHARLES B. DRISCOLL
BECAUSE OF HIS
FAITH IN THESE WORKS

BEFORE THE CURTAIN

Recently I have been collecting from wild animals various statements and opinions of wild life and tame men; and of all interesting zoological researches, I know of nothing else that surpasses this line of endeavor.

Of course every intelligent reader knows that it is possible to communicate with animals in other ways than by the spoken word. Any naturalist who is worth his salt can determine the thoughts and feelings of mammals, birds, and reptiles by the sign language, by facial and bodily expression, and by telepathy; and afterward he can easily translate the whole interview product into outdoor English for the benefit of the reading classes.

Some persons may call these stories "fiction"; to which we do not at all object. In case there arises a doubt or suspicion regarding the accuracy of the translation of an interview, the author will call to the witness-stand the animal concerned, and cheerfully submit it as a material witness for cross-examination. In pursuing these researches, we have learned a great deal that we never knew before, and my only regret is that they were undertaken too late to be of any real service to the animals concerned.

Neither the youngsters nor the oldsters of to-day are fully aware of the breadth and depth of the wild animal mind, the wonderful scope of its reasoning, or the high quality of its conclusions. I have said before that the wild animal must think or die; but now I will add that it is the fate of all the wild beasts, birds, and reptiles, of both the temperate and the frigid zones, to think and to die quickly at the hands of the savages of civilization.

I am very much peeved by two unavoidable conditions. I am dismayed by the constant outcrops of evidence of civilized man's devilish meanness, cruelty, and persistent murdering of wild creatures, the wicked wastefulness and folly of it, and the dead certainty of the extermination of the best wild life of the world, *pronto*.

But I protest that these interviews were not written out to point morals or adorn tales; because they were started agoing solely to entertain and amuse the populace if-and-when all other polite literature falls down or blows up. The author disclaims all responsibility for the opinions of his animal friends who knock on the moral quality of the alleged lords of creation, and for the use of the outdoor language that invariably is employed in such interviews.

W. T. H.

The Anchorage,
Stamford, Conn.,
July 1, 1928.

CONTENTS

	PAGE
A Grizzly Bear Demands the Ballot	3
The Pack-Rat's Amazing Jokes	10
The Pika Tells How He Lives	19
The Mountain Goat's Point of View	27
Road-Runner, the Feathered Elf of the Desert	35
The Bad Wolverine's Other Side	41
The Secretary Bird Shows How He Kills Snakes	50
The Big Orang Tells His Story	56
The Big Python Explains His Mistake	63
What Makes the Wild Goose Wild and Tame	70
The Lion of Luxor	82
The Bird That Lives Nearest to God	89
The Kick of a Wild Ostrich	96
Two Sage Grouse Flocks Entertain Visitors	102
A Wild Duck's Point of View	114
The Step-Mother Elephant	121
A Quail Visits Us	128
A Chimpanzee's View of the Descent of Man	136
Why the Gray Squirrel Is in Hard Luck	144
The Wise Old Buffalo Who Transfers Himself	151
The Prong-Horn Who Poses on the Knoll	158

CONTENTS

	PAGE
KING PENGUIN GIVES AN AUDIENCE	165
THE TALE OF A FLORIDA CROCODILE	172
A HEART-TO-HEART TALK WITH A SKUNK	179
BORNEO'S NEVER-SEEN NOSE-MONKEY	186
THE ALMOST-GONE WHOOPING CRANE	193
A GIANT TORTOISE RECALLS THE PAST	200
AFRICA'S MOST WONDERFUL BIRD ARRIVES	206
THOSE GIANT LIZARDS OF KOMODO	213
CORDIAL RELATIONS WITH A KUDU	220
PLAIN TALK TO A FOOL-HEN	227
THE HOME LIFE OF THE YOUNG LADY TIGER, AND THE END OF IT	235
MARY GIRAFFE AND HER BABY	246
THOSE RIVAL WILD BABIES,—ZEBRA AND GIRAFFE	253
CLARENCE, THE WART-HOG	260
THE YAK FROM THE WORLD'S ROOF	267
THE ARRESTED DEVELOPMENT OF THE SLOTH	275
THE CONFESSION OF THE SPOTTED TERROR	282
THE GRAY WOLF REFUSES TO BE CROSS-EXAMINED	289
THE GOLDEN BIRD-OF-PARADISE	296
THE AMAZING PLATYPUS THAT CAME TO US	303

ILLUSTRATIONS

	PAGE
The Grizzly Bear	5
The Pack-Rat	15
The Pika	23
The White Mountain Goat	29
The Road-Runner	39
The Wolverine	43
The Secretary Bird	53
The Orang-Utan	57
The Regal Python	67
The Canada Goose	73
Jack Miner's Wild-Goose Sanctuary	77
The Lion	85
The Willow Ptarmigan	93
The Ostrich	99
A Normal Sage Grouse	105
The Sage Grouse Strutting	111
The Pintail Duck	115
The Pygmy Elephant Baby	125
The Bob-White Quail	131
The Chimpanzee	139
The Gray Squirrel	145
The Buffalo	153
The Prong-Horned Antelope	161

ILLUSTRATIONS

	PAGE
The King Penguin	167
The Florida Crocodile	177
The Northern Skunk	181
The Nose-Monkey	189
The Whooping Crane	197
The Giant Tortoise	201
The Whale-Headed Stork	211
The Giant Lizard	217
The Greater Kudu	225
The Fool-Hen	229
The Tigress	237
The Giraffes	251
The Zebras	257
The Wart-Hog	265
The Yak	269
The Three-Toed Sloth	279
The Leopard	285
The Gray Wolf	293
Golden Bird of Paradise	299
The Platypus	305

WILD ANIMAL INTERVIEWS

A GRIZZLY BEAR DEMANDS THE BALLOT

I HAVE just had a surprise. While visiting a zoo here in the East, I came upon a four-year-old silver-tip grizzly bear in a new temporary cage, only ten feet square. He was restlessly padding to and fro, panting at intervals, evidently nervous and irritated. Said I to myself, "I'll bet you this is a newly caught bear."

When I gave him a good close-up he startled me. He was as handsome as a picture. His long, waving, grizzly-gray coat looked as if just then combed and brushed. His face was unusually light-colored for a grizzly, to an extent of lightness that is rare. Now *where* have I seen that face? Ah! I have it!

"Hello, Baldy," says I, quite familiar like. "When did you come out of the Yellowstone Park?"

The bear stopped with a jerk, rose on his hind legs, and stared at me. (My! How I wished for a camera!) He was dumfounded; and at first he just silently stared at me, to size me up.

"Oh, yes. I know you," said I. "You used to live in the pine woods just back of the Canyon Hotel. I saw you there last June. With the sun only half an hour high, and the mosquitoes on that ridge biting us like the mischief, you suddenly popped out of the evergreen timber of the middle distance, and galloped straight forward across the green grass for two hundred yards, with your hair rolling all over you in great waves. Then you went to work, along with five other grizzlies, on the hotel scrap-heap to stuff yourself."

"Righto! But how do you recognize me now"?

"By your bald face. I could recognize you and swear to you, even if I saw you at the South Pole."

"Well, I was at the Canyon last June, all right; and I wish I were there now."

"Why did the Park Rangers pick you out and make you It?"

"Well, it was this way." A pause, and very evident embarrassment: "At the Canyon Hotel I was all right. But I went off up to Yellowstone Lake to the woods back of that ranger station, and there I forgot myself. The fact is—well, I guess I got a little too fresh at the cafeteria and the tourist camp. Chief Ranger Sam Woodring posted me in the club as a nuisance and a pest; and the next thing I know I was in a steel shipping-cage, with my baggage checked for Washington."

"And just what was it that you did, Baldy?" I inquired, registering sympathy.

"Well, it was nothing much. I just took some bacon and eggs, and a little bread, from that tourist camp; and once I broke into the cafeteria, to get a good feed of chocolate from the showcase. But that stuff was trifling. I don't think Sam cared a rap about the value of it; but in getting that bacon from a touring-car, I frightened the tourists all up, and that made Woodring sore on me. You see," continued Baldy, "a stingy old cafeteria is no Canyon Hotel; and when I looked for a high-class scrap-heap there wasn't any! No, not

THE GRIZZLY BEAR.

"I broke into the cafeteria at Yellowstone to get a good feed of chocolate from that show-case."

even a second or third class one. And now look at me! —but, say; do you think I'm in for life?" (Great concern registered here.)

"Surely not in this bum cage, Baldy. This is only one remove from solitary confinement. You will get a fine large cage by and by, in which you can be quite comfortable and happy."

"Thanks. Will you just speak to the big chief about it? It's a delicate subject for me—without references where I came from. You understandwottimean."

I assured him that I did, and would, ifandwhen I could.

"Baldy, I want to ask you something. Just what do the wild animals think of Yellowstone Park?"

"In summer they think it's what men call a paradise; but in winter it's different. To get through then, you must know the ropes. And let me tell you that when the hotels suddenly close there is no more high living on table scraps. Then us bears have to scatter out and live on our own until *the middle of the next year*—and, gee whiz! It gives us an awful kick in the ribs. We're opposed to that lightning-quick shut-off being worked on us thataway. It ain't right."

"It is tough, Baldy, when the hotels close. You bears ought to be put on government rations until near denning-time. But who's going to foot the bill?"

"Ain't we the wards of the nation—just as much as the dog-goned Indians? And don't we earn some grub and consideration by the shows we put up all over the place every summer for the entertainment of the visiting proletariat? You take a straw vote on it among the U. S. tourists and see if they don't every one of 'em vote for the old bears and an appropriation. Why, gosh darn it" (caution by visitor registered here). "Well—confound it, we ought to have back pay!"

And here was Baldy, fresh from the untainted air of the Continental Divide, already actually snorting with indignation over his fancied wrongs, and his claims upon Congress—quite in the style of the dear-departed William Haywood. I had no idea that a perfectly healthy wild grizzly could be so quickly upset and communized by the air of Washington; but you never can tell.

"Baldy," said I, kindly, "the one Big Thing that every wild animal and wild bird now needs, and needs most of all, is a VOTE! Yes, sir. A vote in the primaries, and a vote on election day at the poor old battered ballot-box."

As this great idea entered Baldy's system, and began to grip his class consciousness, he nearly had a fit.

"That's it!" he bawled, jumping high in air and raking his big claws across the cage-floor whenever he lit. "You've said it, at last! That is IT! Why did you not think of it before? Yessir! We want votes! Give us the ballot! Votes for bears, and forbears! Nothing could make things any worse than they are now—with the two-legged wild animals voting like they do. Look at the Yahoos of all nations that in every election march up——"

Here I hurriedly interposed.

"Hush, Baldy! For goodness' sake, hush! Don't say too much or we may be arrested. You are now on dangerous ground. This is the Home of Democracy, the Idol of all nations, for which and whom the world must be made safe. Keep still! If you want to start something, do it at night, and quietly at the offgo; and then, if you keep at it, you will go far. I'm with you about ballots for bears. Plenty of wild animals have 'em now, so why shouldn't good, honest native American bears get theirs?"

Bald-Face was right, and his rightness went far beyond himself. The wild animals and the wild birds need votes; they need them to-day, and they need them very much indeed. One leather-lunged constituent can put up a vast howl to a lawmaker for more killing privileges, affecting, or intended to affect thousands of wild creatures for life or for death, when not one of the intended victims can even whisper a protest or file a demurrer. And worse than that, it may easily happen that, through apathy, fear, laziness, or "the expense," not a single voice will be raised for helpless wild creatures. The sportsmen claim that the game is theirs, and they assume and exercise the privilege (not the right) to dictate what its fate shall be. Once in a wild-life conservation meeting my wise friend Daniel Carter Beard made this little speech to his fellow conspirators:

"Gentlemen, in trying to dictate what the laws shall be for the killing or the protection of game, we are like a lot of criminals legislating for the suppression of crime."

And the worst of it is that now, with "game" in a well-nigh hopeless state as to survival, the sportsmen are just as savage as ever about killing it, and the people who do not kill are rapidly becoming utterly indifferent to its fate.

Yes, this subject is tiresome now; but it will be still more so twenty years from now, when only "specimens" of the game and song birds remain.

THE PACK-RAT'S AMAZING JOKES

ONCE upon a time that I had in the Rocky Mountains, I took a modest little pack on my back, and hiked from our camp on Elk River about ten miles to the cabin of a nice young trapper on Bull River, who had invited me to pay him a visit. I forgot to phone him that I was coming, and one day at sunset when I saw his smokeless chimney, and knocked on his silent-looking door, I'm blest if I didn't find him out. But he was a thoughtful Johnny, and just as a precaution had left on his rough pole table these comforting words: "On trap line. Back to-morrow night. Make yourself at home, but wash your dirty dishes."

On looking for Johnny's matches, I found none; which seemed mighty queer. Going and coming, trappers usually are outrageously careful about their match supply. However, I dug up some of my own, and soon had a fire going. Carelessly leaving half a dozen spare matches on the table, I took the water pail, and set out to find the water-works. Yes, it was a spring all right, a small one, under a big rock, and its water certainly was good.

Back in the cabin, I reached for one of my matches, to light the lamp; and no matches were there! I could have sworn that I left three or four on the table; and I just hate "mysteries." Some of them give a fellow a

THE PACK-RAT'S AMAZING JOKES

kind of crazy feeling. Digging once more for a match, I made a light, and cooked a light supper. I couldn't find a spoon about the place, high or low; which again seemed mighty queer. However, with my own patent combination of knife, fork and spoon I was sufficiently outfitted for table activities. Johnny's mule-deer steaks, bacon fat and coffee were just all right.

I had finished a good supper, and was feeling fine over it—in spite of my disappointment over the absence of Johnny, when out of the dead silence of the cabin a faint rustling sound came from the wall at my right, where the two bunks were. Yes, it was "made by some animal," and no hummingbird.

Slowly turning my head, hunter fashion, I saw a pair of big, beady black eyes looking at me, a pair of big, erect ears, and a thick and furry gray body. It was a rat, of some large kind, and presumably mean and savage.

Now, I don't like house rats the most of all wild animals. I have lain awake at night two hundred and fifty times to hate them, and to plan how to kill That One. I would love to club all the house rats in the world, but I am not so hot about the wild ones. They have not been brutalized by long association with man.

The rat I saw now not only looked at me, but for a long minute he actually inspected and appraised me, just as cavalry officers do new horses. Would he condemn me, and run away? To my astonishment he scrambled up to a log, and came gingerly ambling along its sloping side, right up to the corner of the table. Pausing only for an instant, he calmly hopped down to the pole surface, sat up on his hindquarters, squirrel fashion, and gave me a long and searching look.

"Well, well!" I exclaimed. "You're a Pack Rat all right, and a big one. It's Bushy-Tailed Pack Rat for you."

"I'm lonesome," says he, as soon as he had finished giving me the once over.

"Now I know who took those three matches from this table. You did it! And where did you put them?"

"Just where I always put matches—in a safe place. They're under Johnny's pillow, in that bunk."

"Just wait a minute."

I got up and looked, and, believe me or not—there they were! As I sat down again, I pointed an accusing finger at the Trading Rat, and said very severely:

"Packy, in a way you are all right. But all the same, you are the fellow who sometimes drives trappers and prospectors half crazy with wondering who has stolen their things. You do these things all the way from here to Florida and Mexico; and sometimes you are very trying!"

"Yes," said the Pack Rat, gravely. "A prospector friend of mine down in the Sonoran Desert once quarreled with his partner over the loss of his spoon. He said his partner took it. They had an awful row about it, and Partner left him, to let him live all the rest of the time alone. Well, that spoon was honestly traded for by a member of my family. He left a perfectly good cactus fruit in its place; but the spoon-man was so mad he never noticed it until the next day; and even then, he was that ignorant he didn't know what it meant. My folks heard that it was not until forty years afterward that a wise old guy told him who took his spoon; and then he nearly cried about that quarrel."

"Packy," said I, "I sure don't love many rats; but you are different. I've heard a lot about you and your folks, and that has made me want to know more. Now, why is it that you hang around men's camps and cabins the way you do?"

"Well," said Packy, looking quite grave, "I hate to say it, but not all of rat society is thoroughly genteel. Some of it is rather low down. Now, confidentially, I have a poor opinion of your house rat. He is too lazy to do any honest work; and the way he destroys valuable property just gets on my nerves. We hate waste and destruction; but he just loves it. He says, 'The world owes me a living,' and so he gets it by all kinds of stealing instead of by honest labor. And then his tastes are so low. Why, he will eat garbage any time rather than go out and dig nice, clean roots and gather beautiful nuts, as we do."

"Yes," I said, "the house rat is a terrible waster. If he gnaws his way into your room and doesn't find any food in it, as like as not he will chew your best clothes full of holes, and even gnaw your furniture."

"I think," said the Pack Rat earnestly, "that the waste of any good thing is a crime, and it ought to be stopped. Now, there's that wolverine, who lives right here on this same trap-line. He is a natural born hellion for destroying things. A wolverine will break into a trapper's cabin, like this one for instance, where the trapper man keeps his little stock of flour, and bacon and coffee and syrup and sugar, and what he can't eat he will mess all up so that nobody can eat it. Now, that isn't right; it's against the law of these woods!"

"The wolverine," I agreed, "is a sure-enough devil. I've heard a lot about him; and honestly, I'd like to get his point of view. And that reminds me. Why do you fellows come to men's cabins, risk getting killed, and do all this troublesome trading business that sometimes makes men so mad?"

"Well," said Pack, politely picking a crumb from the table, "in the first place, the men and women of my family were born industrious. We just naturally love to be doing something. But we don't harm a soul," he added hastily. "We eat a little of Johnny Trapper's food now and then, but we destroy nothing. You know how we make our burrows, don't you?"

"Yes, I have seen some, down in the Southwest, that were like castles and fortresses of spiny cactus joints, reinforced with sticks and stones. They sure are great. Your intelligence in home defense is nothing less than wonderful,—far beyond that of savage man."

"That's to make the rascally coyotes and skunks keep off our grass. Up here, the winters are so lo—ng and so dul—l that we get bored stiff with keeping our own company, and we are glad of a cabin and a live man to play with. No, the danger isn't so great. The trappers don't hate us. They hardly ever get really mad and try to beat us. I kinda think they themselves get lonesome, and at times they almost like to have us around. But just now Johnny Trapper is awfully mad about his pet spoon."

"I say, Pack. You had better bring it back. He needs

THE PACK-RAT.

"The trappers don't hate us. They hardly ever get really mad and try to beat us."

it; and just now I needed it myself. Go on. Be a sport and a go-getter. I'll trade you this match-box for it."

"All right," said Pack genially. "Since you put it that way, I will. Just excuse me a minute."

Pack disappeared toward the bunks, rummaged a moment in the top one, then quickly ran along his log highway. Carrying in his small jaws a dull-white teaspoon, he politely landed himself in the middle of the table, and delivered the goods.

"Thank you, Pack," said I, "Johnny will be obliged to you. Here's your match-box. But I say, Packy, who are your worst enemies up here?"

"Well, there's Bear, Wolverine, Wolf, Weasel, Skunk, Marten and Fisher; and there are the owls, hawks and eagles. Can you beat that lot for wickedness?"

"Truly, you must be mighty wise, or you could not for long escape that gang of cutthroats. And now will you tell me who your best friends are, and what they are like. I'd like right well to have you make up a Who's Who of the Summits."

"I never thought of that before, but your idea germ interests me," said Pack gravely. "In the first place I must mention the red squirrel, the Columbia ground-squirrel, the golden-mantled ground-squirrel, and that solemn old graybeard, the whistling marmot, who takes himself so seriously. Did you ever see one at noon, lying on a big chunk of slide-rock, sunning himself? Say, that's a picture of Solid Comfort, believe me."

"Yes, I've seen the old whistler more than once. He is handsome, but dumb."

THE PACK-RAT'S AMAZING JOKES

"Then," pursued Packy, "there is the little pika,—but I advise you to interview him at length. He is worth it. Honestly, I cannot see how he carries on. Yes; I know about his hay-making; but that can't be all of it. The white goat and mountain sheep we often see, but they are not very neighborly. They are busy with troubles of their own. Then there are those old camp-followers, the Clark's nutcracker and the Canada jay; and the ptarmigan and the fool-hen. In addition to the bad ones, that is about all of our neighbors who come into my mind just now. On the whole, for one reason and another, they are a migh-tee fine and interesting lot, and I doubt whether very much is known about their lives, or anything else than their skins."

"I thank you, kindly," said I, "and I see ahead of me great possibilities in making new friends. Once I begged a nice young man with a big bank roll and a budding ambition to come up here, build a cabin and spend a winter here, studying the lives of the animals of the summits; but he shied at it. He preferred to stay down and just write. He said, 'There's too much cold, and wind, and rough stuff about that scheme.' The real trouble was,—it was too far from Broadway!"

That night the Pack Rat was very busy. Every time I awoke I heard him at work, and when I rose in the morning I found that the cunning little rascal, with a perfectly wonderful mind in his small skull, had taken particular pains to make things interesting for me. He had taken my cake of soap from a shelf, and put it into a pocket of my buckskin shirt; and he had taken my eyeglasses from a stool near my bunk, and put them on the shelf where the soap had been. One of my socks was under Billy's cookstove, and the other under the pillow of the lower bunk. I am sure Pack was somewhere watching, and was vastly amused while I hunted all about to re-assemble my property.

THE PIKA TELLS HOW HE LIVES

ONCE upon a time I went out alone in the Rocky Mountains of Canada, just to see what I could see.

It was a grand exhibition of mountains both steep and high, V-shaped valleys plunging down, evergreen timber up to the 2500-foot line, rock, precipices galore, and great fields of slide-rock until you couldn't rest. The steepest mountain-sides were scored from summit to base by the long, naked roads traveled over by the avalanches of snow, ice, slide-rock, and tree-trunks, and in their open season (May), you had to mind your step, and keep out of their way.

We were camped at timberline, on Goat Pass. Rain that fell on the east side of our tents ran madly down Goat creek into Elk River; and the dampness of our west side slid down into Bull River. The view from the top of Bird Mountain, above our camp, disclosed a magnificent cyclorama of mountain peaks, ridges, hog-backs and valleys, cliffs of clean, gray limestone, and such miles of broken slide-rock as I never saw, before nor since.

> Oh, puny man, woulds't thou atone
> For years of swelling ego heart?
> Go, tread the mountain-top alone,
> And learn how very small thou art.

I was fascinated by the way the toiling hand of Nature was breaking off (by extremes of heat and cold) the faces of those tremendous cliffs of gray stone, throwing down the pieces as nice, clean slide-rock, and spreading it out in terrible sloping acres with a pitch of from 20 or 30 degrees, or more. The fresh workings were absolutely clean of soil, grass and bushes, and you could eat off of most any big chunk of stone, anywhere.

As one looks in silent awe at those great exhibits of the Toil of Nature, and sees how those peaks and cliffs are being broken down to fill up those V-shaped valleys; and as one hears the sharp crack and rattle of the falling fragments of those slide-rock factories, it gives one a feeling of awe and littleness. What is more, it takes out of the hunter a lot of his thirst for the blood of the wild creatures that elect to live amid those grand, gloomy and peculiar surroundings.

We climbed a lot in those mountains, and all that we shot or cared to shoot, was four animals,—even though there were plenty of them. It was about fifty times more interesting to see them, and talk with them, alive and unafraid. That place had *not* been spoiled by hunters, and the wild animals were not so very wild. On our first afternoon on Goat Pass three white mountain goats ran through our camp, and no one fired a shot at them.

A certain bright and sunny noonday found me on a field of massive slide-rock of clean, gray stone, walled in on three sides by sheer cliffs a hundred feet high. It was from those walls that all the limestone had broken off and fallen down.

Tired from climbing and hungry from an early breakfast, I selected an arm-chair sort of a place on a soft,

THE PIKA TELLS HOW HE LIVES

clean stone, and sat down to rest and eat my luncheon. From the depths of the great stonepile around me came a queer little drawling wild-animal cry.

It said, "Chee-e-p! Chee-p!" and a little later "Cheep" quite sharply and near at hand. And there, as I live and breathe, on the right-hand chunk of my stone arm-chair perched a droll little animal the size of a half-grown rabbit, with a gray-brown coat of fur and a white rim around each ear.

"Why, hello," said I genially. "You must be Pika, the little Haymaker of the Slide-Rock."

"Never heard the name before; but, anyhow, I'm no piker, if that is what you mean. I earn an honest living; I take care of myself and I'm no expense to anybody."

"No offense. Pika is your name, and you ought to be in the Rabbit family, but you're not."

"It's a family tradition that our forefathers and aunts' sisters were distantly related to the Rabbits."

"Well, tell me, Pika," said I, "however did your people happen to come away up here and settle on these awful summits?"

"Awful summits!" sniffed Pika indignantly. "I think they're the finest summits in the world. Where are there any finer ones?"

"Well, as summits go, they are all right, in a way; but why did you do it?"

"It was this way," said Pika, with a glance at the sun. "When we lived down below in the Elk River Valley, we had to live in holes in the ground or in brush piles, as those foolish rabbits do. It was easy for the weasels to catch us inside, for the skunks to get us outside, and for the bears to do us up both going and coming. At last we got tired of those wild animal pests, and we came up here, where slide rock is plentiful and cheap and the chunks are so big that no animal can dig us out. We can run all through these fields of big stones, and neither the mountain lion nor the wolf can get at us. We're just as safe from harm as we'd be in a Zoo."

"Well, Pike, what are you afraid of? The grizzly? The black bear?"

"No, not on your life. The grizzly can dig out those foolish little Mikes that live over yonder in holes in the ground"——

"Ground squirrels?"

"Yes. They're so stupid I guess they never will learn to come up here and play safe in the slide-rock along with us. The grizzlies dig them out, just as you dig celery in your garden in winter. Why, I even offered to show 'em how to make hay! But they don't savvy our game at all. But, gosh! It makes the fat old grizzlies blow and pant to dig them out of that hard and stony ground! They'd better go to a good zoo and live high without work."

"Are there any bad people up here, Pike?"

"No—that is, none worth mentioning," said Pike proudly. "Still we take mighty few chances. The weasels could get us in our burrows; that is, if those murderous little wretches could live up here; but they can't. The Columbia River ground squirrel is our good friend. In winter there are other people up here, and the company below stairs is very select."

THE PIKA.

"Yes, we make our hay while the sun shines. We cut all kinds of small plants that are good to eat."

"I hear that you and your relatives are great workers, Pikey."

"Yes, we're that, all right," answered the little one, airily. "We make our hay while the sun shines. We cut all kinds of small plants that are good to eat and pile them up in the sun to dry out enough that they won't spoil on us when we take them down below and stow them away for winter use."

"I know. You're wise little guys. You know enough to turn your hay piles in curing them, and carry them from shade to sunlight, don't you?"

"Yes, we have to do it. Do you see that pile over yonder?"—pointing with his right paw—"Well, I cut that two days ago, over there among the bushes. I've turned that pile four times, and in three days more it will be ready to take down below."

"How do you tell a good plant from a bad one?"

"Well," said Pikey with a wise air, "we try 'em out. We take a bite, to try it. If it tastes good, we swallow it—and then wait to see what happens. If it makes you sick, or kills you, that's a sign that it's not good food. But, pshaw! All these plants up here are good; though some do taste better than others."

"Now tell me, Pikey, how in the world do you and your folks ever get through the long and cold winters that blow and howl around so up here, and pile up such awful drifts? Why, the snow on this slide-rock must be ten or twenty feet deep in winter! And it must be banked up on you for fully six months!"

"Well," said the Little One, gravely, "there are some winters up here, and no mistake. Late in the fall, before we go in, the winds are something awful. They blow from the northwest, they blow steady, and they blow all day.

"The Clark crows and jays and magpies fly lower down. The grizzlies den up tight. The sheep and goats all work down into the timber, and on into the valleys and bad lands, to find shelter and perhaps a little food."

"And you?"

"Oh, we go far down in the crevices of these big rocks, and we find rooms that the cold winds can't reach. We carry our hay to them, and then with grass and leaves we stop up the doors as tightly as ever we can. No 'fresh air' for us in winter! No siree. When the first big snow comes, we are sealed up for the whole long winter. Little by little we eat our hay, and then we go to sleep. If we wake up when we shouldn't, we eat a little more hay, then sleep again. Comfortable? You bet your life we are!

"Yes, there is one thing that makes us sort of unhappy. It's our thoughts of our friends the mountain goats, mountain sheep, elk and deer that are out in the open all winter, battling with the snow, the ice and the storms."

Suddenly Pike stopped abruptly, cast one startled, hasty glance over his left shoulder, and without stopping to say "Aye," "Yes," or "By your leave," he dived head first into the mouth of his burrow. My slow mind was just getting ready to wonder what had so frightened him, when——

"Whish!" came a loud snort like hissing steam, and "Bang!" came a hoof-stamp upon a stone.

I roused up and pulled myself together. With kicks

and flounders I sprawled out of my hard stone chair and scrambled to get my feet on some kind of decent footing.

And there, not quite ten feet away, was the big, hairy form of an animal friend of quite another story.

THE MOUNTAIN GOAT'S POINT OF VIEW

On dizzy ledge of mountain wall, above the timber-line,
I hear the riven slide-rock fall toward the stunted pine.
Upon the paths I tread secure, no foot dares follow me,
For I am master of the crags, and march above the scree.

THE snow-white, shaggy-coated animal that suddenly came upon me in my stone arm-chair of the slide-rock from which I had been talking with Pika was a huge old Rocky Mountain billy goat with a beard much longer than mine ever was at its worst.

He snorted and stamped in his first outburst of alarm, then he wheeled about and, bobbing absurdly, dashed away downhill over the chaos of broken limestone, to secure safety first on the cliffs of Goat Creek.

"Hi there, Billy!" I shouted, "come back here. Nobody's going to hurt you. I want to see you."

Billy paused and glared back over his shoulder.

"You're hunting billy goats," he cried, resentfully.

"I am not! I'm through. I'll never shoot another one, honor bright."

"Well, then, what do you want? What's your idea?"

"I want to interview you, and I want to tell you something. Come on back here."

"Not on your life will I. If you leave that old gun, and come down to these pines, I'll see you."

We met on Billy's terms under a flag of truce. With another snort and stamp he opened up on me very severely.

"You've been hunting billies, and I'm sore on you!"

"It's not so bad as it looks. I could have downed three yesterday, and another big one this morning; but I'm through, I tell you. Two are enough for any man."

"Well, then, what can I do for you?"

"First, I want you to answer a foolish question. Do any of you goat people ever 'leap from crag to crag?'"

"Not on your life! We are not fools. And goats have no airplanes, nor even wings. Who ever said that we could fly?"

"Only people who never saw goats on crags. Let's forget it. But tell me something about your ups and downs, Billy. Who are your enemies up here?"

"We have no bad enemies except men with guns, like you and the other Indians. The bad Man-with-a-Gun gives us no show. He can spy us out and shoot us a quarter of a mile away, and we can't escape him. I tell you it's tough."

"This place is going to be made a billy-goat heaven," said I.

"What do you mean by that?"

"All shooting here is going to be stopped, and after that you won't need to be afraid of anything but bad wild animals."

"I want to know! But, say. The bad wild animals don't bother us much. The wolves don't get up here; the mountain lions are afraid to tackle us, and ever since my

THE WHITE MOUNTAIN GOAT.

"We have no bad enemies except men with guns, like you and the other Indians. The bad Man-with-a-Gun gives us no show."

granddad killed that old he-grizzly bear that was tackling him the silver-tips let us alone."

"How was that, Billy?"

"Easy enough," said Billy, with a proud air. "The old silver-tip came suddenly upon my granddad, on a level spot of grass at the top of a cliff. Grizzly, thinking he could put one over, jumped the old gentleman, to break his neck and eat him. As he came on, granddad gave him one big horn-punch, right behind the fore leg, and punctured his tire. Grizzly finally broke grandsire's neck, but then he soon bled to death himself. You know what our sharp little horns can do in a fight."

"Yes; and I'm mighty glad you've got 'em, and know how to use 'em."

"Thanks. I'm sure we need 'em in our business up here."

"Do you not often go cold and hungry in winter up here?"

"Indeed we do. Honestly, I wonder that the Nannies and the young goats stick it out as well as they do. On these summits the cold winds are something awful. Often for days and days together we can't find one mouthful of food. If it were not for the danger of being killed, we would go down to Bull River Valley to live in winter, but as things are now we just don't dare."

"Tell me, Billy. Do you and your folk ever fight with each other, or fight with the sheep, about pastures or anything?"

"Indeed we do NOT!" cried Billy. "How foolish that would be! It's against the first law of the wild folk. Only men quarrel over pastures. I guess all wild animals

THE MOUNTAIN GOAT'S POINT OF VIEW

know better, don't they? The wild folks have more sense than to fight each other, and steal. There's always territory enough for all."

"You and your folks have to meet many dangers up here, Billy—from blizzards, from snow-slides, from bad animals and golden eagles, and from men who kill. Now tell me this. Of all the laws of the wild herds, which one is most important in saving your flocks from danger?"

"Oh, by all means, the law of quick and perfect obedience to herd leaders. The young and the weak members must obey or die! When danger threatens, and the alarm signal is given, there is no time to ask foolish questions, or to explain anything. The young ones must rush to obey the order of the leader, and keep on a-doing it."

My next question I asked with some hesitation.

"Well, Billy, if it's no secret, who is it who usually does the leading in your herd?"

"It's like this: In the summer and fall the Nannies and kids flock by themselves; and then, of course, it is the wisest and most masterful Nanny that does the leading. In the winter, when the whole herd comes together, it is some Billy like myself who tells the others what to do. We Billies are not sleepy and stupid as the old buffalo bulls were in the days when the cows did the leading. Up here, stupidity means death."

This last statement was made with pardonable pride, and there is no reason for it to be suppressed.

"And now," said Billy, "I'd like to ask you a question. You've seen a good deal of us by this time. Now what do YOU think is the one thing that does the most for our safety on these summits?"

"Well," I said, after a pause for reflection, "it surely is your steady nerves. You fellows don't know what it is to get panicky. Your best bet is cool judgment in the face of danger, and your straight thinking. On these points I rank you high; and, honestly, so far as I know, you can't be beaten on any of them by anything that wears hoofs."

"I thank you very much," said Billy, bowing politely. "I will tell that to all the white flocks on these mountains and it will cheer them up a lot. Now, tell me, what more can we goats do to promote safety first? I'll own up that I'm getting scared about our future. The long-range rifles are giving us hell."

"Well, you may tell your flocks about the game sanctuary that this place will be pretty soon. It's coming, sure. After this season you'll never see nor hear any more shooting in these Elk River Mountains."

"What! Never?"

"Yes, never!"

"You almost bowl me over!" said Billy slowly.

"Well, now I just thought you didn't quite catch on when I mentioned it before!"

And then a mighty queer thing happened.

Billy slowly sat down on his hind quarters, dog-fashion, and dazed-like. The wind blew through his long white chin whiskers and waved them. He looked at me, then he looked at the cliffs and finally up at the sky. Plainly, the big idea had jolted him some, and he was trying to change from low gear to high.

Presently he jumped up, and came forward for a close-up. Looking up into my face he said, slowly:

"It's wonderful! It seems too good to be true! I never dreamed that any of us would live to see anything like that done for us! We have been looking forward to being shot one by one, or two or three at a time, until we were all gone. But, surely now, you wouldn't fool a poor old goat about it, would you?"

"No siree! No more men with guns for you after next Christmas, honor bright."

"Well, the world isn't so wholly bad after all, is it? I sure am pleased to have made your acquaintance."

And once more bowing politely, Billy turned and without a trace of doubt or fear solemnly marched off down Goat Creek and faded out of my view.

Truly, it thrilled me profoundly to thus come in close touch with a fine, big, representative member of North America's most wonderful species of big wild animals of the mountains. As the average visitor sees a white mountain goat quietly chewing red clover hay in a corral of a large zoo, of course he does not seem so terribly wonderful; but if you could only know all about him as you look at him, he would seem to you like a prize animal.

As you see him in his Rocky Mountain home, anywhere from the Bitter Root Mountains to the head of Cook's Inlet, Alaska, he is (at least every fall) as white as snow. He is "chunky" in build, and very hairy and shaggy-coated. He wears fine, wool-like hair next his skin to keep him warm, through which grows the long, coarse shaggy hair that is intended to shed rain and snow. He seems to have on his back two humps, one on his shoulders and another on his hips; but they are made up only of long, coarse hair standing straight up.

His legs are short, thick and ungraceful, and of little use in leaping, but with their big and powerful black hoofs, of combined rubber-ball and sharp knife-edge, he can climb to beat the world. No, indeed he does *not* "leap from crag to crag"; but he can climb up the face of a cliff of bare rock in ways that are amazing. No other American animal can equal him on the cliffs, but at the same time he is no jumper, and he never will be. He climbs up and down deadly places just as mountaineering men do,—safety first,—slowly and foot by foot.

Billy's head is small, hung low like that of a buffalo, his neck is short, and in going across the face of a cliff, on a ledge two feet wide, he pegs along stiffly like a mechanical toy. He does this to make sure of each step. His horns are very small, black, curved, and as sharp on the ends as skewers. In summer he lives on the highest summits, either at or above timberline, but in winter he goes lower down. His meat is not considered good, his fur coat is quite worthless (it has no wearing qualities whatever), and his little black horns ten or eleven inches long are not prized as trophies. For all of these negative qualities we are most thankful, for we wish nothing but safety, good food and long life to the Crag-master of the Rockies.

ROAD-RUNNER, THE FEATHERED ELF OF THE DESERT

WHENEVER you wish to find out things from shy people, keep still about yourself; ask a few harmless but leading questions about their daily life, and try to be a good listener. Usually you will run the risk of being bored to death, but such hazards must be counted as coming all in the day's work.

I have been thinking of the queerest, most erratic, most intelligent and most shy bird of the Sonoran Desert wonderland of southern Arizona and elsewhere. "That is a large order," did you say? Yes, it is; but I am thinking about the Road-Runner, Chapparal Cock, or "Snake Killer"; to which queer names I now add another much more genteel—the Feathered Elf of the Desert. He is a brown-and-speckled bird, small-bodied, loose-jointed, and built for surpassing agility and speed.

Have men ever made careful studies of the mind and manners of this amazing bird? Not on your life. I wish they would.

The first road-runner I ever met personally was a new arrival in one of the long, outside cages of New York's big bird house. There was a dead tree standing at one end for birds to perch upon. As I looked in, a smallish, long-legged, and very long-tailed bird ran nimbly over the sanded floor of the cage, and zip! It shot up into the air about six feet, as if thrown up by a steel spring; and seemingly without one wing-flit landed neatly upon a perch.

I think my lower jaw must well nigh have fallen off, from surprise and admiration.

It was not long after that introduction that Fortune kindly loosened up her grip sufficiently to permit me to break into the ancestral home of this queer bird. It was the Sonoran Desert, of southern Arizona, that has all the other deserts of this world beaten by miles. Direct comparisons are odorous, and I will refrain from instituting any.

But, please bear in mind that I am *not* talking about the desert exhibit of northern Arizona, above the spine-defended Southern Pacific Railway. For canyons, and plateaus, and painted rocks and cliffs, northern Arizona is *all right;* but as for upright and downright sharp-pointedness, for weirdness of scenery, for queer yet beautiful *arboreal* deserts, and a regular riot of cacti of scores of different shapes, sizes and kinds, let me offer you *southern* Arizona. You can take your pick of cacti, all the way from cannon-ball shapes and sizes up to candelabra trees sixty feet high.

Yes, the home of the feathered elf of the desert in the Sonoran tract is a wonderland, no less. It is so fascinating that even intelligent horses and dogs appreciate its vast level floor spaces, and its theatrical-property mountains, set here and there just where they best fit into the picture. You struggle to grasp (in your mind), the bizarre cacti, creosote bushes, mesquites, palo verdes and white brittle bushes until you are bewildered by the overpowering oddity of the most wonderful desert flora in the world.

Naturally, you expect to find queer animals, odd birds

and strange reptiles in an outlandish place like that; and you do.

You have the Gila monster, the Gambel quail that won't rise on the wing to be shot, the croaking raven, the exquisite little kangaroo rat, the wise pack-rat, the heat-defying mountain sheep, the thirst-defying pronghorned antelope, and what more would you have?

The Road-Runner was born to live in a country where good roads and runways are plentiful and cheap. That is what they are everywhere in the Sonoran Desert, no sand, and the roads smooth as telford and hard as wood. He scorns to fly, and his legs cheerfully do all the work. If a trotting horse scares him into action he takes to the middle of the trail, and without seeming to do more than open up into high and step on the gas, he runs like a brown streak ahead of that devoted horse, as if he loved the chance to show off. He runs for yards, rods and furlongs, until he comes to a sharp turn, which gives him a running high jump of ten feet or so into the bushy oblivion of the desert.

If you see anywhere a Road-Runner on the ground, he is surely running; and if there is any jumping to be done, he is always ready to oblige.

Once when I was in the Sonoran Desert, along came a Road-Runner who halted in amazement at the sight of me. Next thing, he pulled off a standing high jump, and landed in a choya cactus tree that presented to the world not less than 30,000 spines.

"Hello, Runner," I whipped out. "Wait just a minute. I want to ask you something."

The bird gave his head a twist of friendly interrogation, sized me up with one big and searching eye, and by his manner plainly said:

"Well, what is it?"

The legs of that bird, a cuckoo sort of a fowl, were long and slender, but powerful. Its enormously long tail was longer than all of the body and head, and among little lizards and baby snakes, that long, spear-like beak is a formidable weapon. Clearly, that bird's horsepower was far beyond the weight and bulk of his tonneau, as racers often are designed.

"Well, Elf," said I, hurriedly, "I want to know where you build your nest, and hatch your young. I've not found out yet; and this is my second trip into these parts. How do you hide your nests on the ground, so as to escape the coyotes, and foxes, and skunks, and bob-cats, et cetera?"

"On the ground?" echoed Runner scornfully. "We don't nest on the ground, ever. What an idea! There, we never could rear a brood; no, nor could we even save our own bacon. We nest in choya cactus trees, like this one, defended by all these lovely spines. In here we are safe, for no wild animal, and no limb of Satan except man, can possibly get at us. Our eggs? Oh, anything from four to eight."

"And what is your favorite food?"

"For our baby birds, little lizards are the best. They are easy to catch. For our grown selves we eat small snakes, bugs, meat if we can get it, eggs and so on."

"You sometimes fight with rattlesnakes, do you not?"

"Yes, but confidentially, it's usually for sport. We tease and worry them a lot, to make them afraid of us,

THE ROAD-RUNNER.

"You sometimes fight with rattlesnakes, do you not?"
"Yes; but confidentially, it's usually for sport."

and not because we always intend to kill the tough old reps."

"Runner," said I, craftily, "I'm afraid that if you run all the time, and don't use your wings a lot more than you now do, those little wings will become smaller, and smaller, and finally become utterly useless for flight."

"Really?" said Runner. I saw that he was a bit startled. "You give me a jolt. Of course we can't afford to have our wings die on us. We need them in our business. I'll think it over."

"Do," I warned. "In this world it is distinctly in bad form for any bird to be without wings, and unable to fly. New enemies may spring up any year to pursue you on the ground, on the jump, and the run; and really, you ought to be able right now to fly a lot better than you do. These are perilous times for birds."

"Truly, they are. You have given me food for thought, and till we meet again friend, I'll chew upon this."

"Well," said I. "So long. I know you love your happy home, but as for comfort all the year round, it has some limitations."

"Your desert is fine in November;
In May it is lovely to see,
But from its hot breath in midsummer,
Good Lord, please eliminate me."

THE BAD WOLVERINE'S OTHER SIDE

TAKE them pound for pound, and you will find mighty few wild animals that will weigh up to the devilish cunning and savage industry of the wolverine of the north country. Even though I am his friend—in a way—I must allow that his reputation would be all the better by a washing.

If you start wolverine talk with a Canadian trapper who is a regular feller, in a very short time he begins to cuss and swear. He will say:

"Well, sir! Of all the cunning, the contriving, the murderous and the mean devils going on four feet, he is the worst. Why, he is that mean that he does things for pure cussedness. He destroys what he can't eat! He can dig, he can climb, he can travel all over creation, and at times he works as steady as a beaver."

The Rocky Mountain Indians fearsomely call him the "Mountain Devil," and the early naturalists wrote him down as the "Glutton."

Out in the wilds nobody has a chance to interview a wolverine, save under such strained circumstances that the yield is nothing. An angry or hurt animal is not a good story-teller. At last, however, a settled animal came to our place from British Columbia, and with him came my chance to get next to his point of view. Once as he sat on his porch, comfortably enjoying the morning sun, he warmed up and thoughtfully gave me this story:

"Yes," said he, "I'll allow that my reputation is none of the best; but times were hard when I was born and I came up fighting for my life. All my days until now I have had to live among savage grizzly bears, black bears, wolves, mountain lions, Stoney Indians and hard-boiled trappers. If I had been born a little saint, like Mary's lamb, where would my hide be to-day? On me? No, sir! It would be on some fur-bearing lady.

"Yes, I do belong to the marten family, but I don't attend the annual meetings. My jaws are powerful and my jaw teeth are big, because I need to have them that way. But for all o' that, I give the bears and mountain lions right of way. What sense is there in rushing head-long into sudden death? Peace promotes long life and prosperity.

"The thing that gives me the bulk of my bad reputation is my success in getting food and sidestepping my enemies. Why, man, I can follow up a trap line as well as Mack Norboe himself, and never miss a bait. I do it by following the tracks of the trapper.

"But I abhor any waste of good meat. When I find four or five trapped mink or marten close together, it is utterly impossible for me to eat all of them. What can I do except to destroy them or bury them in secret places?

"I am very fond of foxes, especially in the spring just before the young cubs leave their nest. I can smell a fox den across a creek. When I break into a den they are all scared out of their wits, and I kill all of them, the old ones first. Mighty good eating, young foxes are.

THE WOLVERINE.

"Why, man, I can follow up a trap-line as well as Mack Norboe himself, and never miss a bait."

"Raiding trappers' cabins? Yes, I do, occasionally. I do it partly for bacon and partly for amusement.

"I did one thing that I'm sorry for. I broke into Charlie Smith's cabin just after he had packed in a little sack of flour and a side of bacon, and he was out on his trap-line. Of course I ate that side of bacon and it was good! Then I tackled the sack of flour and ripped it open, but I just couldn't do a thing with it. It was so dry and dusty that I couldn't swallow it. All I did with it was to scatter it on the floor and roll in it, and I came out a white wolverine, if you can imagine such a thing. I was amused at myself, but it was lucky for me that I made my get-away before Charlie came back.

"Some people say that I take steel traps off of a trap-line and throw them into rivers, but that is untrue. I never do foolish things like that. All that I do with traps is to bury them in snowbanks and roll over the places to make it impossible to find them. It's very amusing to hide and watch the trapper go hunting everywhere except in the right place. Even a wolverine must have a little fun now and then.

"What is our greatest sport? Our greatest sport is in hunting for caches of food and then breaking into them. You know that the hunter or trapper who has too much food always tries to get ahead of us by making a cache that we cannot break open.

"First away, the trappers tried burying their food under big piles of wood, but to us wolverines that was only a joke. Then they tried hiding it in caves and shutting us out with big stones. A good idea, but it seldom worked. Almost always we found a way to go to it.

THE BAD WOLVERINE'S OTHER SIDE

"Up in the open country of the Far North, where white men don't like to live, they have been making caches high up on four posts or tree trunks, sometimes building up there a good little log house with a door. My great grand-daddy was famous for his agility in climbing up to those caches and breaking into them quickly. Then those brutal trappers began to carry huge fish hooks and nail them to the posts half-way up. And believe me, those inhuman contrivances have bothered us an awful lot. But even so, those little log houses high up are worse. We just despise them.

"I saw by the papers in Charlie Smith's cabin that away back in early days an awful lot of silly stuff was printed in queer old books about the big animals we regularly killed, the amount we would eat, how savage we always were and the wiser-than-man things that we did. But those days of foolish talk are now quite over. Men are learning that beyond being strong and tough citizens, able to fight and live off the country on the small game, we are very much like other members of our family. You can see for yourself that I am no fiend. If you were to come in here with me, as the keeper does, I wouldn't fly at you and bite you. Take a baby wolverine and bring him up in a genteel family and he would make a perfectly good and decent pet—while young. Most flesh-eating animals get too fresh when they are full grown.

"I will say, however," said the wolverine with an air of pride, "that both in our hunting and in keeping out of traps we are—well, outstanding members of society. We can outwit and live upon wild mice, rats, ground squirrels, ptarmigan, grouse, rabbits, hares and foxes. Of course we can, and sometimes do, kill young goats, sheep, elk and deer, when we can catch them away from their daddies and mammas, but we don't specialize on them.

"Traps? Yes, we object to all traps aimed at us, and I certainly must hand it to my mother for the way she showed us how to keep out of log and box traps of every kind, especially deadfalls. But the concealed steel trap, with a bait carelessly hung up over it, does cause the best of us to forget sometimes. When we are caught it is nearly always a steel trap that is to blame. Sometimes, when a trapper is real mad at one of us for raiding his cabin, he springs down a sapling and fastens the trap chain to the end of it. When he makes a catch in that cruel and unlawful way, that sapling spring-up leaves no room for argument.

"Who, me? Oh, well, I was caught by two toes only, in Charlie Smith's steel trap, and they held me until Charlie found me. You bet I was hot about it, it was so blamed trivial. Yes, I know, I could have bitten off those two toes and escaped, but I expected to escape without that. And but for one mistake, I would have made a getaway all right. I underestimated Charlie. In the first place, I didn't believe that Charlie could tie me up, single-handed as he was, and I was sure that even if he did tie me up, he couldn't carry me out to his cabin on his back."

Here I registered keen attention.

"Are you really interested? Well, I don't mind telling you about it. You see, we were on Avalanche Creek, and six long, hard and rough miles from his cabin. The trail led over slide-rock and through down timber that was enough to break a trapper's heart, but that never discouraged Charlie any."

"The first thing he did was to tie up my jaws, and we sure did have a dispute over that. I used my teeth and my big, white claws for all they were worth, but Charlie won at last. He lashed my jaws together with a muzzle hitch, then one by one he tied my legs so that I couldn't scratch. Finally, he made me up into a package,—*me!* —a live, old-he mountain devil! And he strapped me onto his back, just as if I had been an old smoked ham. Oh! It makes me angry even now to think of the indignity of it."

"But I came mighty near to winning out, after all. Yes, sir, I did. You see, as soon as Charlie backed me like that, and started out with me, stumbling over the trail, and fighting his way along, I quietly set to work to get free. And believe me, I kept right at it. At last I got one front paw sufficiently free that I could reach the thongs that bound my jaws together. Instead of scratching Charlie with those claws, I just worked on my head-gear.

"By and by, those thongs began to loosen up, and I decided that when I got my head free, I would seize Charlie by the back of his neck, and kill him if I possibly could. And I figured that even if I failed to kill him at once, by chewing his neck, I would disable him so badly that I would have a fine chance to complete my escape.

"Well, sir, just then a mighty queer thing happened. Something or other warned Charlie of danger! Suddenly he threw off his shoulder straps, and with an awful jolt dumped me upon the frozen ground. He did it just at the very instant I got my jaws free! Wasn't that queer? With my jaws all free and ready for business, Charlie looked at me, and I looked at him, and I don't know which one of us was the most surprised.

" 'Well, you son-of-a-gun!' said Charlie, panting for breath. 'You nearly got me, didn't you!'

"I was so surprised, and so disappointed, that just then I couldn't say anything. When Charlie again set to work to tie up my jaws, I just lay still and took it. I saw that the man was bound to win.

"Oh, yes, Charlie carried me on down to the cabin all right, and he kept me there until Mack Norboe, his partner, got back from Michel. Then they set to work with their axes, cut tough tips of dead Jack pines, and made a strong cage for me. In that rough cage they carried me out on their shoulders, five miles, to the wagon trail,; and it was an awful job. From there I was hauled in to Michel, and here I am.

"Do I wish I had bitten off those two toes, and escaped from the trap? Yes, I do. Life on Avalanche Creek beats this dull place. I don't care for people, and I'm never allowed to kill anything. . . . But I'll escape yet, and when I do, believe me, there will be one busy day here."

. . . .

No, he did not escape. He finally settled down in his spruce log lean-to, with an open yard in front of it, and after having in his own picturesque person shown about

THE BAD WOLVERINE'S OTHER SIDE 49

5,000,000 New Yorkers what a Rocky Mountain Wolverine looks like he died in his bed, and was sent to the American Museum to be translated to a state of perpetuity behind plate glass, where the wicked cease from troubling.

THE SECRETARY BIRD SHOWS HOW HE KILLS SNAKES

TAKE it physically, mentally or morally, and from whatever angle you please, you will find that the Secretary Bird is the champion queer bird of all Africa. Also, if Mother Nature did not build and equip him for the special job of destroying poisonous snakes, then why is he?

Consider him now as he proudly marches about in his private park. Is he not a spectacle? He is so queer that no bird amateur can place him without help. He stands high up on very long and slender legs; but he is neither crane nor heron.

He is an outlandish and unbelievable *ground hawk!* He stands four feet high, he loves Mother Earth, and he seldom leaves her for long. He lives upon the ground, and eats snakes! As a snake-killer, Rikki-Tikki-Tavi has nothing whatever on him! He is good for the deadly whip-like mamba, the plethoric puff-adder, the black cobra, rattlesnake and copperhead; but we would hesitate about entering him in a fight with a king cobra. As a killer and eater of rats, which he beats to death with his feet, and swallows whole, he deserves the freedom of every city and town in the civilized world.

A view of the front elevation of this rare bird is rather startling. The legs are fastened to the body much too far apart for grace and aplomb, but they are all right for poise and action. Viewed from the side, the Secretary is handsome enough for all practical purposes; and the quill pens over his ears, pointing backward, are very jaunty. It is because of this reminder of an English "clark," or eke a secretary, that his given name was bestowed.

The legs stand very high and they are much more respectably dressed than those of some people we have seen. The hardy American "bathing beauty" (who sometimes really bathes?) completely outstrips him in the race for the public eye. Now he wears black velvet knee-breeches, a nice gray coat with a claw-hammer tail effect, and the pert and jaunty side-plumes to his head fairly rival those of the harpy eagle.

It is a pity that the Secretary Bird is so rare a visitant to our shore; but as a foreign celebrity he is great. Soon after our first pair arrived, and settled down in their grass-grown front yard, I went to call upon them at lunch time. In principle, such a call is always a misdemeanor, and previous to that one I was not guilty; but that one was a special case.

"Hello, Mr. Secretary," said I glibly, as became a man accustomed to the society of cabinet officers. "Did you bring me some notes from the veldt?" (This was meant as a joke.)

"Of course you know," said the Secretary quite seriously, putting his quill pen carefully over his right ear, point foremost, "that I have only just now arrived from Cape Town, U. S. A. . . . No, that does not stand for the U. S. of America. It's Union of South Africa. However, I can offer you a note on the new Kruger National Park. . . . Ah! I thought that would intrigue you."

"It interests me; but it does not intrigue me any. Up here, we refuse to be intrigued. But do produce your note on that Park. I'm sold on it in advance."

"All right, then. Now listen." And then he read the following:

"The Kruger National Park is not yet a going concern. It's born, but it can't walk yet. It needs $35,000 a year from America. It contains more and handsomer big game animals than you white folks ever saw. It's got 500 lions, and they are needed to keep down the surplus of zebras. It has buffaloes, elands, sable antelopes, waterbucks, kudus, gemsbucks, wildebeests, kongonies and——"

"Yes, yes," I interposed. "They are all there, and America ought to do something right now to cheer up the Union of South Africa about making that animal wonderland available. It's a whale of a big place, you know. . . . Have you got any notes on the ostrich-feather industry of South Africa?"

"No. The ostrich business is down and out, killed by that huzzy Fashion, who hangs out in Paris to make guys of women and girls all over the world. 'No more ostrich plumes' was her order, and out they went; but that can't last forever. Aha!" continued the Secretary with animation. "Here comes our luncheon. Do you wish to see us eat?"

"Righto. Please do your best."

"Well, our meals here are all right. Now, here comes one of your pilot black-snakes—a big and bad tree-climber that lives on little birds whenever the nesting open-season is on. Now watch me, and I'll show you

THE SECRETARY BIRD.

"Have you any notes on the ostrich-feather industry of South Africa?"
"No. The ostrich business is down and out, killed by that huzzy Fashion."

what some people would like to have us do to all bad snakes."

A small but bad pilot blacksnake—and truly a persistent nest-robber—was flung into the middle of the yard. At once the Secretary Bird nimbly stalked up to it, and sized it up. He maneuvred to a position within a foot of the snake's head, and the snake struck at him. The bird dodged, and gave way slightly. The snake grew angry, and swiftly struck, again and again. The Bird jumped sideways and avoided. He held his wings slightly open, to aid his movements.

Presently the blacksnake turned, to crawl away from the Bird. Then the Bird darted forward, and with astounding quickness lifted high his right foot and brought down a smashing blow upon the serpent's head.

The snake was severely jolted, but moved out to defend himself when bang! came another blow—and in mighty quick succession two or three more. Each one landed upon the snake's head. Both the method and the execution were wonderful. The serpent never recovered from those fierce, banging blows with a big, bony foot that was like a club. Presently the Bird seized the snake by the head, gripped it firmly in its powerful beak, and between beak and feet stretched all the kinks out of the serpent. It was the queerest action I ever saw with a snake.

And then, starting in at the head, that amazing bird began to swallow that snake,—whole! And when these birds kill rats, by beating them to death with their feet, they swallow them whole, also.

From that moment I have wished for a Secretary

Bird as a household pet, for the benefit of our rat-killing industry. More than that, I would like to see a pair of them on each farm, and in every cellar, in America. Is it not a pity that they are so expensive, and so hard to come by?

My wish that every country home might have a Social-Secretary Bird as a household pet is not idle pleasantry. I mean it. In some parts of Africa it is a common thing for them to be kept by the farmers as pets, and the birds take kindly to that part. They are voracious eaters, and devour meat, bread, vegetables and fruit of approved kinds, eggs, and all the chicks they can catch that are small enough to swallow.

THE BIG ORANG TELLS HIS STORY

FOR twelve cold seasons I have been the Official Orang of this Zoo. My flat, expanded cheeks show you that I am no fresh kid. Happy? Well, yes, I am. Only a few people in this crazy human jungle have rooms as large, well-lighted, well-ventilated and carefully heated as this one of mine. It was built to make me comfortable, not merely to rent for $30 or $40 a month, and "your money or your life."

I was born in a big nest of green branches in the top of a young tapang tree, on the shore of Padang Lake, in the territory of the white Rajah of Sarawak, Borneo.

My father's face was thirteen inches wide, and he was a fighting giant. Yet, believe me, we had our full share of enemies and trouble. We were afraid of big snakes, bears and clouded leopards. Always and always, even in the treetops, we were afraid of those naked brown men of the jungle. Sometimes they brought white men with fire-sticks to roar at us and bring us crashing down. More often the brown men chopped down our trees, killed our old ones and caught the orang boys and girls and babies alive. But once they caught a mother and her baby; and right there was where I came in.

When I was a very little chap my mother got so tired of feeding me on nothing but milk that one day she took me across her hip, and started on a trip through the treetops to a mangosteen tree that she knew about. It was

THE ORANG–UTAN.

"When I was a very little chap my mother took me across her hip, and started on a trip through the tree-tops to a mangosteen tree that she knew about."

about time for the fruit to get ripe, and mother just had to take a chance. That was a hard trip for her, hungry as she was, and all run down. But I helped by clinging to her body hair, leaving her arms free.

She swung and swung, under miles of big branches; and in crossing from tree to tree it was awfully scary and dangerous. At last we came to a little Dyak field in the forest; and a very good mangosteen tree stood out at one edge of it. Mother said afterward that tree was left that way just as a trap, to catch some of us.

Well, mother was leery about that lone tree, with only one small jungle connection; but we were desperately hungry, the mangosteens looked good enough to eat, and she decided to risk it. The fruit was ripe and mighty good; and daylight came and found us there, still eating. It was my first good feed of ripe fruit.

And then a terrible thing happened. A lot of those light-brown Dyak men suddenly got between our tree and the jungle, cut off our retreat and made us prisoners in that one treetop. Then they went to work like bees, with their vicious little axes, to cut down our tree!

Yes, we were scared; but what could we do? At last, down crashed our tree. It hit with a tremendous wallop on the rough floor of the clearing, knocked the breath out of poor mother and kept her from fighting. She was too tired to put up a big fight; but, even if she had fought ever so hard, she would have been killed.

As it was, mother was mastered, and so quickly bound hand and foot that she had to give up. The Dyaks thought they had done a terribly big thing in catching a mother orang alive and unhurt, and to their village

THE BIG ORANG TELLS HIS STORY

many, many Dyaks came to see us. When they looked at mother, some of them said, "Chut! She will die."

But my mother loved me so much that I kept her alive! Yes; it was very odd. Instead of despairing, and refusing food and fighting for death, for my sake she ate plenty of fruit, especially bananas, and finally boiled rice. I, too, began to eat every kind of food that mother did; and when the Dyaks built a big bamboo cage for us and put us into it, I declare we were quite comfortable. Mother didn't seem to care what happened as long as I was with her.

After a long time, when we were settled down, a round-faced man with a light yellow skin and a long, long braid of black hair, came to our village. He made a deal for us, and by great labor took us in a small, new traveling cage to the town where the white Rajah lives, in a white Astana. There we were put on a big, black boat, taken out on a smooth warm sea, and in two days landed in a flat and rainy city where there are many men who have go-downs and compounds, and buy and sell all kinds of wild animals, beautiful birds and big snakes. They called it Sing-a-poor, or something like that.

We were left in a compound yard, under a shed, surrounded by cages upon cages of monkeys, savage cats, tapirs, wild hogs, squirrels, big birds, little birds, good and bad birds, pretty birds and ugly birds, and the biggest snakes you ever saw! Out in the middle of the yard were great, gray, wrinkled wild-animal mountains, to us strange and terrible, with a tail at one end and a big gray snake-like thing at the other. We never learned their name. What do you think they were?

Men came from everywhere to buy and take things away from that compound. Mother never knew there were so many different kinds of men in the world, black, brown, yellow, and white. One day a big white man came to our cage, and our yellow man hopped around lively to show him what we looked like.

"Take him out," said the white man.

Our yellow man carefully reached in and took me out, and put me down on the stone floor. I whimpered—because I was scared stiff, and I looked at the ring of queer faces far above me, to see if I could find a friendly one. When I looked up at the big white man, he looked down at me, right at my eyes, and to me he looked good. I ambled up to him, and climbed up one of his long legs, clear to his breast, where I stopped and hung on by his shirt. At once he put his arms around me, and began to laugh.

"Well, you funny little tyke," sezzee, and laughed loudly.

I liked him from the first.

"I'll take this little fellow," he said, "but not the big one. She won't live long."

I held out one hand toward my mother, because I was scared; and I asked for her.

"Noh, noh, noh!" cried my Chinaman. "No can! No can take loose! Baby go,—mammy awlight! She no die quick."

Finally, the tall white man bought both my mother and me, and many other beasts, birds and snakes. He crowded us all into one big room in a ship, and we rolled

THE BIG ORANG TELLS HIS STORY

and pitched, and were sick. At last, with everybody quite tired out, we came to this big place—swarming with ships, and people and noise.

Straight to this big palace we came, and oh, my! what a relief it was to get here! We were washed in warm water in a tub, our hair was combed and brushed, our teeth were cleaned and we were given deep beds of clean soft straw. It was wonderful.

Mother and I were adopted by two of the kindest men we ever had seen. There was nothing they wouldn't do for us. They gave us this lovely big room, with a big, black devil as our next door neighbor, and we had food as good as folks get.

"Give them a rich Irish stew twice a week. It will do them good," said a worried-looking man. And, oh, man! That stew was good! We all get it regularly.

By and by warm weather came. And then we were let out, into a cage outdoors, so big that we seemed to be free; and before us was a beautiful green jungle! It was wonderful. Then an artist white man came and painted a picture of mother and me.

All that was years and years ago, when I was nothing but a little red-haired orang-utan baby. I grew fast, and mother lived a good long time; but finally she went to sleep and never woke up; and then she was taken away.

Yes, they say I am the largest one in captivity. If there is one anywhere else larger than I am, or happier than I am, or with wider cheeks, I would just like to have his name and post office address.

Do I ever wish I was free again and back in Borneo?

Not on your life. The place where the wicked cease from troubling is right here.

What's that? The most interesting occurrence since I came here? Why, it was those things that I was taught to do in public, to show how much I know. It was you, yourself, who started it, and worked up the show. Don't you remember how I learned in four lessons how to ride a tricycle? I could go anywhere on a level. And then those roller skates. How I loved to dash around on Baird Court with them! You don't let me do it now, and I think it is because you are afraid I would get gay, and either bite a scared visitor, or run away. Honestly. I would do none of those things. I'm not looking for trouble as men are.

And then there was that table stunt. How the crowds did enjoy it! And so did I. I put on that keeper's uniform, and those socks and shoes, and then climbed up the step-ladder to the high platform where the table was. I climbed into my chair and sat down, opened my napkin, and tucked a corner of it in my neck, and I ate with my knife just like other men. I handled my fork and spoon correctly, poured tea, drank from a teacup, ate my sliced bananas with a fork, and used a tooth-pick *most* politely.

No; I am not allowed to smoke cigarettes, because it might lead the other apes and monks into bad habits. But honestly, I could have smoked, just as correctly as any clubman or flapper in this town. I like acting. It is so easy to amuse idle people.

There; that is all. Now I will make up my bed, and have my noonday nap.

THE BIG PYTHON EXPLAINS HIS MISTAKE

AND speaking of snakes, here is a snake story that happened to me; but I expect no one save my very best friends to believe it. Had I not seen it, I would not believe it myself.

When I was a barefooted country boy about eight years old, one hot day in midsummer I had occasion to walk all alone along the dusty wagon-track of a country lane. Suddenly, and prompted by no cause whatever, this strange idea popped into my small head:

"I'll just take a real *long* step!"

With no pause to reason why, I promptly did so.

As I stepped out nearly a foot farther than usual, I hope to die if a garter snake didn't start from the dusty grass at the right hand side of the road, and wildly wriggle across it, *between my bare feet!* And now no one will believe it; but it is as true as the Gospel according to St. John.

Many times since that day, when in really snaky jungles I have wished hard that other snakes would wriggle between my feet; but none ever have done so. I have been disappointed, surprised, and finally disgusted by the scarcity and the absence of snakes, little and big, from the places where snakes should have been. This has bred in me so colossal a feeling of contempt for wild snakes that in the rattlesnake sage-brush of Montana, the cobra country of India and the bushmaster jungles of South America, I have lain me down to sleep with no more thought of hostile snakes than if they were nonexistent. I regret to say that, to the best of my knowledge and belief, real snake adventures in the jungles of this world are almost as rare as angels' visits. All the snake-bite accidents with which I ever came in touch had happened to men who were fussing with captive snakes.

If you let wild snakes alone, the chances are that they will return the compliment. Do not try to catch and "handle" venomous wild snakes, unless you thoroughly know how, and have at hand the means with which to take first money. "Like to like, as the devil said to the collier, and every sow to her own trough."

Owing to the difficulties that lie in the path of Observation, mighty little is known of the minds and manners of snakes. The wild snake is keenly anxious about his getaway, and the human who all suddenly blunders close up to one is equally anxious about his. Unless the big stick is present, usually they meet only to part pronto.

On the whole, the very best place in which to study the intelligence and the reasoning powers of snakes is in a large and well-stocked reptile house,—the keepers of which are not "afraid" of snakes. The very first fact that you learn there is the wonderful pacifism of nearly all the serpents of the world, except the blasted vicious cobras. With most other snakes, you can put dozens or scores into one cage together, and be amazed by the absence of bullying, quarrelling and fighting. Far better than the men of this world, the snakes know that peace promotes long life and happiness, and that war is all that General Sherman said it was.

After I had watched seven of our men patiently peel 22 feet of dead and dry skin off our biggest and newest Malay Python, because to save his soul he couldn't shed the old coat himself, I had a lot of new respect for snake thought and reason. He was only six weeks out of the jungle of the Malay Peninsula, and the last four of them had been spent in a tight box, with only one pailful of friendly water to keep his skin moist.

Through a crack at the rear door of his spacious Reptile House apartment, (with a private bath), I once got close up to him; and after a patient half an hour he gave me the high sign.

"How did you feel, Krimp, before the peeling?" I said, feelingly.

Krimp breathed deeply,—ever so deeply; and eight feet of him swelled out like a flat tire that is going up on free air.

"I felt as if I were in a coil of tin pipe that was four sizes too small for me."

"My word! You must have been some uncomfortable."

" 'Uncomfortable' was it? It was like war."

There was a long pause. The longer the snake, the slower it thinks. At last, being stumped like, I said, "Well?"

"Yes. And when your savages blinded me by squirting that cold water into my face, and then grabbed hold of me and straightened me out, I thought I was surely going to be killed and eaten right there. But where in the world did you ever find all the men that I see around here?"

"They spring up just like asparagus. But our reptile men were rather nice to you, were they not?"

"The best ever! They were wonderfully skilful."

"After a little while you lay as still as a sick lamb."

"Yes. As soon as I saw that they were not going to kill me, I gave up. That was all that I could do to help them. I'll never fight your men again."

"I say, Krimp. Just how was it that you were caught?"

"Well, sir, it was all done by what men call an 'accident.' A Malay pirate named Lamu Din had a little hut, a garden and a pig-pen away off in the heart of the Big Black Jungle of Selangor. He had his own reasons for not wanting to see people. All around his hut and his clearing he built a tall fence of peeled poles, to keep out all of the jungle folk. To keep out the tigers and the sambar deer he built it seven feet high, and sharpened the stakes at the top. It annoyed the tigers a lot. The best of them could manage to jump and climb over it, and hastily eat a little pig inside; but no tiger could jump out with a big pig in his mouth."

"But how did any of that keep you out?"

"Well, he set the stakes so close together that he thought I couldn't find a crack big enough to let me in. It was a foolish idea, don't you think? A snake that has had no food for a long time can slip through almost any native fence. It is wire-netting and glass that gets our goat. I'm dead against their use; and both ought to be prohibited by law."

THE REGAL PYTHON.

"Well, I swallowed that pig, right in the pen; and I forgot all about the small crack by which I squeezed in. Then morning came, and Lanu Din the Malay had me."

"I quite agree with you,—that is, from the snake point of view. But *how* did you get caught,—smart as you are?"

"Not having made a big catch in a long time, I grew very thin. Then I went to Lamu Din's place, and easily found a place where I could squeeze through between two stakes. One dark night I went in. The pigs and the chickens close by made a great row, but I picked the biggest and best shoat that I could find, and ate it."

"How much did it weigh?"

"Not nearly so much as a big old jungle pig. The biggest python has to hump himself to swallow one of those old rounders."

"Did you swallow it alive?" I asked, for a rise. It came quickly.

"Certainly not. How can *you* ask such a question? I killed it very quickly, by squeezing it in my coil. When I fling just two turns of my body around a pig, it is quickly dead. We rarely swallow anything alive. For the animal, it is all over in a minute. There are no snakes or tigers in our jungle who eat things alive. The idea is horrible,—to a humane snake. But we must eat, you know; and the jungle people must be kept down, or there would be no living with them."

"What do you think of our plan, of killing the food animals before serving them?"

"That is perfectly satisfactory to us snakes; but really we pythons and the boa constrictors can kill our food just about as quickly as your men can kill it for us. Did you ever see a big python throw his coils?"

THE PYTHON EXPLAINS HIS MISTAKE

"Yes,—once. That was quite enough for me. But we never let visitors see it."

"Why not?"

"It is wrong to exhibit crime or cruelty in public. Its effect on the public mind is bad. But I say, Krimp. You have not yet told me how you were caught."

"Oh, yes. Well, I swallowed that pig right in the pen; because I *couldn't* carry it away. And I forgot all about the small crack by which I squeezed in. Now, that pig swelled up a bunch on me as big around as your body; and it surely did feel good. My biliary dux, my pancreas, and my uric-acid generator went to work on it right away. But morning came; and Lamu Din. Then I roused up and tried to slide out; but gosh! I could as easily have gone through the eye of a needle as through the crack by which I came in. The Malay had me. So after a hectic half hour I gave up, and let him noose me, and drag me into a box that he seemed to have all ready. . . . I have a horrible suspicion that Malay pirate had done that trick before. I think that all such bandits and hold-up men should be suppressed by law, don't you?"

"To us, Krimp, they are a sort of necessary evil."

"Well, anyhow, through him, and a Chinaman, and Singapore, and Captain Collier and the *Mogul*, I landed here. And really, I might have gone farther and fared worse."

WHAT MAKES THE WILD GOOSE WILD AND TAME

I

THE UNSQUARE DEAL

"Vainly the fowler's eye
Might mark thy distant flight to do thee wrong,
As, darkly seen against the crimson sky,
Thy figure floats along."

"All day thy wings have fanned
At that far height, the cold thin atmosphere,
Yet stoop not, weary, to the welcome land,
Though the dark night is near."
—BRYANT.

ONCE upon a time when the Zoological Park was quite new, we gave the freedom of our Wild-Fowl Pond to a nice flock of Canada Geese. To discourage that flock from migrating north to the Hudson Bay country, as our first pair did in early spring, literally before our horrified eyes, its members were skillfully pinioned. They took possession of the pond, declared that it was good, settled there, and went to housekeeping.

One bright Sunday forenoon in the next period of bird migration southward, out of the sky from the north there came a V-shaped flock of eight honkers, cheerfully honking their "All's-well" as they flew along over our tree-tops. Our birds heard them coming, and called to them. They said:

"Ah-honk! All's well down here, too! No guns! no traps! nothing mean! Good food and good society. Ah-honk! Come on down. The water's fine!"

Their lingo was just as plain as print; and after sailing two circles around that pond, steadily dropping lower in their beautiful spiral, I'm blest if those eight birds didn't land on the level ground on the east side of the pond, close to our own flock.

Then followed considerable conversation between the strange geese and ours; and because you easily can guess the nature of it, I need not follow it up. Our geese invited the strangers to stay and take pot luck with them; and the strangers said they would consider it.

Now, rather near to those two bunches of geese stood a big wire cage, the size of a moving van, but seemingly as innocent and harmless as a hay-rack. Because our bird men wished to catch some ducks, to pinion them, there was a lure of shelled corn at the bottom, and the drop door at one end was up, and all set!

The visiting geese were hungry, for that was before their devoted friend, Jack Miner, had started his wonderful Wild Goose Road House, at Kingsville, Ontario. Of that I will tell you something later on in this chapter.

Those eight geese went into that trap for corn and while they were having the time of their lives, somebody pulled the string and caught the whole flock. They were in that trap-cage the remainder of that Sunday, and early the next morning I called to see them. At first they were horribly frightened at being caught, thinking they would all be killed for the game-market down on Canal Street.

"You don't understand," said I to the big, old fighting gander, who surely was the leader, and the most upset. "You are not to be killed! No one would harm a feather of you, except that little wing-tip that will be taken off to put you beyond the reach of the temptation to fly away from us. We wish you to stay here, and cheer and instruct the cliff-dwellers of New York. Now, are you willing to talk a bit for publication?"

"Oh, yes. We have nothing to conceal: and we have some grievances to register."

"Good! Now speaking of grievances, Honker, tell me: Just what is it that makes the Wild Goose wild?"

"Honk! Ah-honk! Truly, I'll be glad to tell you," cried the leader, and at that the other geese gathered around and lent their ears. *"We are wild about the cruel way in which we are deceived and killed by men like you!"*

This hit me hard; for I was no goose hunter whatever, and I had a perfectly good alibi. However, to avoid interrupting a good interview I wisely said nothing about it. We must not be too finical about protecting our egos.

"Tell me all about that. It will be news to millions of friendly people."

"Well, sir," said Honker, coming close up to the netting. "We're all down on the use of *live geese as decoys.* to help bum sportsmen to kill geese. You just ought to know what is being done in Massachusetts, and Virginia, and North Carolina, and Florida. Why, some men keep live geese to hire out by the day, for decoys. We call those men Hessians!"

THE CANADA GOOSE.

"Speaking of grievances, Honker, tell me: What is it that makes the Wild Goose wild?"

"We are wild about the cruel way in which we are deceived and killed by men like you."

"Where is the worst of it done?" I inquired with some hesitation, for Honker's complaint had made me some ashamed and sore. And really, I could *not* defend the live-decoy practice, now very common.

"Well, the worst of it is done in Massachusetts, around Duxbury, for instance. Have you ever seen what the goose-hunters do there?"

"I am glad to say I have *not!*" said I, boldly; but the next instant I felt secretly ashamed, because it had been very fully reported to me in writing, *by a Duxbury man!*

"Well," said Honker, "those fellows have studied and bought land, and built things for years, all to get the best of us. Their 'blinds' are really tight board fences, built hundreds of feet long, to connect with their club houses; and they are cut full of narrow holes so that the sportsmen can shoot through them at the geese that happen to swim close to shore, or come upon the shore itself, only a *few yards* away! They keep flocks of live geese, in pens, and they send them out on the water, with a long string tied to one leg of each goose.

"They let those decoy geese swim away out, in natural formation, and those tame birds honk and honk, to fool the wild geese, and call the flocks down to them. When a wild flock 'lights among the decoys, the decoys are slowly pulled back to shore, until they get close up, and then, through those holes in the fence the sportsmen turn loose a big volley *at close range!* Then the slaughter is awful!"

"Shocking! Most unfair! Most unethical!" I exclaimed hotly enough.

"Unfair, is it? Then wait for the next one; for I haven't told you the worst. In the fall those same men keep with them at their goose slaughter-pens, (for that is what they really are!) *flocks of goslings just old enough to fly;* and then turn them loose, and make them fly out over the water for short distances and back again, to fool the wild flocks that can't be fooled by the old live decoys. What do you think of it?" angrily demanded Honker.

His black eyes glared at me; and several of the geese around him opened their beaks, thrust them forward in fighting position, and hissed at me.

"Both in principle and practice," I stormed out, "it is not fair. The men who do it ought to reform. Everybody else will say so. You just wait and see if they don't."

But, thank heaven, there are a few men who do just the reverse of the live-decoy "hunters"; as the next interview will show you.

II

A SQUARE DEAL

Did you ever stand all alone on a vast virgin prairie of the West, with not a steer, a horse or a fence in sight, and see flocks of migrating wild geese cleave the sky in V-shaped formation, on their way south in the fall? Have you ever heard aloft and far distant, that first faint "Honk" that fixes attention to the sky, before the brave winged voyagers came in sight?

Have you never been thrilled by a huge flying V of wild geese—mixed black, white and gray—sailing as straight as a ship through a boundless ocean of blue? Every now and then the members of the flock talk briefly to each other, do they not? The old leader says:

"Ah-Honk? How is it? How goes it back there?"

And the medley of voices replying, says,

"Honk! A-honk! All's well! Doing fine!"

And then, as you turned your face squarely up to the sky, and the well-drilled formation purred over you with machine-like synchronism of wing-beats, were you not thrilled and awed? I warrant that this was your mental question:

"Who gave those wonderful birds all that wisdom? And who shows them their way through the uncharted skies, through thousands of miles of unerring flight?"

> "He who, from zone to zone,
>   Guides through the boundless sky thy certain flight,
> In the long way that I must tread alone,
>   Will lead my steps aright."

Wise birds! Brave birds! Wonderful birds!

—And yet! There are millions of men with guns who see nothing in a wild goose save a bird to be killed—somehow; brought crashing to earth as a poor, dead thing, and hung up in a perfectly legal daily string of eight big, heavy carcasses, from the shoulders of the one Man-With-a-Gun.

"Honk, sir! Ah-honk. I greet you," said an old Mother Goose, coming straight up to me and looking me

JACK MINER'S WILD-GOOSE SANCTUARY.

fearlessly eye to eye at a distance of only seven feet. And she was nominally a "wild" goose, at that.

"Howdy, old lady," said I, friendly like. "I'm certainly pleased to meet you, and to meet you here is a double joy."

We met on the gently sloping hinterland of Jack Miner's amazing goose-pond, between his house and his drain-tile factory, near Kingsville, Ontario, fourteen miles northeast of Detroit. For three years I had been trying to get there in the goose, duck and swan migrating season.

"Isn't this place just wonderful!" exclaimed Mother Goose.

"It is all that," said I, "and much more. As an object lesson to men who have both brains and hearts, it is a world-beater."

Close around us lay hundreds of ears of corn. The five acres of open ground surrounding the pond were fairly paved with it. And those same acres were garnished with about 2,000 wild geese, leisurely feeding and visiting, or else just resting on the ground. On the surface of the pond there floated, like so many stuffed geese on a glass pond in a museum case, about 500 more geese—more or less.

And the big joke of it all was—all those lazy, luxuriating, perfectly fearless geese were all classable as "wild!" A little queer, is it not?

"Do you know how Friend Jack did all this?" asked Mother Goose, edging a little nearer to me.

"Well, no—that is, not from your point of view. How do you figure it out, anyway?"

"In the first place," said Ma Goose, pointing one wing at me for accentuation, "Friend Jack knows us birds—better than any other living man does, or ever did. He has an enormous heart, but not one selfish muscle in his whole body. Then, too, in all this giving away of thousands of dollars of Jack's money in corn for us to eat, he has been backed up all along by the most wonderful wife and son that ever happened. Ah-honk! I mean every word of it."

"Goosie, I subscribe to everything you say; because I know it, also!"

"But," pursued the keen old Bird, "the gaining of the confidence this-a-way of the whole wild goose population of eastern North America was not as easy as falling off a log. No siree! Ah-honk, not! Friend Jack worked for years with tame geese on this pond, and corn on shore, to induce the wild flocks to believe that he was Genuine! Slowly at first, very slowly I guess Jack thought, we learned that this man is different from all other men. In this game there are half a dozen rich men who give for bird food a little out of much, but Jack, a poor man, gives too much out of a little.

"And then the geese began to stop here spring and fall—to rest, and fill up on Miner's corn, before going on. Now nearly all the geese of the Atlantic coast come here twice a year. Don't that beat you?"

"Yes, and the corn they eat is something umbrageous," said I, hotly. "The goose and duck hunters of the eastern third of the United States ought to give Mr. Miner $3,000 a year for corn; but all I could get out of them toward a fund of $2,000 a year for three years was a measly $1,400 all told. It was disgusting."

"Ah-honk!" cried Mother Goose, loudly and indignantly. "What d' I tell you? All that the goose-killers want of us is eight dead geese each day, and eight brant, and let the birds get their food when and where they can, or go without it. But now the Canadian government is helping out, and so are two fine Americans in Detroit."

"Yes," I bit off sarcastically, "and Mr. Miner goes around lecturing for money to spend in buying more corn to feed you fellows from Hudson's Bay and Currituck Sound—to provide more 'sport' for goose-killers. That's a great note! But that can't go on forever, mind you. Some day this combination will break down."

At this point Mother Goose posed in the act of listening, looked up at the sky, then stretched her shapely neck skyward and screamed in piercing tones:

"Honk! Ah-Honk! Honk! Honk!"

A perfect chorus of distant "honks" broke out of the sky, and it was answered by a roar of honks from the geese on pond and shore. Mother Goose stretched her neck far up, and joyously beat the air with her wings. And then above the pond there came a sight of sights.

It looked as if a dozen wild goose flocks, all heading for that goose paradise, had suddenly melted together over Kingsville; for here came a mighty flock that contained 500 geese if it had one. I never, never before saw such a sight in bird migration. The air above and below was indescribable. I guess the geese at rest were as much surprised by that huge arrival as we were.

Down swept that great seething wild goose mass. About a third of it alighted on the pond, with a loud splash and dash, and the two-thirds chose the corn-littered shores.

Clearly, many of those geese had been there before; for they never jockeyed for position, nor hesitated for an instant. They just plumped down, into the lap of Affection, Protection and Luxury that the great hearts and strong right arms of two wonderful men and one amazing woman had created out of nothing for God's own wild geese and ducks. And it was given to the birds without the toll of one single drop of blood, or one ounce of meat. Can you believe what I am telling you?

Slowly I faced about, looked toward the modest farmhouse nestling amongst its green trees and shrubs, and took off my hat.

THE LION OF LUXOR

FIFTEEN years ago we kept the Emerson McMillin gift collection of Alaskan heads and horns in the laboratory of the Lion House. During the course of our work upon it, my secretary and I often passed through the full length of the building, and that was what, quite unexpectedly, yielded this incident.

It was during that time that we received from Luxor, away up the Nile, a very superior Barbary Lion. He was big, hairy, dignified, and so handsome in face, form and pelage that the painters and sculptors flocked to him. Twice Rungius painted his portrait, Proctor reproduced him in marble, *12 feet long*, for the McKinley Monument at Buffalo, and Eli Harvey sculped him several times.

His name was Sultan I, and he looked it. You know Sultans are long on dignity. Once when a keeper suddenly found himself (by a bad mistake) in that lion's cage and at close quarters with Sultan, with only a penitentiary broom between them, Sultan proudly refused to seize the opportunity to kill the keeper. The keeper always had been square and kind with him; it was beneath his royal dignity to take a mean advantage of a mistake, and so the old chap just calmly looked at Schwartz, and never even snarled. But if it had been another big lion instead of the man we would have seen something. Once I saw him become enraged against a perfectly innocent felt mat an inch thick, and fiercely tear it limb from limb. We had specially procured it, as a divan for the old lion, to keep him off the hard wooden floor.

It was wholly by accident that Miss Secretary tripped along beside me on that particular morning, notebook and pencil in hand, at the witching hour of eleven-thirty. All the cages were clean, and the lions and tigers and leopards and everything were at parade rest. You know, the doing of morning housework always makes one tired enough to sit down for a few minutes.

We paused in front of Sultan, who posed at ease, in the pose of the Sphinx.

"Isn't he a glorious animal!" exclaimed the lady, glowing with appreciation.

"He is marvellously fine and perfect," said I. "Never before have I seen a lion with so many fine points."

"How I wish we could know all of his history," said the Secretary. "I'm sure it would be most interesting."

"Yes. It is too bad that we cannot secure it."

At this point Sultan turned his face toward us, and looked at us with strange intentness of regard. Then we were astounded by hearing deep and solemn tones, saying:

"I am the Lion of Luxor. I look backward through five hundred generations of desert history."

"Oh, my goodness," excitedly exclaimed Miss Secretary, "I must take down what he says!"

"Do, by all means," said I, "and don't miss a word."

"My home," continued the Voice, "was within sight of the ruined Temple that stands on the west bank of the Nile," said Sultan. "My Saharan ancestors roared in the streets of Carthage within one month after it became a ruin. Toward the far south, my forbears knew all the secrets of Zimbabwe, the wonderful stone city of Rhodesia. My grandsires were the rulers of the deserts of middle Egypt. They saw the stone quarried for the pyramids of Gizeh, and the Sphinx was modeled from one of my great-grandmothers. They knew the quarries of the Mokattam Hills, as I knew the fields of Luxor."

"I say, Sultan!" said I, very gently. "Why did not your people exterminate all the early Egyptians? I think they easily could have done so."

"There was no reason, no incentive. It would have meant a great waste of raw human material, and from the beginning of the Age of Lions we never have killed more food than we could eat, and never wastefully. On the game plains of the poor old Africa of today, each full-grown lion kills only two zebras, or two antelopes, each week. What sense is there in being wasteful? Do we not preserve the balance of Nature, by keeping the hoofed animals down to reasonable numbers?"

"That is all perfectly true. We learned it first from the very keen game-rangers of Kenia and Tanganyika."

"Good!" muttered Sultan. "And you hear very little about the killing of people. After hunting and feeding upon big game, the hunting of men and women seems mighty trivial. It is no sport for kings, I assure you. And then, too, men have so many diseases! That subject is so painful that we lions rarely discuss it, and never when our children are present. Man's troubles in Africa are as numerous and as great as the troubles of

THE LION.

"My grandsire saw the stones quarried for the Pyramids of Gizeh; and the Sphinx was modeled from one of my great-grandmothers."

the wild animals. Would you like to have me tell you something about the future of Africa?"

"Oh, yes! Some of it is very puzzling, and not very satisfactory. Will the big wild animals of Africa all be killed by men?"

"No, not all of them,—until the great End."

"He means the end of the Age of Mammals!" said the Secretary in an awe-struck whisper.

"The bad little tsetse fly is our one last and invincible protector. There are vast regions in which the fly will not permit domestic animals to live. Men cannot keep domestic animals in those regions, nor cultivate the soil without them. Where man cannot live wild animals are safe. Man is our one deadly enemy. The white and the black men soon will be fighting for supremacy and killing one another. When the blacks obtain plenty of guns and cartridges, the great race war will begin, and the game will go. No game can find a retreat where a native hunter cannot follow."

"O, yes they can," I cheerfully broke in. "There are the big game preserves, the sanctuaries you know, wherein wise Africanders are making huge homes, and many of them, just for the game."

"With no shooting allowed?" queried the Sultan, doubtfully.

"Absolutely none! A game refuge wherein any game shooting is permitted is no more a 'sanctuary' than a penitentiary is a sanitarium."

"Well," conceded the Lion of Luxor. "That is a royal idea, and worthy of big men. It will save much African game that otherwise would disappear. But I fear the greed of the Man of Futurity."

"So do I, Sultan. But it is yet possible that a reform may come in time to save something. However, this is a gloomy subject. Did you ever hear of the Man-Eaters of Savo?"

"To be sure I have," said the Sultan, regretfully I thought. "Their evil fame went all over the lion countries of Africa. You know, of course, that our home now exists only in shreds and patches, a little here and a little there. Well, those two wicked lionesses of Savo were a disgrace to our race. The lions of Savo should have stopped them. Those females were poor sports, to a disgusting degree. Just think of killing a lot of poor, ignorant, utterly defenseless blacks one after another, just like shelling beans——"

"Or shooting hungry ducks, on baited waters, with live decoys," spitefully broke in my Secretary, who really knew a lot about the different brands of sportsmanship.

"I have no personal knowledge," said Sultan with dignity, "of anything so trivial and primitive."

"What is your opinion of America?" said I, but my Secretary instantly looked at me, so surprised, and so reproachful, that I was sorry I made the break.

"Well," said his Majesty, reflectively. "I am most surprised by the number of your white and near-white people, and the heterogeneous array of mixed bloods and patchwork nations that they represent. You must have raked them together from the four corners of the earth. Honestly, I never before saw such a human mixture; and as for the babel of tongues,—why, the races of the Sudan are out of all comparison. Lower Egypt must have been like this in the days of the Pharaohs, and the building of the Pyramids."

"How do you like your apartment, Sultan?"

"It is beautiful, and at all times very comfortable, both indoors and out. I will be quite happy here, and live long. Really, I know of nothing in Africa equal to it; but I must admit that these Sundays of yours are rather trying to the nerves. There are far too many egos in this cosmos."

"In a limited sense, Sultan, they are a necessary evil; and we just have to take them as coming all in the day's work."

And then, being crowded away from the rail by a rude avalanche of visitors, we had to pull our freight and seek parking space elsewhere.

THE BIRD THAT LIVES NEAREST TO GOD

FORTUNATE indeed is the person or the personage who knows, and who goes to, places that are more wonderful and instructive than even the wild creatures who inhabit them. Yes; it is possible to find landscapes and floras that eclipse in interest the birds and beasts that occupy them, and call them "home." But for one thing, I could write a most interesting book about "The Summit Dwellers of the Mountains." I do not know half enough about them.

All young people should be taught that there are mountains and mountains. There are a hundred and one different kinds; possibly more. The mountains of the tropics that are heavily forest-clad clear to their summits are good as mass productions, but in details they are impossible. The mountains like the Altai, of huge, rounded and uneventful ridges, are only mildly interesting. It is the naked, steep-sided, bold and insolent mountains, bluffing you and daring you to come on, that are so fascinating you just can't let them alone. When you take a lot of impudent and daring peaks, and garnish them with plunging streams, emerald lakes, lovely patches and blankets of green timber, and rim-rock cornices hanging over all, you have got some mountains worth while.

No person who possesses as much intelligence as a

shepherd dog can fail to be deeply interested in the beasts and birds that "choose to run" in those risky summit homes, and who also have the wit and the industry to spend their winters there, instead of giving up beaten and hiking south every fall. We admire anything that knows how to make good, and hold its fort in the face of the enemy.

Slowly, and one by one, the trained zoologists of the natural history museums are working out the life histories, the haunts and the habits of the summit dwellers of the Rocky Mountains, and of the countries lower down. The subject animals are well worth the effort, and we wish them well.

Only fifty years ago, outside of burned-out countries like Egypt, China and Asia Minor, nearly every square mile accessible to man was found stocked by prodigal Nature with interesting and valuable wild life. But for three things, I would write a thrillingly interesting book about that. Unfortunately, (1) this is the age of Frivolity; (2) the interest of the masses in wild life is now not any more than skin deep, and (3) I would have to pay the printer myself.

Back in the days before the feet of the young men had been dedicated to jazz, I went into a fine sector of the Canadian Rockies, to see what I could see. Our perfectly ideal party scrambled up to the top of Goat Pass, and from that base spread over the landscape. It was glorious. On one never-to-be-forgotten morning, solely to view the landscape o'er, we climbed up to the bald and rock-strewn summit of a peak that rose northward of our tented camp.

And the view was worth it! Below us, the world was unrolled like a map. Go to it, and you will say that the grandeur of that display of mountain peaks, passes and valleys, and its uplift to the soul of man, is overwhelming. I can testify that that sixty-mile wide cyclorama took many kilowatts of conceit out of the storage batteries of at least one member of that party.

And even up there, far above the bed-grounds and sky pastures of the white mountain goats, we found a flock of birds in permanent possession. They were Willow Ptarmigan; and very few people of low altitudes know them personally.

The bald top of the peak, a thousand feet above timberline, was covered with clean and angular broken limestone, and in that field of scrambled rock those birds hid and harmonized so well that it was not until they flew, almost from under our feet, that we discovered them. No wonder the golden eagles pass them by unnoticed.

When flushed, they flew just a few yards, and calmly settled once more. They were amazingly unafraid of us, quite after the fatal manner of the fool-hen. Naturally, we were both interested and excited by those ignorant but trustful dwellers in the clouds, and for a time even Mr. Phillip's Peak was forgotten. At that time, however, there was no chance for a private interview; not in the least; but we laid out a perfectly good plan.

One week later my chance came. I went off all alone for a day with Nature, and lost not a moment in swarming up to the top of the summit of the range between our Avalanche Creek and Bull River. Part of that summit was precisely at timberline, and part was above it;

and on a rounded spot of the latter, to my sincere joy I discovered another flock of ptarmigan.

For that day, even in the presence of killable white goats, my more-or-less trusty rifle was merely so much personal furniture, and no more. On that armistice basis those birds sat still, and permitted me to approach within four feet of the nearest one! Now, was not that a golden opportunity?

"It's all right." I said in my velvet voice, "I wouldn't hurt one of you for anything."

"Well then, tell us why you have come to us?" said a low voice from the flock.

"It is solely to meet the birds that choose to live up here, nearest to the Great Unseen Power that men call God. This is the most like holy ground of any that I ever trod. The sins of this world seem far below. I feel a moral uplift."

"We cannot live down below," solemnly said the voice. "There are too many bad men, bad animals and savage birds that wish to kill us, and eat us. Up here, all is peace, and we are very happy here."

As the biting cold west wind whistled over those broken rocks, and I looked back at the twisted and wind-whipped dwarf pines and cedars, only four feet high, that I had examined only the previous hour, I had to smile at the delightful optimism of those brave birds.

"But surely," said I, "you do not live up here in the dead of winter! It seems impossible. The storms and cold up here must then be something awful."

"Yes, we live on this summit all winter. On that slope over there, there are many little bushes that are just

THE WILLOW PTARMIGAN.

"Yes, we live on this summit all winter. Over on that slope there are many little bushes just loaded with teeney-weeney little huckleberries."

loaded with teeny-weeny little huckleberries. The West Wind keeps the snow from burying them, and we feed upon them all winter long. How fine it is that they were planted there just for us!"

"Well, well!" I said, in wonder. "I saw those little blueberries, and I ate a lot of them; but I was so dull-witted it never occured to me that Nature had planted them there just for you."

"Yes, honestly, she did. We love them, and we love her still more."

"But how do you keep from being seen up here, and killed and eaten, by eagles, and owls and wolverines?"

"Mother Nature has kindly arranged for our safety," said the Voice, with a touch of pride. "In springtime, just before the end of the snow our feathers turn brown, just like these rocks; and when we shelter here in these little rooms, it is impossible for our enemies to see us. In the fall, just before the snow comes, our feathers change back to white, which is our favorite color, you know, and then the snow protects us."

"How perfectly amazing are the ways of Nature!" I said, really to myself.

"What is it to be amazing?" queried the bird.

"I am thinking of the wonderful wisdom and forethought of Nature in caring for her wild children. Under her care, they seem to be secure against destruction—until man, the arch destroyer, comes along with his great array of killing machines, and murder in his heart."

"That is tough on all of us wild ones. Can you not do something about it for us?"

"It's a mighty tough job; and lonesome, too; but I

will go down to the big battle-ground, try once more, and see what else I can do, if anything. But I'm afraid it's all too late."

"Go, man! Go, and do your best, win or lose!"

And with mingled feelings of solemnity and soreness, I slowly picked my way onward over the rugged rocks.

THE KICK OF A WILD OSTRICH

WHEN I visited the Park incognito three weeks ago, upon Audubon Court I heard a distant "hello." Looking, I saw Ostrich-Keeper Snyder in the offing, waving at me, and then running toward me. I hurried to meet him.

"Sir," he said, hastily setting his food-pail at parade rest, "we've got a new Ostrich, a big black fella from South Africa. His mind seems all upset like, and I just can't make out what's the matter with 'im. I wish you would give him the once-over, and see what it is."

To save time, we decided not to take along the Secretary Bird, to record our observations; so we came about, and started for the large Ostrich Corrals at the foot of Antelope Hill, where the new one was hanging out.

He was a whale of a bird for size—black as ink where black he should be; his white wing and tail plumes were spotlessly clean and white, and for a wonder his whole suit of feathers was in fine condition. When we first caught sight of him he was alternately walking and running up, down and across his corral, frequently opening his beak and snapping it together, just like a forgetful lady with her shopping-bag.

"If it's safe to go into his corral, I would like to get a close-up interview," said I. "Out here there are too many people, and I have no standing."

"It's a little chancey," said the Keeper, "but I guess we can risk it, once."

He opened the gate, and we went in; but the country near the gate looked good enough for me. Promptly I took out my loose-leaf note-book, to be ready; and even while I was striking the key-note, the big black fellow ran toward me, truculently, and stopped short at rather close range.

"Look out, sir!" cried the Keeper, "I believe he means mischief." And then—bang! The old bird launched a kick that caught my note-book fairly, sent it flying through the air, and jarred my sore thumb umbrageously.

"You old cuss! What did you do that for?" said I, rather warmly. "You just missed my face. What in time are you kicking about, anyhow?"

As the horrified keeper sprang between us, using strange language, the bird snapped his beak some more, and threateningly backed off a yard or two. Plainly, he was what the boys call "het up" about something.

"I've been wanting to get at a writer!" he hissed, savagely. "I have been aching to get square with you and the others—all of you!"

"What for, you skinny old lunatic? What have I ever done against you?"

"For a hundred years you have been saying that when a wild ostrich is chased, and frightened, he sticks his head into the sand, and thinks that he is hiding so that no one can see him."

"As to me, it's false. I never once said so. I can prove an alibi. I always have known that ostrichs have more sense than that."

"Well, if you didn't say it yourself, others like you

have done so. It's an insult to my whole tribe, and it must stop."

"Shall we go out, Mr. Snyder?" said I, kindly. "I'm afraid my presence is provocative to this noble bird."

"No, I'll fix him. I keep a rake-handle here, and I'll make the old party behave himself. We mustn't give up to the black devil, or there'll be no living with him. He must play our game."

Back ambled the Ostrich to our territory. If anything, he looked more angry than ever; but the poised rake-handle gave him pause.

"Why have you ruined the ostrich business?" snarled the bird.

"I have ruined nothing, you bald-headed fanatic. What's biting you this time?" By then I felt some petulant.

"Clap-clap-clap" went his bill. And "Oom! Oom," he bellowed, way down in his skinny old neck.

"You know, if you know anything, that our ostrich feather business is ruined,—yessir,—ruined! Ostrich farms worth millions have been put out of business. Look at the feather market and the live ostrich market to-day. Flat! And all of us birds are done for, except to look at."

"I know it, confound you," I broke in, "and I'm properly sorry for it. But you needn't blame me for it, even if there are fifteen hundred thousand dollars worth of fine ostrich plumes right here in New York to-day that can't be sold at any price. We fixed things so that the trade in your plumes would not be interfered with. It's the fortune of trade."

THE OSTRICH.

"For a hundred years you have been saying that when a wild ostrich is chased, and frightened, he sticks his head in the sand and thinks that he is hiding so that no one can see him."

"As to me, it's false. I can prove an alibi."

"It is not!" cried the Ostrich. "It's the fault of those blank milliners of Paris, and the copy-cats of New York."

"Oh, come now," said I. "If you crack on like that, people will think you are crazy. Don't talk like that in public. Women will wear anything that originates in Paree, no matter how it looks, nor how they look in it. We can't mend that, and we will just have to bear it the best we can, until the next change comes. Cheer up! That Paris Fashion huzzy may to-morrow order up dresses trimmed with ostrich feathers, and send your ostrich-farm stock right up to the peak."

"Never. We are done for."

"Well, then, what is the matter with wild life on the veldt?"

"Nothing in it any more. The hyenas now are making a special drive at our eggs and chicks, and where those ugly brutes are plentiful I give you my word that only one wild nest out of every ten escapes alive. The farmers are not feeding or protecting us as they did in the days when we were valuable. The lions are killed too much, and the zebras not enough. Up north the zebras are increasing too much, and eating up too much ostrich grass. Something has got to be done about those surplus zebras. They are a nuisance to the farmers."

"Do not the sportsmen kill them any more?"

"Yes, but not half as much as they should. Sportsmen never kill what you want them to. You ought to give us homes on your wild lands here in America."

"You couldn't stick it in winter. You lack feathers

and fat. In America the best ostrich country is in the big zoos."

At that the black one lowered his head, bowed his neck down, and silently walked away, as if thinking.

TWO SAGE GROUSE FLOCKS ENTERTAIN VISITORS

I

MONTANA

I HAVE so liked and admired the big and handsome Sage Grouse, or "Cock-of-the-Plains," that eight years ago I worked overtime trying to induce eight western legislatures to pass new laws protecting those birds in their different home states, for five years. Five of those states rose to the occasion, and made good, but now I have a horrible fear that some of them may have fallen from grace so far as to again permit some killings.

Early on a certain crisp October morn not so very long ago, I rode Easter Lily out northward from our Montana camp at the ruins of LU-bar ranch house, (of blessed memory!), toward the Hell Creek badlands. It chanced that I started out alone, and slowly rode ahead of the outfit, in order to commune for a half hour with the sage-brush and the big short-grass country, and have a good, long think. We were right in the heart of the range that only a short time previously had been the home of the buffalo millions of the great northern herd.

While riding along the dim wagon-trail, meandering across a flat that was handsomely planted with sage-brush, I came full upon a flock of twenty-four "sage-hens," as the cowboys call them. They were slowly and majestically marching through the sage-brush, and crossing the trail. They saw me; and I took stock of them. To my surprise the flock did not at once explode into the air, beat the ozone to a froth with its wings, and heavily speed away for safety. "How very queer!" thought I.

Just as an experiment, I slowly rode forward, and finally arrived within *thirty steps* of the flock. Then those birds just calmly stopped, and looked at me; and it was so astonishing that I almost fell off my horse. I drew rein, stopped, and for minutes just sat there spellbound, gazing at those birds, and wishing hard for a camera.

Yes; I had a gun; and I certainly could have shot one or two of them; but what is a *dead* bird worth, anyway, in comparison with a live one? As another experiment I decided to try talking to them.

The sage grouse is by far the largest and the handsomest of all the North American grouse species, being fully twice as large as any other! And he is handsome, too. His black, white and gray colors just compel you to admire him. And then the poise and carriage of him! Why, each of those twenty-four birds posed and strutted as if he, or she, were as proud as any old Lucifer.

"Tell me, King Bird of the Plains, said I to the leader of the flock, "why are you not afraid of me? I'm armed!"

"I know you. I've seen you before. If you were a cowpuncher or a doughboy (soldier), we wouldn't wait here three seconds. No sir! But since you are yourself, I am stopping to ask you for a square deal, for myself and my people!"

"That's funny!" said I, "I've just been thinking a lot about you fellows. But first tell me what's in that wise old head of yours. Just what is it that you want?"

"*We want the cowboys to stop shooting us up just for fun.* There's mighty little fun in it for them, and none at all for us. Are there *no* men who can look at a bird without wanting to kill it!"

"Migh-tee few, old Bird! And just look what the killers have done to the antelope herds! I've not seen one yet."

"All gone! All gone!" cried the King Grouse. "As you go on north you will see thousands of sheep, and just one lonesome old buck antelope. He's all alone; and you'll see him away off, standing on the top of a butte, watching for his enemies. He's awfully smart about spotting men before they spot him. But for that he would have been killed long, long ago."

"How long have you known him?"

"For more snows than I can tell. The 'lopes used to live on this buffalo-range in thousands. In the early winter they would herd up day by day until there would be valleys full of them. It was fine. And little did I think that I would live to see them all killed but one!"

"Well, what other wild neighbors do you remember?"

"Oh, the buffalo! The buffalo! I never can make anybody understand how many there were, everywhere on this range, all at the same time, covering everything. Thousands of buffalo skulls have been gathered and sold, or you'd see them everywhere. The buffs kept the wolves away from us, sometimes. How big, and black and hairy they were! We learned how to hide our nests

A NORMAL SAGE GROUSE.

"Just what is it that you want?"
"We want the cowboys to stop shooting us up just for fun."

so that they wouldn't trample our eggs in spring, or kill our chicks when they were too young to run. And we just loved their little red calves!"

"And then what happened?" (I knew the answer; but I wanted the Old Bird's point of view. Before answering he slowly turned completely around.)

"Then came those awful, awful men. With big guns they killed and killed, at an awful rate. Then they flayed, and spat, and shouted at each other. Finally the wagons came, and hauled away the hides, leaving all the meat to spoil, or to feed the big gray wolves and the coyotes. It made us sick, sick, sick! Soon, *very* soon, all the buffalo were gone; and none came back. Say, where are they now? Do you know?"

"They are dead, all save a very few that are kept in corrals like cattle. I hate to think of it. But how about elk? Do you ever see any?"

"A very, very few," said the King Bird, reflectively. "I don't seem to remember them very well."

"Of course not. But I think there were some here. I never saw one on the plains myself. Did you ever see a wild mountain sheep?"

"Him with the curling horns?"

"Yes. That's it. How well you remember," said I hopefully.

"I do remember some. They were on the tall bluffs and buttes along the river; and sometimes in the badlands. I'll tell you a secret," he said, with a quick glance at the approaching buggy with old Judy, Mr. Huffman and the camera fixings,—"if you'll promise not to tell."

"Oh, Laton's all right! He'll keep it safe; and we'll not tell the cook."

"Well, there are a few sheep right now in those deep and awful badlands of Hell Creek, farther north! But there's a hunter from Texas up there. He kills wolves, and he may kill those sheep."

"We'll find him, and try to talk him out of it. And——"

But just here Mr. Huffman arrived opposite me, and suddenly stopped.

"Well," he demanded, "who in Time were you talking to, old man? I've been hearing your voice ever since away back yonder. Have you been making a speech to yourself?"

"Oh, no. I've been talking to this big badlands Bird. He's an old-timer, Layton, just like you. He was born just about the time that you discovered Fort Keogh that day at sunset, by its bugle-horn. He has told me a lot about the big game of this country,—what's left of it."

"There go your birds," said Layton. "Perhaps they are suspicious of me. Can't you tell them that I am on the square?"

"I have, old man. But for that they would have quit the flat before you arrived."

At this point the cook drove up with the chuck wagon. Layton went right on:

"Yes, they are fine birds to look at; but they are not fit to eat." As he announced this rather loudly, he looked at me, and winked craftily.

"No," I answered truculently. "They taste too

strongly of the sage-brush leaves that they feed upon. It's a waste of cartridges to shoot them!"

Having thus contributed to the general understanding of the cattle-country regarding the bad flavor of its finest bird, we resumed our trek northward.

II

OREGON

The story of the sage-grouse now shifts abruptly to another stage, and other actors. Please envision, in the far Northwest, the arid and volcanic strand of Lake Warner, in southeastern Oregon. It is a land of lava, antelope, sage-grouse, cattle and sheep; and being remote, it is only the most hardy perennials among artists and bird-men who point out for it, and win to it. But this tale is worth the telling:

"Stealthily and carefully," said Bruce Horsefall, the wonderful wild-bird-and-animal artist, "we picked our way across the mud flat, and finally peered through the bars of a gate in a fence of rough lava rock." The place was in southeastern Oregon, the time was May, 1917.

"There they are!" burst from our lips as we caught the glint of white spots a few hundred yards beyond. In the open and bare flood plain before us, at intervals of twenty-five to fifty feet, were sixty magnificent sage-cocks, strutting around with puffed out chests, and tails

SAGE GROUSE ENTERTAIN VISITORS

spread like miniature turkey-gobblers, making sounds for all the world like the popping of corks on the pier at Atlantic City."

The artist and his comrades had traveled far to see that performance, and on finding the curtain up, and the show actually going on, his heart leaped within him. For a hundred years and more of man's occupancy of Oregon and other lands of the Sage Grouse, that astonishing performance had remained undiscovered by a man qualified to picture it, describe it, and make it clear. We firmly hold that the honor of "discovery" belongs to the man who finds something undescribed and practically unknown, and by means of his wit and his industry first makes it really known to the civilized world. This is precisely what Mr. Horsfall did with the display phenomenon of the great Sage Grouse, or Cock-of-the-Plains.

"Come over here!" softly called the artist to the performer that was nearest him. "Come over here! I want to paint a picture of you."

The feathered egotist paused, struck an attitude registering "Attention," and haughtily exclaimed:

"What for?"

"I want to show how you do it. Be a good sport, and come on over."

The appeal to ego has captured more men and women than birds. For reply the bird reefed his wings, furled his tail, and slowly stalked to close-up distance in front of the gate. The other strutting birds were so hard at work showing off, and wallowing in self-esteem, that the new departure went unnoticed by them.

"Thank you, old chap," said the artist, genially.

"You're real kind, and I'll speak about you to the game warden."

"Game warden? Game warden? Who's that? I never saw one," said the bird a bit peevishly.

"They're the good fellows who keep the Basque sheep-herders from shooting you up. You may not see much of them, but they and their friends on these ranches are on the lookout for your enemies, just the same."

"Well, now that you are really here," said the bird, amiably, "what can I do for you?"

"I'm already making a picture of you," said the busy artist, "and I would like it a lot if you would just give me a benefit performance." (Here the bird registered "suspicion" and "alarm.") "I mean, just show me from start to finish how you do it."

"Oh! All right," said the bird, affably. "I'll oblige you,—seeing that you are making a picture of Me."

At that he bowed deeply to the artist, and raked the bare earth with one foot. Down dropped the flight feathers of his wings, the rest close reefed. Up went his tail, and—whisk! Like the flirt of a coquette's fan, it flew wide open.

Stiffly held in a semicircle, each tail-feather pointed out like a Spanish bayonet spear, all were spaced accurately, and they literally speared 180 degrees of the air. The artist gasped with surprise when he caught the wonderful details of it, and saw for the first time the ray-like radiation and sharpness of those feathers. *Why* had no one pictured it before!

Thus garnished the bird proudly marched in solitary

THE SAGE GROUSE STRUTTING.

procession two or three times across the stage, while the hand of the artist flew like the hands of a lady with many diamond rings knitting in the Subway.

"Fine!" cried the artist. "Go right on, old bird! I'll put you down in history."

"Oh," said the sage grouse, airily, "that's nothing much. Now see me inflate my air-cushion."

Pointing his open beak at the sky, he began to emit a series of polite little grunts, each time pumping in some air. Very soon, on his breast a ghostly shape began to rise; it made the artist think of a rubber tire-tube going up. In quick time there hung from the neck of that strange bird a perfectly amazing air-cooled double-barreled pouch that extended from the neck half-way down to the legs. But pshaw! It is useless to try to describe it in words. Nothing but a picture can give a correct idea of the outlandish and almost impossible Thing that hangs from the neck of a strutting Sage-Cock doing its act.

Finally, with its air-pouch well filled, the bird took a short run, then suddenly stopped, flung its tail wide open and pointing its beak straight upward, threw back its head, and with a forward hunch from the wings, and a toss with the breast muscles, that amazing air-cushion flew up in the air,—and fell back upon the breast with a "plop" just like the drawing of a cork from my neighbor's bottle of booze!

Almost speechless from amazement, both at the stage properties and the performance, the artist cried out:

"Why do you do that? What's the idea? Are you courting the hens?"

"Courting nothing!" sniffed the bird, very scornfully. "This is no mating season. There are no hens here! What do we care for the old hens, anyway!" (Which sounded some disrespectful!)

And then away went the bird on another performance. Viewed from some points, that amazing and ridiculous air-cushion, covered with short white feathers, looked a bit like a white-fox boa worn in a quite new way; but it's lucky that the Man Who Saw could also Draw; for no words on earth can describe it to the seeing point. It takes a Horsfall picture, or a copy of one.

And after all, that Bird never did tell the artist why he did it. On that bare three-acre plain there were about sixty other male Sage Grouse, each one preserving his distance on his own square of ground, and very busily going through with that same air-pumping, strutting, tossing and plopping performance. Mr. Turber, the game warden, said that those birds had assembled from miles around on that one bare and level spot, to strut and carry on in the presence of each other; and they keep it up at intervals "from early in March until the first of June,"—which truly is not the courting season at all.

"Poor as I am," I would give any of those birds a hundred dollars a week for six weeks if he would contract to do that stunt every day in our Zoological Park. Wouldn't you?

A WILD DUCK'S POINT OF VIEW

BELIEVE me, until it is killed, every wild duck that comes into this country in fall or winter leads a dog's life. I hate these United States; and I come here in winter only because I must."

Thus bitterly spoke a beautiful Pintail Duck, standing on one leg only, because the other one had been shot away. Early in November we heard a report from a lawless gun; and that drake fell, wing-tipped and with one leg gone, into Lake Agassiz. Head-Keeper Stacey and Keeper Atkin rowed out and rescued him, cut off the shattered wing-tip and leg, dressed them carefully, and then he became a life member of that sanctuary, but unable to fly away.

"You are perfectly right," said I, "and that is only the beginning of what might be said about our treatment of our wild ducks and geese."

The drake flapped his wings in frantic excitement.

"From the day we come in from Canada, where eighty per cent of us are born, the guns begin to roar at us. Some begin at dawn, and by sunrise it's a barrage. The guns surround all ponds and marshes that are suitable for ducks. There's a gun for every rod of rushes or tall grass, there are blinds and sink-boxes to burn, and they pound us all day long. If there is wild rice anywhere, or corn on the bottom, there's a cartridge for every grain. It's barbarous!"

"Honestly," said Sam Stacey, "I don't see how in the

THE PINTAIL DUCK.

"The guns surround all ponds and marshes that are suitable for ducks. . . . There are sink-boxes to burn, and if there's corn on the bottom there's a cartridge for every grain."

living world you ducks ever do get enough food to carry you through. It's a shame, I say!"

"There are days, and weeks, when we can get no food save by diving for it in black darkness. Now, what do you think of that as a means of support?" cried the Pintail.

"It seems incredible; and it is unspeakably cruel. But in some places there are rest days,—are there not, —two or three per week?"

"Rest nothing!" scornfully exclaimed the drake. "Half the time those tricky rest days deceive us, and do us more harm than good. On those rest days the duck-club members bait the water close in front of their blinds, with shelled corn. At last, when faint with hunger, we find it; but by the time we get fairly started at feeding upon it, thickly massed together,—'slam! bang!' The guns rake us unmercifully. But often we are so fearfully hungry we just can't leave that corn, and the poorest shot in the club usually gets his twenty-five of us before noon. Finally, when half the ducks are dead, the rest give it up and fly away,—to be shot in other places. What's that? No; it's no exaggeration whatever. Ask any real duck-hunter."

"That's unfair business," said I, "feeding ducks near blinds in order to murder them."

"Well, that's what many and many of them do. Don't think for a moment that any more than one duck-hunter out of every hundred cares to give us a square deal."

"Well, why don't you keep away from our hostile waters?"

"'Keep away? Keep away', is it?" cried the drake

scornfully. "And where would we keep to? Don't those ducking clubs command the very waters that we most need, and must have? We must come here every winter, in order to keep alive. And why do you game-protectors permit the killers to kill *so many* of us in one day? Do you think we can stand up forever against the guns that are as thick as the ducks, and each one out to get twenty-five of us every day?"

"It is a shame and a disgrace," I confessed. "Here in the East, the South and in California the killers are having things all their own way. It's a long story. There's a bitter fight on about it, but I'm afraid that before it's finished all the ducks and geese will be dead. A few men say that there are 'millions' of ducks here on this coast, but,——"

"Millions? Rot! Millions of hunters, they should say, but not of ducks. I say that now there are two duck hunters for every duck in the United States; and my word is just exactly as good as theirs. That 'millions' idea is just guesswork, founded on nothing but more ducks than people can count. And then those awful pump and automatic guns! Do you think we can stand up and carry on in spite of them?"

"No," I exclaimed. "Most—decidedly—I—do—NOT! It is wildly and utterly impossible. I have said so for years, and——"

"Well, those guns will give you your final revenge on the men who make them, and on the men who use them."

"How do you figure that out?"

"By their killing all the game birds of America, exterminating their own sport, and ruining their own market for guns and cartridges. Mark my word, you will soon have your revenge. The day will come when you can say to pump and automatic gunners, 'I told you so. It serves you right.'"

"I think you are quite right. And as the ducks and geese go, so will go the woodcock, snipe, quail, grouse, turkey, and many species of the song-birds as well. They are going now at express-train speed, by local extinction."

"Well," said the Pintail, reflectively, "after all, that was a lucky shot that brought me down in this place. Here I will be safe from the guns and gunners who know no such thing as justice and mercy to game; but I do pity my poor relations who already have gone south to be treated as gun-fodder."

I decided to change that gloomy and hopeless subject.

"My dear Pin, I do not wish to puff you all up, or make you vain, but I will say that I think you are just about the most beautiful duck that Mother Nature ever made."

At that bold announcement, the bird gave a startled flop into the edge of the pond, then swung around to look at me. Evidently it gave him quite a jolt; being unused to complimentary truth.

"Yes; I mean it; and I am ready to back it up. For shape, the finest yacht ever designed had nothing on you. Your hull is absolutely perfect, and that perky long tail of yours is enough to make a blue bird of paradise turn green with envy. The soft and rich harmonies of your buff and gray color scheme backs the gaudy wood duck into a corner, and the chicness of your style beats the French."

"Well, you are no duck-hunter,—I can see that. Do you think that any bloody duck-shooter ever looks at us with eyes that see our beauty? No, siree! All that they think of is a splash in the water, a well-flattered ego and six ounces of fishy meat on a greasy plate."

There was that infernal old subject again!

To get away from it, I left my parking space and drifted along the edge of the Wild-Fowl Pond, to have a look at the redheads and mallards, the canvasbacks and Canada honkers.

How fine they did look! And how happy they were. I know a lady mallard who made her nest between two spur-roots of an oak tree, facing a walk that was not more than ten feet away! I thought it fair dangerous; but she blended so perfectly with her dead-leaf and woodland surroundings that hundreds of thousands of visitors passed by without seeing her. Now that was what we might call real "protective coloration."

While I looked at those happy and carefree ducks (all of which do well in captivity,—if it is right,), my mind threw back to the famous fight for the "Bayne Law," to stop forever the sale of wild game in the great state of New York, by bottling up America's biggest and best dead-game market. What a fight that was; and what a sweeping victory! It took our lawyer two weeks at Albany to pick up the right men to introduce the bill,—don't you remember,—Senator Bayne and Assemblyman Blauvelt? And all those anxious days the wise men of Gotham were saying: "You can't do it! It can't be done!" and et cetera.

It was a long and hard, but perfectly clean, fight. There was not one compromise with our enemies, the market-gunners and game-dealers. Our campaign started with nothing, and soon became an avalanche that absorbed the apathetic and buried the opposition. Beginning with no votes, our bill ended on its final passage with every vote of that whole legislature, save one.

And then how the "rich duck-hunters" of the Atlantic coast clubs rejoiced,—over the fact that a quarter of a million of Atlantic coast ducks would every year be saved from commercial slaughter. It put three-fourths of the eastern market killers out of business; and the visible duck supply at once began to increase. It was considered "great,"—because it was the other fellow's ox who was being gored!

And now, with the duck supply again going down, and a demand for a hunter's daily limit of 15, instead of 25, do you think those same "rich duck-hunters" will stand for it?

Not—on—your—life!

And our ducks and geese, and Canada's geese and ducks, are doomed to go like the heath hen, the passenger pigeon, buffalo, and others too numerous to mention.

Can nothing save them? No; I think not. It is too late. The killers are overwhelmingly powerful, and "free shooting" in America is killing itself.

THE STEP–MOTHER ELEPHANT

MY personal acquaintance with the elephants of the world began when I was a small boy, with old Tippoo Sahib, in the little river town of Eddyville, Iowa. He was a big one; and not only that, he had the grandest pair of tusks that I ever saw or heard of in a living elephant. When he walked, their tips often touched the ground.

Skipping over many others, I knew Jumbo, first in the London Zoo. When he was in Washington, D. C., with P. T. Barnum the Great, Mr. Barnum gave me his card with a provisionary written "permission to measure Jumbo," and when I showed it to his boss, J. A. Bailey, —Mr. Bailey almost had a fit.

"Wha-at? *Measure Jumbo?*' Well, young man,—I guess—NOT!"

Jumbo's selling height to the people was 12 feet 6 inches; but twenty years after that Mr. Robert Gilfort, who, with the help of Elder, the pole-jumper, secretly measured Jumbo, told me that his real height was 10 feet 9 inches.

Then there was Gunda,—poor old passion-racked Gunda, who tore our nerves to tatters for three years or more; and Kartoum the Destroyer; and Congo; through fifteen hectic years erratic Alice; and finally darling little Tiny.

Alice did not come from a ricey and spicey Indian jungle, full of waving palms and turbans and what not.

She was the storm-tost waif of Coney Island, and like that classic isle her cosmos was composed of many strata, with numerous geological faults, dips and strikes.

If anywhere in this world there is a lady who was once an unmitigated cuss, Alice is it. Our adventures with her would make a book that would rival Alice in Wonderland. The standing wonder of fifteen years has been the fact that throughout all the mazes and windings of her cussedness, that erring female never has turned vicious, and never has even attempted to hurt anybody. On a record like that,—of neglected opportunities,—much else may be forgiven.

Alice has more voice language than any of our male elephants ever displayed. When carrying a temperature, she freely lifts up her voice and says things. When begging, she squeals on high C. If discoursing, she trumpets musically. If irritated she squalls, and when swearing mad at the world she roars and bawls like a bull of Bashan. It was a long, long time, however, before she consented to talk freely for publication; which shows the wide gulf between her and the human animal who loves every printer like a brother.

One time I heard, and presently saw, Charming Alice marching around her private park, blaring and bawling out rank discontent. When I politely asked her for particulars, she came up close to the inside fence, and began a regular tirade.

"I think Dick is just the con-demndest, aggravatingest, and provokingest cuss that ever keepered anywhere. I won't stand it any longer! I'll resign!"

"What's the matter now, Alice? Shall I put Dick out

of the way for you?" (This was a bluff, to try her affections.)

"Well, no. Not just yet, anyway. But I do wish you would beat him, and make him give me that little Tiny elephant for mine. I want to be a mother to something, and that cunning little tyke is just right. Will you do it, in memory of old times?"

"Humph! Alice dear," I said cattishly, "speaking of 'old times,' if I did anything in memory of the times I have had with you, you would get the biggest licking any lady elephant ever got. I'm thinking of——"

"Now! Now! No rakings up!" cried Alice. "I withdraw that reference to the past, and I ask you without it. The question is, will you?"

"Alice, there is no blinking the fact that you are a Lady with a Past. You have a police record, and it cannot be shoved away. You have been an erratic and erring female, and you may be again. I can't forget how you broke into the Reptile House, and smashed thirteen cases, and cast thirteen live rattlesnakes upon the floor. If you had little Tiny in your cage, you might get angry at her, and do her a lot of mischief."

"It is very ungallant in you to rake up a lady's past that way. Since I came to this elephant palace I have reformed."

"Oh, do you remember Sweet Alice how you came to this building from the Elk House up yonder? Yes; you can protest all you like; but it was at the end of a long rope with twenty men pulling at one end while the other end was tied around your right front foot. You were acting so badly that finally you had to be yanked to this building, a yard at a time; and you have not been allowed to quit these quarters even once since then. That is why you have not broken into more buildings."

"But what has that got to do with my affections? Are not they all right? I never get mad at any person, do I? Ask Dick and Walter. And look at my visitor-carrying business."

"That is true, Alice. You have been very decent toward your keepers, and toward visitors. I will try to be just with you, even if you have been some erratic. Now, just what is your basic idea about Tiny, the baby Pygmy Elephant?"

"Well, you see I've never married, but I want to know what it is to have a child to love, and that will call me 'mother.' Every right-minded human woman wants to be called 'Mother,' don't she? My life is barren. I give the world everything that I have, but I get nothing save hay, vegetables, bread and water, and a place to sleep. I can't even see the other elephants; and I want a companion that I can call my own child. Of course I'll never be anything but a step-mother, but that will be better than nothing."

"Alice," said I, touched by a feeling for her infirmities, "you shall have Tiny for your step-child; and she may live with you as long as both of you are happy together."

The next day, the papers of adoption were made out, and executed. Alice was too happy for words, and no wonder. Of all the lovely and "cute" and interesting baby elephants that ever came down the pike, the new little-girl from West Africa was It.

THE PYGMY ELEPHANT BABY.
She was a lesson to American girls and boys in Contentment.

With astonishing appropriateness, her capture and her coming to us was all due to our appeal to a young lady of London. I said to Miss Cunningham, (John Gorilla's saviour), "Won't you and your brother *please* bring us from Fernam Vaz a baby Pygmy Elephant?"

She promised across her heart that she would. At the right moment, Capt. Cunningham remarked, "Well, it's a fine day. I think I'll go out and catch that baby elephant," and he did, just offhand and carelessly like that; quite as if he had been in the habit of finding and catching small elephants for people while they wait.

Never was there a more merry or amusing elephant baby than Tiny. The way she enjoyed life with us, and loved her own beautiful little park garnished with big shady maples and grass and sunlight to order, was a lesson to American boys and girls in contentment. No one could see her spread out her ears, stick up her funny little tail, and run joy-races across her park, squealing and laughing shrilly, without laughing at the droll spectacle. She acted as if she was too happy for words.

And "Mother" Alice! She mothered that rollicksome, care-free child as an old hen conserves one chicken. An elephant's trunk is a great thing for the delivery of caresses,—if you are not fussy about your best clothes. But to Alice it was a real disappointment that her trunk was not long enough to completely enwrap the whole body of her step-baby. It was a great joy to the mother when her baby learned to amuse itself, and make visitors laugh, by quickly running to and fro under its mother's mighty body.

But at times Alice was jealous about her baby! When-

THE STEP-MOTHER ELEPHANT

ever she thought keepers or people were wearing out Tiny with too much attention, she would promptly interpose her own bulk, and force her child into a state of refuge on the other side of her personality.

When Tiny had been four years a step-child, another baby elephant suddenly arrived at the Park, and was parked beside Alice. But do you think that Alice took kindly to the new and littlest waif? No, indeed! She would have nothing to do with it! This was out of all reason; and it showed once more the strangely warped and erratic mind of our storm-tossed Alice.

A QUAIL VISITS US

ONE lovely Sunday forenoon in June, my small grandson rushed into the bosom of his family with the news that he had heard the call of a Bob-White from the grounds of our neighbor across the street. This created a sensation; because, in about 20,000 miles of motoring through the lovely meadows, woodlands and lakelands of Connecticut and southern New York we had up to that time actually seen only one quail. Naturally, quail shooting around us had become a dead sport.

Of course we hoped that some day that last Bob-White would come across the street to our place; and very soon he did. It was a great thing to have a sure-enough wild quail come upon our grounds, and give his clarion call from the sheltering rose hedge of the garden. At once I gingerly stole out to find the owner of the voice.

"Well, Bob," I said softly, "this is a fine surprise! For years we had not ventured to hope ever to see another wild quail in Connecticut; and here you are, actually at our door. However did you dare to risk it?"

"There are no cats around here now," was the prompt answer.

That was true. A year previous, some heartless wretch had put out a fearful lot of poison, and every bird-hunting cat for blocks around just quietly disappeared. Previous to that, the ugly, blear-eyed and savage old yellow Toms and Tabbies swarmed over our

A QUAIL VISITS US

place, and harbored under the very rose hedge that now sheltered Bob-White! Funny, wasn't it? We had a house cat then, who dared not even look hard at a bird or a squirrel; but our Jett also went down in the holocaust of the Borgia of Mill River.

"You were quick on the draw, Bob, in finding out that these places are catless," said I.

"Oh, that was easy enough," said Bob, a bit airily I thought. "We can see cats and dogs farther than they can see us. If it were not for the keen noses of the horrid hunting dogs, we could laugh at the hunters, and grow fat. It's very unfair for men to hunt us with dogs, to assist hunters who are not smart enough to find us without dog help. Great sports, men are! They have to hire all kinds of help in order to get any game. To us it looks just like unarmed foot travelers being hunted by well-armed bandits in automobiles."

"Bob, I am dreadfully afraid that what you say is true; but I don't dare to admit it."

"Well, why don't you dare?"

"It's a delicate matter," said I, blushing horribly. "The sportsmen who are so crazy to kill quail all claim they not only are your best friends, but your only friends, and——"

"How do they figure that out?" broke in Bob-White, impatiently.

"Why, they say, 'No one but sportsmen feed quail in winter; and if we don't feed them, they'll have no places to sleep, and all of them will freeze to death, et cetera.'"

"That's all bosh," snorted Bob, visibly swelling up with indignation. "It's silly!"

"And some of them also say, Bob, that it's a good thing to shoot up coveys every fall, and scatter them, to prevent the quail from dying out from high living, and inbreeding, and other dreadful diseases."

"What nonsense!" cried the quail. "Do they think that scattered quail are such imbeciles they do not know how to get together within twelve hours? Do they think that the scattered pieces of a covey take root where they light, and grow there like burdocks? It's bad enough to be hunted by dogs, and the owners of dogs, and shot with choke-bore guns with extra-strong smokeless powder; but that libel on our intelligence is more maddening to us than being hunted."

"Who shot up your coveys before white men came along?" said I.

"That's what I would like to know. When nobody but Indians lived here, we lived high; and there were millions of us. Why, in the open places that were not swampy, we were just everywhere. Of course the hawks and owls, the foxes and lynxes, got a lot of us; but the ones eaten that-a-way never were missed. And the first white men—with buckskin clothes, coonskin caps and long rifles with tiny little bullets like peas—they never bothered us, either. We lived right along with them, and they didn't hate us at all. And what is more, it is not the farmers who are the worst on us now; nor the hawks 'n owls 'n foxes."

"Then who is it, Bob?"

"It's the sports that swarm out from the cities and towns, with automobiles and dogs, with the finest guns you ever saw, and loads of high-power cartridges. They

THE BOB-WHITE QUAIL.
"If you and your covey will come up here in the fall and winter, we will feed you."

harass us every day during the open season; we can't fly from one bunch of hunters without landing near another one; and we get just no time at all to hunt for our bugs and weed seeds."

"Could you hold up all right if the guns would let you alone?"

"Sure we could!" cried Bob, wagging his handsome head so hard I feared he might loosen it. "We always come back when they stop shooting us—that is, if there is a decent remnant of us left. But, of course, it's a long hard job; and lonesome, too."

"Do the farmers feed you in winter?" I queried.

"They used to; but now they don't very much. They say, 'What is the use of feeding game birds in winter for the hunters to run down and shoot up just as soon as the next season opens? We never get a chance to eat a game bird, no matter how many we feed, or how long.'"

"Do the town sportsmen feed you in winter?"

"Huh!" snorted Bob, registering indignation. "I—should—say—NOT! Some farmers do feed us occasionally; and some of the State Game Wardens do the best for us that they can. But, dear me! There's only one Warden where there ought to be five."

"If you and your covey will come here in the fall and winter, we will feed you."

"We'd like to; but we don't dare come when the leaves are off. The dogs would drive us, and the owls could catch us at night."

"You ought to change your habits now, and take to roosting in evergreen trees. You'd live a lot longer, and not freeze to death so often."

Bob cocked his head sidewise, and looked thoughtful.

"What kind of trees, for instance?" he inquired at last.

"Why, pine trees, cedars, spruces like these, hemlocks—in fact, any of the cone-bearing trees. There are lots and lots of them around the fine country homes, and small-town homes, too; and any man that loves to have such trees on his place surely will be good to quail. Just try it once. Show me a man who loves evergreen trees, and I'll show you a man who loves birds, and is a bird protector."

"Really?" said Bob, excited like. "You've given me a new idea. I'll put it before the covey at our next meeting. Meanwhile, if you don't mind, I'll just stick around here on your place for a little while."

"Righto! Make yourself at home; and bring your friends to eat our wheat screenings. The whole place is yours; and I particularly recommend these thick and prickly Colorado blue spruces as ever present helps in times of trouble. They're cat-proof."

But after all, that solitary Quail made me sad,—because he was solitary,—if you know what that means. I cannot write about the quails of the United States without feeling both rage and sorrow. It is because of their marvelous and widely-spread original abundance, their beauty, their lovable qualities, their actual cash value to agricultural man, and the brutal and foolish way in which civilized man has everywhere handed out to all of them treachery, persecution and death.

The crane, the wild duck, the goose and the sea-shore-bird are long on wings, and if persecuted too much by gunners they can rise and fly five miles, or a hundred. But not so the quail. His plump and heavy body is a perpetual handicap to his small wings, and even a mile of flight tires him. His standard flying stunt is between a quarter and a half of a mile; with the result that he is easily followed up by the gunners and their dogs, and attacked, again and again. Do people *never* think of that? Moreover, the automatic and the pump shotguns, and the hunting automobile make his destruction simple, sure and easy. He has only 5 per cent of the chances for safety that he had forty years ago. Is it not a tragedy?

And then the merciless savagery with which the quail-killers pursue him! It is incredible until seen. Nothing is farther from the mind of a quail-killer than the thought of mercy, and a square deal. He takes every advantage of the handicapped bird that his sportsman-made laws permit him to take, and everywhere in quail-hunting lands he is exterminating both the quails and the sport that he "loves," as if quail-slaughter were a virtue.

No; it now seems quite useless to work for a reform. The sportsmen now are in full control of the game-extermination industry, and they are elaborately careful to preserve their killing privileges. The non-shooting public has become resigned to the idea of game extermination; and many of my readers will find this page tiresome reading. And alackaday! Some of the natural friends and defenders of the quail, like the National Association of Audubon Societies, have formally and publicly decided that "the quail is a game bird, it belongs to the sportsman, and it should not be placed in the list of song birds for permanent protection."

Right soon the foolish and wasteful people of the United States will see the finish of all their quail species.

A CHIMPANZEE'S VIEW OF THE DESCENT OF MAN

DULL indeed is the man who can not learn something from a healthy and vigorous chimpanzee. But wherein could human Solons be more dull than when they talk about the "descent" of man from the apes, when they mean precisely the reverse?

Our biggest, blackest, and brainiest adult male chimpanzee, "Boma," is, so I believe, more wise than some of the people whom he left behind in the Congo country, and also more interesting. There are times when he hilariously goes to work to act out his thoughts, and those make very interesting sessions for me. When I greet him in the morning, by saying in his own language, "Boma! Hoo-ah, Hoo-ah. Wah-hoo," and he thrusts out his lips and says, "Hoo-hoo! Hoo-hoo," in a conversational tone, that is equivalent to saying, "I'm feeling first rate, and ready to talk to you."

At that friendly gesture it is my habit to slip in behind the barrier, and take a position near to Boma,—but just outside of his grabbing distance! He is big, and very powerful; and whenever he feels insulted he flies into a towering rage that makes Ivan the Terrible look like a mourning dove. His raucous screams of rage are thoroughly demoralizing. Beware the seamy side of any big ape.

One bright morning recently, on seeking Boma soon after the finish of his breakfast, I found him feeling fine, and fit for an interview. The wise old ape sat at ease in a front corner of his cage, maliciously spitting through his front teeth at a tough-looking young man outside the wire-netting barrier, whose face should have been painted to represent "The Insolence of Youth." And I soon saw that the ape was a pretty good shot, too; because the young man suddenly swore a few lines, rubbed his face, and moved away.

"Boma," I said, slowly and distinctly, "what is your private opinion of the descent of man?"

"Say that again, please," said Boma, hearkening, but looking puzzled.

"What do you think of the idea that men have descended from apes like you, or worse ones?"

"Oh, that's all right. It's quite true, I assure you. Many men have descended from us, and some of them pretty low. But, while it's true enough, I wonder that so many of them admit it."

"They misuse a good English word, Boma. They mean *as*cend instead of *de*scend."

"Well sir, their word is all right. The most of them *have* descended from us! Just look at the far-down ones that come to see us! They certainly have gone down, not up. But you do not believe that all men descended from the same family tree, do you?" said the Ape, with a meaning wink.

"Look out, Boma," I whispered. "You could easily start a riot now by saying things about the proletariat. A law will be passed next winter making it a penal offense to tell any truth about any objectionable person or people. Already in New York the newspapers are forbidden to publish the nationality of a criminal. With some of the melting-potters it seems to have become a sore subject. Can you guess why?"

Boma looked puzzled; so I changed the subject.

"Boma, it seems to me that you chimps are not making much progress in intelligence. You all seem to be doing things just as you did two thousand years ago. Now, take houses, for example. Your people have seen the black people of Africa build houses for themselves, for a thousand years, and good houses, too; but you fellows don't build anything, not even tree-top nests, such as the orangs build so easily. Your home life has not yet begun. Why don't you do something in that line?"

"Now, baas," said Boma, using the Cape Dutch word for "boss," "if you will think with your head for one moment, you will see one or two reasons why we dare not develop houses and house life. If we were to build houses, it would be to live in them, and take our ease in our inn. That would enable our man enemies to mark down our dwellings, or our villages, and attack us so successfully that we would easily be destroyed. Human robbers always wish to find people who live in towns and cities, so that they can rob and enslave large lots at once. Houses of any kind would lead to our extermination. We dare not make any. It is the law of the jungle that in separation there is the longest life. Why, you have told me yourself how you found orangs in Borneo by their nests!"

That was quite true. I did, sometimes.

"Boma, you have given me a reason. Your chimp logic is sound. But honestly, with the wonderful intelli-

THE CHIMPANZEE.

"What do you think of the idea that men have descended from apes like you, or worse ones?"

"Oh, that's all right. It's quite true, I assure you."

gence, and the physical strength and agility that you chimps have, could you not learn to work like people, and do a whole lot of useful labor?"

"Oh, yes, baas. We could. Indeed we could. Why, we would make tree-top foresters of most superior abilities. Think how I could take your pruning saw, and clear all the dead branches out of the tops of your trees."

"You could, Boma. You certainly could. Now why not try it, just for fun?"

"No, baas! Not I. It would be fatal. If we chimps should consent to work, it would lead to our becoming just such slaves as men are. Do negro slaves gain anything by working? Not one good thing; but they do gain blows and stripes, and hunger and sickness, such as they never know until they are caught in the jungles, and enslaved. For five hundred years we have seen the slave gangs, in slave-forks, and sometimes with chains run through holes in their hands, being driven to the Ivory Coast, from their jungle homes where their villages betrayed them!

"No, baas! We can have no houses in our jungles; but we will not be slaves to man. The native tribes of Africa come and go, but we go on forever. Your people shoot a few of us, and catch a few more, but we are not being exterminated—yet. At home we are happy; but here the sight of the human wage slaves that I have seen all over America has made me unhappy. I'm sorry for them."

"Tell me, Ape. Do you think that the human people of this world are becoming better?"

"W-H-A-T?" shrieked Boma, jumping up. "*Better* is it?"

Then he wrecked his face, and gave two or three blood-curdling yells, ending with his most hectic performance. Under extra great excitement, he would for half a dozen times jump up and down like a huge, black, jumping-jack, and at the finish loudly smack his big feet upon the floor, a dozen times in quick succession. This explosion of fiendish rage and activity always drew a crowd with quick dispatch.

"You know perfectly well" (and the angry ape's accusing index finger pointed his remarks), "that all low-class men, savage and tame, are mean, and cruel, and wicked, and growing more so day by day. Did you ever know any apes, or baboons, or antelopes or deer, or even lions or tigers or wild dogs, that loaf and lie, and steal and waste, and abuse their wives and children as the mean men of all nations do? Show me any animal races whose strong members bully and oppress and rob the weak ones,—aye, and murder them too,—the way mean men do. It simply isn't done by the Wild Ones. Look out for the men who have really 'descended' from us!"

"You are right, Boma. The settlings of the human races are a tough lot, and no mistake."

"Here," said he, "if it were not for the wild animals in front of my cage, it wouldn't be so bad. On Saturdays its tough, but on Sunday afternoons,—it is the limit! Every tenth man is a pest, and unfit to roam at large. I see the pickpockets at work, and the dope fiends and the bootleggers; and it gets on my nerves because I can't make arrests. And look at what they do to us?" continued the Wild One. "They throw lighted matches through two barriers into our cage straw; and three times, in spite of this fine mesh barrier, they have set our cage bedding on fire."

"*We* never break your Park rules; but mean visitors often do so,—when they think they can get away with it. *You* know how you had to build these wire barriers up *nine feet high*, to keep the Yahoos away from us, and to protect *us* from *them!* Whenever they can, they give us lead pencils, tobacco, cigars and cigarettes, rubber bands, pocket mirrors, and pieces of broken glass,— but *never* anything that is good for us!"

Boma's indignation actually had to pause for breath; and then I asked:

"Do not some of your visitors look like you? Do you not see some resemblances?"

"In that there is nothing worth mentioning," answered the Ape with icy indifference. "You have seen for yourself how widely they differ from us. They have descended away from us, and I am glad of it. Let them keep it up. No. I'm thankful to say that men do not much resemble us."

"In a grand fight for your freedom, Boma, how many ordinary men could you whip?"

"Well," said the anthropoid, reflectively, "with all hands bare, I will say about ten. They could strike me, of course, but I could turn somersaults and bite them so savagely and so often that they couldn't stick it."

"How would you like to be a prize-fighter, Boma, and fight men in a ring?"

"Hooray! Yah! Whoop-ee!" he screamed. "Give me

one, and let me show the Yahoos how to fight fair and square."

"Hush, Boma! hush!" I hurriedly butted in, "or you will offend millions of Good People who are being worked for big gate money. When Good People determine to be gudgeons, you must *not* interfere with them. The moment you Apes enter the prize ring you will stir up a hornet's nest with the promoters through being so uncontrollable, and refusing to stand hitched. This educational job is the best thing for you."

At that Boma became so disgusted with mankind that he sprang up, leaped to his balcony, and sat down upon his straw bed to mull over the situation alone.

WHY THE GRAY SQUIRREL IS IN HARD LUCK

FOR twenty-five years I have been savagely criticizing our whole country on account of the outrageous way its squirrels have been treated by the men who shoot them, and also by the Lazy Ones who let them do it. I have talked and printed until I am discouraged, and tempted to become a quitter. Nothing that I have said has seemed to do any good; but the trouble is, the rawness of the deal to the squirrels keeps me on the job.

Here on our home place, we all do our best to protect our squirrels from the lawless dogs, cats, and two-legged enemies of all nations. I try to be cheerful about my end of it, but to tell the truth I am sulky clear through. The troubles of our squirrels keep us riled up, winter and summer.

And what a fight we are having to protect and feed this one squirrel family! Why, if these Stamford squirrels had not been mentally alert every waking moment, as quick on the draw as chain lightning, and swift as thought in delivery, every squirrel in town would have been killed long ago.

It was my daughter's special pet, Little Mammy, who gave me this interview, and set us all thinking anew. She said:

"That house you fixed for me, in the forks of the biggest maple, is too small for my family, and too cold.

THE GRAY SQUIRREL.
"The troubles of our squirrels keep us riled up, winter and summer."

That is why my four babies were born in the roof of the porch. It is the only other safe and dry place for them anywhere around here. The good nest holes in the trees are all gone. I'm awfully obliged to you for refusing to have that roof hole repaired, and stopped up. That would have just finished me and my babies."

"I'm sorry," I said, "that I was so mortally slow in finding out that you needed that bean-pole to connect your tree with the porch roof. I'll try to do better next time."

"That pole surely is a great help. It saves me a seven-foot jump every time I come home; and that ladder down to the ground is great."

"Tell me, Little Mammy, when you come and stand on my girl's window-sill, and put your paws up against the glass, does that mean that you are without food, and hungry?"

"It certainly does. That is my sign language for 'up against it.' And if little Lady Bountiful had not understood my signs to her, believe me, in that long, cold and bitter spring we would all of us have just starved. No, in those snowy and icy times, there was not a thing to be had by us anywhere else. My babies were in hard luck this year, and the Lady pulled us all through, except Little Pete, the one who was killed by a falling limb."

"That white dog nearly killed you last March, did he not? What an awful mauling that was. That hole in your side looks as if it is not fully healed, even yet. Your Lady just wept when you crawled up to her window, to tell her, and collapsed on the sill. We were all afraid you would die, but we didn't dare to take you from your babies."

"Oh, that was awful," said Little Mammy. "The dog caught me on a stretch of bare ground, and I thought I was done for. But I fought him! My, but I tried hard to bite him! When he gave me that awful bite in the side, I got him by the end of his nose, and bit and bit for my life. I gave it to him good! He opened his mouth to yell, and he was so upset that I managed to get away. But honestly, that big hole in my side *almost* killed me. And can you guess what cured it?"

"No. Tell us the answer."

"Peanuts! Nothing else but peanuts, and on this very roof! I couldn't possibly have gone out and found food. Without them, we would have died."

"Tell me, Mammy. Which are the worst enemies of squirrels? And which do you fear and dread most, the dogs, cats, or men?"

"Boys! Bad boys are the worst of all. But dogs and cats are bad enough, goodness knows. They love to hunt us wherever we are; but by watching for them every minute when we are hunting food on the ground, we can save ourselves pretty well."

"I know how you do it. Your big, black eyes are keen, your little brains and legs act together like forked lightning, and by the time a dog gets his idea of you, and unlimbers his long legs to get into action, you are half way to your safety tree."

"Yes, that's it. The slow squirrels don't live long in a town, do they?"

"No. And speaking of boys, I am afraid of 'em all."

"Oh, but they're not all bad. There are the Boy Scouts, you know."

"Yes, but with the badges and uniforms off, how am I to tell a Scout from any other boy? A squirrel can't take a chance on any boy until he has been tried out. I call them our worst enemies, because of their little 22 rifles, their air guns, and their sling-shots. Boys can hunt us all the time, and get away with it."

"Well, between the boys and the cheap sportsmen, the squirrels are nearly all gone from the Northern forests, and here there are far more squirrels in the suburbs of the towns than there are in the country woods."

"Yes, we've got to be fed now, and helped along, or we can't hold out. The woods are nearly all saplings and young trees, with no nest holes in 'em. There are few acorns, and just about no nuts at all. The trees are too young. Now, how can anybody expect us to live under such conditions as those, escape the regular shot-gun squirrel hunters, and the boys besides?"

"You just can't do it. And you're not doing it. The whole American people, so boastful about 'fair play' and 'conservation,' are giving the squirrels of this whole country a raw deal. I hate their folly and their unfairness, and I don't care who knows it."

"I'm glad you feel that way. It makes me feel some better in my mind."

"Well, more than that, Little Mammy, I'm going to turn over a new leaf myself, and treat you and your kiddies better. Before next winter you shall have better ladders for your home in the porch roof, and a bigger and warmer house in the big maple tree."

GRAY SQUIRREL IN HARD LUCK

"Thank you, ever so much; and if you forget, I'll climb up to your window-sill, and remind you."

The gray and fox squirrels of the United States are our most beautiful, most interesting and most companionable of the small wild animals. Give one of them half a chance to feel that you are his friend and protector, and he will eat out of your hand. As you sit on a park bench he will climb up into your lap. Keep your devilish cats and dogs from him, and he will come up to your doors and windows when hungry, and ask you for food.

Either on the lawn, or in your big trees, the gray squirrel is a gay and graceful little elf. His astounding quickness of eye, ear and limb is a source of perpetual interest and admiration. The lightning quickness of his thoughts and movements make us think of electric activity. I know of no other animal on earth that is his equal in that. This is the reason, and the sole reason, why gray squirrels can exist in populous city and town suburbs, reeking with worthless dogs and cats, as they do. I could tell wonders, if there were time, of squirrel survival amid deadly perils.

Some very mean things are done regularly by the mean men of all nations. I think that aside from actual banditry and other major crimes, the meanest lawful acts done by Americans (next to the nagging of wives) is the way thousands of Americans each year hunt down and mercilessly shoot all the squirrels that they can kill under our rotten laws. One would think that the salvation of their souls depends upon the number of squirrels they can shoot.

And they *eat* them, too! The smelly, catty flesh of the friendly little squirrel is, in America, cooked and eaten, and Americans are the *only* white people on earth who do it! I am no saint, and I am not by a long shot "chicken-hearted"; but just about sixty years ago I made up my mind that it is not fair to hunt squirrels with a gun, because they can't escape; that squirrel hunting is so one-sided and so easy it is no "sport" whatever; that only a poor sport can come down to potting helpless squirrels; and that squirrels are not good to eat, anyhow.

But, outside the cities and towns, our gray and fox squirrels are doomed to extermination. In the north, they are nearly at that point now. The sportsmen control the laws, they are coldly determined to shoot "something" as long as anything remains alive, and there we are. If the town and city people do not save some squirrels, by means of city ordinances against firing guns within the "city limits," none will be saved. Therefore, I call upon the town and city dwellers to put up commodious squirrel boxes, dispense squirrel food, curb the dogs and kill the wild marauding cats that are so deadly to song birds and squirrels.

THE WISE OLD BUFFALO WHO TRANSFERS HIMSELF

ORDINARILY one can not tell what thought work is going on in the shaggy head of an American Buffalo, any more than we can guess the mind of a stone image. It takes manifestations to reveal animal thought to the dull mind of man. However, if a man travels industriously, and keeps his eyes open at least one-half the time, he will see many queer things.

When I was last in the Yellowstone Park, running around loose to see what needed to be seen, on the road between Mammoth Hot Springs and the Lamar Valley I met a real personage. It was in spring; warm enough to set all the wild folk agoing, and to put an outdoor urge into winter-weary men. I was walking in the glorious sunshine, to see what wild animals were stirring, headed eastward from the Mammoth Hot Springs Hotel, and only about five miles from that vast Palace of Comfort.

Out of the sparkling distance, and following the broad and smooth Park road as it swung around curves and breasted slopes, there appeared a strange object, black and big. Now what can travel over this highway that is so big and so black?

As the moving mass rounded a point, and started to traverse a sharp curve in the road, my game eye recognized a big and shaggy-haired bull Buffalo! There was no mistake about it. He marched in single file, at a steady, brisk and purposeful gait, going somewhere. It was "eyes front," and "little-finger-on-the-seam-of-the-pants," in a way that bespoke either military training, a military atmosphere, or both. Ah! I have it! He must be going to Fort Yellowstone, at the Mammoth Springs.

Being conscious of our dual personal rectitudes, the bull and I marched on with serene confidence and sang-froid,—until we met. Face to face we came, close up, and mutually halted to take stock of each other.

"Hello, Buff," I offered, in my patronizing tone, "where do you think you are from?"

"I'm from the Bison Corrals, up in Lamar Valley, where Mack is," rumbled he.

"Do you mean Warden McComb?"

"Uh-huh," grunted the big one.

"But is there nobody driving you, nor even showing you the way?"

"No. I'm all alone!"

"Well, great Scott, bull! Are you running away from the herd, or what? Did you break out of the range?"

"None whatever. They gave me a transfer, turned me loose, and I do all the rest. This is what I do every spring. Have you not yet heard of me?" (He said this with a reproachful air; and right away I felt condemned.)

"No, I'm blest if I ever have. I have just come in, and I don't know much. Now, be a good fellow, and tell me all about this mystery. You've got me guessing."

"Well," said the bull, clearing the bubbles from his throat, "since you put it that way, I will. I'm the Buffalo Bull who twice a year transfers himself twenty-nine miles all alone, with no guide nor anything. I know the

THE BUFFALO.

"Well, great Scott, bull. Are you running away from the herd?"

road between the Hot Springs and the Bison Corrals in Lamar Valley, just as well as any ranger in the Park; and better than the young ones, maybe. I winter at the corrals, and in summer I'm on exhibition at the Springs. When spring comes up there at the Corrals they open the gate for me, and let me out. I march down the Cook City road, and keep agoing until I come to where it strikes this road. There I keep to the right, and follow this road right on down to Mammoth Hot Springs. Down there the tourist effectives all flock to see me, and I stay there until fall. They're all just crazy to see some wild animals."

"Well, of all the queer outcrops of Bison intelligence! And what happens in the fall? Do you just reverse your gears?"

"Humph! I reverse nothing. In the fall I go back to Mack's herd at the Corrals, and find everybody glad to see me again."

"Have you never wandered off the road, never played truant, never got lost, nor anything?"

"No," grunted the Bull. "No nonsense; just plain business. I was brought up at the Post, and I'm for strict military discipline. It's my duty to live up to the Park regulations," he added with evident pride.

"Well, old Bison, you are a wise one, and a prize winner for brain and personality."

"But say, man. Did you never hear of our company of bulls that wouldn't be discharged and mustered out?"

"I never did, from *your* point of view. Tell me all about it."

"It was this way," said the Bull, after a look backward, to see if any troublesome busses were coming. "Up at the corrals our buffalo herd grew and grew, until it outgrew the corrals. Then McComb said, 'We've just got to discharge some of these old coffee-coolers that we don't need any more, and let them go off and be wild.' 'All right,' said the surplus. 'We'll set up a free wild herd.'

"They were turned out; and then it seemed like they had no place to go.

" 'Oh, botheration,' said Mack. 'We'll just drive you where you ought to go.'

"And they did. But to those buffs, where they went, the feed didn't look good. There was no hot-and-cold water, and no hay-racks full of grub. And winter was coming pronto. The next day, the whole discard turned up at the corral gate, and wanted to re-enlist.

" 'No, sir!' said Mack, firmly. 'You fellows have got to get out o' here, and be wild.'

"Again he drove them away; and that time still farther. In another two days, back they came, all a-begging to come in and sign up again with the herd. Mack was disgusted and sore; but he just had to take 'em in. They were so spoiled by luxury and laziness that it looked as if they didn't know how to rustle any more."

"Those are the twin curses of the human race, Buff. Look out that they don't light on you."

"Well, I must be moving. So long," said Buff; and with a huge nod of his vast and shaggy head he heaved past me, and in perfectly good formation ponderously marched on down the road. He went to his summer engagement at the Springs, as a Visual Educational Exhibit,—or words to that effect.

Now that trifling incident recalled to mind a really huge one of the same tenor and date, (i. e. the present), that has been taking place in Canada. Incidentally, it drives home and clinches the success that Canada and the United States have severally achieved in atoning for some of the sins of the past, and bringing back the bison. Canada has not only done a big part in "bringing back the buffalo" as a captive and half-domestic animal, but also in restoring it as a wild one.

Canada has sent from her captive herd at Wainwright, Alberta, nearly 3,000 young bison, far northward by rail and by steamer, up to the wild Peace River country, west of Ft. Smith, and turned them loose to rustle for themselves. And the joke is on those buffs; because they are so fearfully far from the home ranch that they cannot possibly trek back to Wainwright, and ask to re-enlist in that pampered herd. No, sir! They have got to stay put, and be "wild." Having found this completely out, like good buffs they have settled down to housekeeping, and even after two winters are reported to be doing well. Even the calf crop seems to be satisfactory.

It is highly probable that from time to time other shipments of buffaloes will be made from the parent herd,—and we will watch with mighty keen interest to see how soon there will be a black wave of very robust wild bison slowly moving southward from the Peace River country, invading northern Alberta.

Aside from about 120 head in the Yellowstone Park,

the only *wild* bison now living are the members of the two original herds of northern Canada, directly south of Great Slave Lake, and extending down to the Peace River. In that vast and inhospitable wilderness, of thin, stunted timber and grass, there are two herds of bison that have existed there ever since the end of the great extermination farther south in Canada, and in the United States. The northern army of those originals is believed by the Canadian authorities to contain about 500 head, and the southern army is credited with 1,000 or more, all broken up into small bands, and seemingly breeding faster than the wolves can kill the calves. All these "wood bison," as they are called for distinguishment, have for years past been carefully protected against slaughter, by the Canadian Mounted Police, and now their entire range has been established by Canada as a National Wood Buffalo Park.

In the Yellowstone Park, the Montana National Bison Range and the Wichita (Oklahoma) National Bison Range, the herds are breeding so successfully that surplus bison are constantly being sold to purchasers whose objects are approved, or presented to public zoos. The United States now owns nine national herds. There are in the world as a whole 16,517 living specimens of the American Bison, and the future of the species against extermination is absolutely secure for the next hundred years.

In 1889 there were in North America only 256 head in captivity, and 635 running wild.

THE PRONG–HORN WHO POSES ON THE KNOLL

THE first wild Prong-Horn that I ever approached to a half-way close-up, stood precariously on the narrow summit of one of the cone-shaped Red Buttes, forty miles north of Miles City, Montana, while I occupied the other. It seems contrary to nature; but the solitary prong-horn loves cycloramic scenery, and he frequently chooses a rounded hill-top from which to survey it. It is good to know personally a wild animal that actually is fond of big landscapes, just as mountain goats and sheep assuredly are.

During the past six years in particular I have done time, and spent over $5,000 of The Fund's money, in helping to prevent the wonderful prong-horn from going down and out before the guns. I began twenty-five years ago; but we will forget those early years.

Ever since the Yellowstone Park was born, in 1871, it has contained a slender stock of antelope that fled there for shelter from the deadly rifles of the plains and foothills. Assuredly none but hard-pressed plains animals ever would climb up to that 7,000-foot plateau, and in winter fight for life in all that snow and cold.

A year ago last June, Chief Park Ranger Sam T. Woodring kindly permitted me to ride with him up the Lamar Valley, to the Buffalo Range and Soda Butte. It was a glorious day, and the Yellowstone Wonderland was every foot a paradise. Never have I seen in any land

THE PRONG-HORN WHO POSES

a more resplendent and entrancing mountain flora, or finer color schemes, than we saw in that most perfect week. I never elsewhere saw feathery sage-brush, green grass, mountain flowers and green timber as brilliant and beautiful as those that adorned the whole Yellowstone Park in that last week of June, 1925.

Naturally I was Argus-eyed for wild animals, and not in vain. A little way beyond the beaver dams of Beaver Creek, we drove up real near to a big and solitary buck antelope who posed like a statue on a beautifully modeled knoll on the right. The ground around him was quite bare, except for a carpet of green grass sprinkled with about 350 great, hulking, pinkey-white mountain lilies in full and perfect bloom. (This sounds like a fake description! It really does! But I can prove every word of it by Chief Woodring, who cannot tell a lie without violating the Park Regulations.)

As we drove up, the Chief stopped his car at the point nearest to the statue antelope, and the 'lope stared at us fixedly, without batting an eye. At once I gave him the grand hailing signal.

"Come down here, Lope! I want to tell you something!"

At that the antelope, who was only just beginning to shed his winter coat, and still looked quite fine, broke his pose and jauntily marched down to fair speaking distance.

"Well then," said he, "what is it?"

"You 'lope are not going to be exterminated after all; or at least not just now."

"Really? You surprise me a lot. Tell me all about it."

"There are more than 30,000 of you; badly scattered, and in a lot of danger; but more and more is being done for you each year. New preserves are being made, new herds are being started, and nobody is allowed to kill one of you,—by law."

"Well, I want to know!" exclaimed the 'lope, dazed like.

"Superintendent Albright is working overtime," said Chief Woodring, "to get a lot of money to buy up all those ranches below Gardiner that you fellows need so much for a winter range, and he's sure to get what he wants." (He got it.)

"You—don't—say—so!" murmured the astonished 'lope. "It seems much too good to be true."

"Well, it is true all right," said the Chief Ranger, cheerfully.

"Tell me," I demanded, "in all these years why have you Park 'lopes not increased more? You ought to have 2,000 in your herds, instead of a paltry 250 or so. What's the answer, anyway?"

"Well," said Lope, "first think of the killings at Gardiner, and just north of the Park boundary; and then the coyotes in spring, sneaking into the Park and eating up the fawns. The worst of all for us has been the deep snows of winter, the awful blizzards, and our weakness and inability to get food. I call it a wonder that any of us here are alive. But that new winter range at Gardiner will save our lives, and help us to build up a real show herd."

"That's right!" cried the Chief. "All the Park visitors are keen to see 'wild animals,' and we must display a

THE PRONG–HORNED ANTELOPE.
We drove up real near to a big and solitary buck antelope, who posed like a statue, on a knoll on the right.

better line of samples. Now, you ought to round up your bunch, and keep it down here where it can be seen, instead of letting it go loafing off to those sky pastures on Specimen Ridge, clear out of sight."

"I see my duty, and I'll try to make good," said the buck, and with that we saluted and drove on.

Now to that trifling little episode there was a most unexpected sequel, and Mr. Bronson Rumsey was my host.

Just three days after that interview we plunged down the steep eastern side of the Absaroka Range, went down the picturesque North Fork of the Shoshone River, passed by the Lake, the Dam and that splendiferous gorge, saluted Buffalo Bill as he posed in bronze on his butte pedestal, and landed in the pleasant town of Cody.

Within two hours thereafter I met the manager and owners of the Pitchfork Ranch, whereon lives the largest prong-horn antelope herd in the world! There are about 1,500 head, and they were eating so much cattle grass that at last the ranch owners were feeling the burden of it, and growing restless. It was plain that encouragement of some kind was needed from without, and of a substantial character.

I said: "Will you, for a fair-sized annual sum in cash, let those antelopes go on eating your grass, and will you guard them from being killed by poachers, as long as the contract remains in force?"

The owners and managers consulted, and promptly said, "We will!"

"It's a go!" said we. "Let's prepare the papers."

THE PRONG-HORN WHO POSES

The next morning, in just one shining hour a solemn business contract was drawn up by the ranch owners, signed up with a Trustee of the Permanent Wild Life Fund, and made immediately effective. It was in satisfactory operation two full years, but now it is time for the State of Wyoming to take over that obligation, and carry on with State funds. Don't you think so yourself? No other state could possibly get so much preserved antelope for so little money as $500 a year.

In zoological characters, our Star Spangled-Antelope is as great an oddity as the mountain goat. For example: Nature handed out to him toward his make-up the amazing and unprecedented feature of *hollow horns growing over a core of bone, which horn case is shed every December, and quickly renewed.* But, while nearly all old-world female antelopes have horns (smaller than those of the male), our female antelope has none.

Nature also gave our animal a unique hair feature of very doubtful value,—more liability than asset. The rear hindquarters of the animal are covered with long and coarse white hair *which can be completely erected at will,* like the bristles on the back of a hog! As a frightened herd runs away, those big patches of white hair stand up conspicuously, and each animal advertises its presence, and attracts bullets and pursuit, by a perfectly worthless ornament that it never should have.

The horn of the Prong-Horn is set directly over the eye; and the animal has no dew-claws. Recently some running antelopes were chased, and paced, by some naturalists in an automobile, and the speed they attained was 40 miles an hour.

Up to five years ago, all friends of the Prong-Horn were alarmed, and for ten years previously had been, by the fear that the species was going out, and soon would disappear. It was about fifteen years ago that all states having antelopes stopped all shooting, and seriously made efforts at protection. The American Bison Society, headed by Mr. Edmund Seymour, toiled early and late at the task of antelope salvage in Oregon, and in reintroduction from Canada to the Wichita National Bison Range. After some discouraging losses, a herd nucleus finally took root in that Range, and now is a going concern.

In 1925 Mr. Edward W. Nelson, Chief of the Biological Survey, set the machinery of the Survey in motion, to take a careful and complete census of all living Prong-horned Antelope. When it was completed, and mapped and tabulated in methodical fashion, Dr. Nelson found that Canada, the United States and Mexico contained 286 herds of 'lopes and a grand total of 30,326 individuals.

This means that for the present our antelope species is safe against extinction. Now there are in some quarters demands for a "short open season"; which are entirely wrong, and also dangerous to the future.

KING PENGUIN GIVES AN AUDIENCE

HAVING interviewed a flock of five King Penguins, all very much alive, I now know why the title "His Serene Highness" was originated. It was invented by an Englishman, to bestow upon King Penguin, of Antarctica. It fits him perfectly, and the poise of it must make many a man king envious.

If ever you are upset in mind, and feel that you must go to a fretting-shop and have some worrying done while you wait, just go instead to the Penguin Rookery at some big zoological park, gaze upon the most serene and unruffled birds of land or sea, and be comforted.

There is only one trouble about this strange interview; and this is,—not a soul who is out from under my control will admit a belief of any more than half of it.

Once upon a time I was scheduled to meet a Real-Man King, and I practised so long upon the modes and tenses of courtly address that when the penguins arrived from the Antarctic Continent I was all set to address them up to date. Picking out the biggest one, whom I felt sure must be the ruling potentate, I thus addressed him:

"Oh, King, may you live forever. Welcome to our— no, no! Not that! I mean,—our hearts grew sore with longing during our twenty-five years of waiting for you, and you are just in time to save our lives."

"All this sounds very preliminary and trivial. Come to the point," said His Majesty, with great dignity.

He pointed his observation straight at me, with a big and powerful beak that easily could have transfixed a codfish. I could not help seeing the point.

"Your Serene Highness," said I, "it is related by the men of the Shackleton Expedition that when his ship's crew landed on Ross Island and coolly set up housekeeping, you marshalled your subjects and calmly marched over to them, to take a close-up, and see what it was all about. Is that right?"

"It is," answered the King with aplomb. "It was a formal but friendly call, from the permanent residents; but I will admit that possibly there was some vulgar curiosity seeking gratification."

"Did you and your court feel no fear of those strange creatures?"

"Fear? Fear? What is that?"

"Well, sensitiveness and modesty about being killed."

"You will deal in mysteries. What do you mean by being killed?"

"Well, sire,—or rather, sir, in your case,—to be killed is to have your head knocked off, or the life beaten out of your devoted body, by a greasy whaler who professionally clubs to death seals, walruses, auks, penguins and other birds of sorts for their paltry oil. He is by profession an Exterminator of God's most harmless and most defenceless creatures, even when they yield mighty little for him."

"Shocking!" murmured His Serene Majesty, with a shudder that shook his portly frame. "I never before heard of such atrocities, such hardness of heart."

"It was indeed fortunate," quoth I, "that Shackleton

THE KING PENGUIN.

"Sir Ernest Shackleton, rest his soul, was a gallant and humane gentleman. He, his men, and his dogs came out all together to receive us."

and his men were not whalers nor oil hunters; for had they been, you and your people surely would have gone to pot, quite literally."

"Sir Ernest Shackleton, rest his soul, was a gallant and humane gentleman. He, his men, and his dogs came out all together to receive us, to talk nicely to us, to take our pictures, and to let us scare their dogs for the amusement of the party. Some of the dogs became too fresh about biting us, and we made some pointed remarks to them that got under their skins."

"And then what happened, Your Majesty?"

"Well, at the end of the call we all bowed urbanely and politely to our strange visitors, and in good formation marched back to the hospitable nests of glacial dornicks that we had been preparing as cradles for our penguin eggs and babies. You know, in all the world there is nothing so good for a King Penguin's royal nest as a big scuttleful of nice, round stones. Each mother penguin goes out and collects her own."

At this point my evil genius prompted me to say:

"Mr. Murray said that some lazy penguins steal stones from the nests near them, while the owners are away collecting more. Is that charge true?"

"Indeed not!" corrected the King with an air of slightly miffed dignity. "My penguins are the most moral, as well as the most intellectual birds in the world. I will prove it to you. Had they been thievish, lazy, immoral or improvident, think you they could long have survived the indescribably cold winters at the South Pole? No, Sir! Of course not. Even if they had been just nervous, or quarrelsome, they would have perished and disappeared. But by practising perfect calmness of mind, coolness of temper, and the stoic disposition that refuses to be stumped by any calamity, or even death, we penguins have been able to survive, increase in size, age by age, and part of the time be actually happy."

"Men talk and fuss a whole lot of what they call philosophy, Your Majesty," said I peevishly, "but believe me, in that line you can give them cards and spades. Why, King, each one of your subjects is a living, breathing, fish-eating monument of ice-cold wisdom touching upon and appertaining to harmonization with tough environments, and the survival of the fittest."

"Pardon me," said the King with ice-cold dignity, "but I think that you are now speaking the jargon of science, and I have to inform your alleged mind that I pass."

"You have a right to be offended, O King. I had no call to do it; for I know only a few words of the lingo myself. Now, if I may do so without giving offense, may I inquire how you manage to endure life on that barren, desolate, ice-bound, wave-lashed, wind-swept, fiercely cold, utterly good-for-nothing and God-forsaken Continent, the No-Man's Land of the World?"

"The country that your glowing words so fitly describe has all of the attractions that you have named, and more. Except when the wind howls, and the cold is the worst ever, it has delightful silence, peace, plenty, and unbroken restfulness. It is too bad that you can not have the same up here, so that you might live longer. We, being coldly appraising but warmly appreciative of the blessings of Nature, call that land Paradise. Of course you know that many of your people have tried to break into it, but unsuccessfully thus far. Nature will not have them there."

"Yes," I said, scornfully. "That is true: and I wonder why. What is the use of discovering and re-discovering, and tri-discovering a South Pole that has no more character than a refrigerator, and that can not be used even when discovered ever so much? It means exploration with a small *e*."

"I have wondered about that myself," said the King, "but for that good-for-nothing icy pole I can't find an answer. Now, as for the Bay of Whales, I get that much all right. The creatures who went there were not like you. They were whalehogs; and they lived on blood and grease. I am strongly opposed to them."

"And well you may be, O King. Some day the Evil Eye of Commerce will alight upon you, and those funny Adele penguins, and the sea-leopards,—or leopard-seals,—whichever side you are on,—and you will all be completely exterminated in one season. I just hope I will not live to see it."

The King shuddered and drew back, as if I had hit him a blow with a sand-bag. He blinked, in dazed astonishment, and possibly nervous shock.

"Dreadful prospect," he muttered. "What awful creatures some men are! Even at the south end of the earth we are not safe."

"And now, Your Majesty, may I ask what you think of America, and the manners and customs of the natives?"

But at this point the royal audience was rudely inter-

KING PENGUIN GIVES AN AUDIENCE

rupted by the arrival of a stony-hearted keeper, staggering between two two-gallon pails of small fish, which at once became the center of gravity.

"He says, 'King's Ex'!" said the keeper sharply. "So you'll just have to excuse him."

And forthwith, taking a skewer from his pocket, Mr. Atkin proceeded deftly to pry open His Majesty's big beak. Then he introduced a small fish head first, and started it on its way to the Interior Department of the royal visitor.

THE TALE OF A FLORIDA CROCODILE

IN the twenty-first year of my abounding youth, I discovered and shot and preserved an old whale of a Florida Crocodile. He was No. 1 for our country; and even to this day he also holds the American championship belt for length, which is 14 feet 2 inches.

The State of Florida contains the only true crocodile species found in the United States. Those formidable reptiles once were fairly numerous in the Big Cypress Swamp above Cape Sable, and on up the East coast here and there, as far north as Lake Worth. My big specimen and his mate were taken from a narrow but deep little Everglade stream called Arch Creek, about a mile below the spot where the highway crosses it on The Arch, and about four miles above Miami.

Take him where you will, a big crocodile alive and well, and able to do damage, is a genuine thriller. Not all species are man-eaters, but please excuse me from going in swimming with any of them, for you never can tell. I have deep-seated objections to being seized by a pair of bony jaws two feet long, set with four rows of stabbing teeth, and being dragged under water and drowned by a scaly old monster with green eyes and a breath like a turkey buzzard. And yet, as museum specimens, all big crocodiles and alligators are good and desirable, at so many desires per foot.

A big Reptile House, in which I once held a block of preferred stock, recently ran out of Florida crocodiles,

TALE OF A FLORIDA CROCODILE

and for a time no mail orders were filled. Advertising was done; but it was two years before a big one showed up. For twenty-five years Alligator Joe had thrilled tourists by crocodile-catching, not wisely, but too well.

The new one came up in summer, in a big, open crate, and mad from snout to tail at the indignity of it. He was ten and a half feet long, and, as crocks go, quite smooth and handsome. His color was olive gray, not black like a 'gator, and his long and slender snout was triangular.

For several days he carried a temperature, but after a week in a comfortable and picturesque crocodile pool his grouch fever came down to normal. Then I approached the presence with an offering of choice horsemeat that quickly established cordial relations.

"How are matters and things in Florida?" I began.

"Fine," was the spirited come-back of the loyal crock. "Bumper crops, two million tourists on the way, and land going up to the sky. A school-teacher from the cold north paid $5,000 for a sunkist lot in the pine woods, and in less than a week she had refused an offer of marriage and $50,000.

"Yes, yes," I cut in, a bit hastily. "I believe all those things, and more. I've just made the grand tour in a friendly car, and we saw the whole lay-out. It's great!"

The crock eyed me suspiciously, and finally murmured: "Oh! You did, did you? Well, did you find the Miami River? Or upper Biscayne Bay? Or any remnants of the Everglades?"

"I saw the ruins of them,—and Crocodile, they made me sick! I was there in 1875, when there were only three houses at Miami, and nothing had been spoiled. A big rattler was caught for me on the site of the Royal Palm Hotel."

"You're sore on the developments, it seems," said he, peevishly.

"Of course I am," said I cattishly. "Look at what they have done to the birds, the game, the fish, and even the turtles and snakes. All gone! Nothing left that amounts to shucks!"

The crocodile nearly had a fit of excitement.

"I hate 'em, too," he hissed. "They make me sore! Why, that infernal causeway across Biscayne Bay is——"

"Look out," I whispered. "Some one might overhear you. You must not say what you really think about Florida,—anywhere south of Quebec. These northern jungles are full of tourists who have been fed up on Florida, and if you talk roughly some of them might do you a mischief."

"Thanks, old man. Even if I can't be pretty I'll try to be discreet. But, say! Didn't the absence of birds, 'n snakes 'n crocks make you feel lonesome?"

"Yes, Crockey. It did just all that. In eleven hundred miles of travel we didn't see enough live birds to stock one bird-house. Lake Okeechobee was there, but inhabited only by mudhens!"

"Well," said Crockey, "mudhens are good! I won't go back on them, ever. In fact, I love 'em. But now there's only one for every fifty that once were there. The turkeys are done for; the raccoons and opossums have been hunted out for their measly fur; the bears are just about every one dead; the lynxes are few and seldom, and a puma is heard of about once in every five years."

"How is it about quail, and ducks, and deer?"

"Going! Going! Mighty little left, and the remnants are being put on the bargain-counter to tempt the northern sports. I know one northern man who hunts quail in the pine woods from his automobile, without getting out. The ducks of Florida are now a joke; and it won't be long before they get the last deer."

"Gee whiz!" I said, "will not that new law, and the new game commission, be able to save something in the shape of game from the wreck?"

"No, sir. I think it's now too late. The voting power of the hunter and game-killer is too strong. The trouble is the people are not organized, the wild creatures can't vote, and the wild game of Florida is gone, never to come back. Too many tourists, and guns, automobiles and developments. In a governor's turkey hunt last year all that the whole staff of the Governor of Florida could find for the Governor of Connecticut was one poor, scared hen-turkey roosting on a limb."

"And how are your own people and the 'gators making out?"

"Making out is it? We're not making out at all! We are all going down and out, pronto! Why, even the baby 'gators two feet long now are being jack-lighted at night, and murdered for their poor little hides. It's clear infanticide, that's what it is. The craze for 'gator skins has broken out again, worse than ever; and the little 'gators don't savvey the hunters at all. If they did, they would live in deep water, and never show up except at burrows in the sandy banks of the creeks and rivers.

with entrances under the water out of sight. And believe me, except when we are hunting for food we stay in our burrows. But do you know how the Alligator Joes get us? They probe down through the sand with long, iron rods, until they find our burrows; then they prod us out. I wouldn't go out for just ordinary prods; and do you know what they finally did to drive me out, and into their noose?"

"No, not I. What was it?"

"They built a fire, and prodded me with hot irons, sir,—*hot* irons! A most unfair thing to do. They ought to be forbidden by law."

"You are right, Crockey; quite right. But even at that, the Alligator Joes would get you, somehow. They would send down depth bombs if necessary. The destroyers are out to get all the mammals and birds, and all the reptiles and fishes of Florida, and the finish is only a question of a little time. It's tough; but it is now too late to worry over it. The desirable wild things are just the same as done for. Mark my word."

"It is tough," moaned the Crock, weeping copiously. It was the first time I ever had seen real crocodile tears; and believe me, those weeps were fully justified by the sorrows of that vanishing reptile.

Even at the risk of being disagreeable, I felt compelled to tell that unhappy Crocodile the naked truth about the game and wild life situation in Florida as I see it. I saw it in 1875, in 1894, in 1901, in 1910, in 1915 and in 1926. In 1901 I made a fine list of all the birds that I saw in a daylight ride from Miami to Sebastian; and at Oak Lodge, ten miles or so above Sebastian. We

THE FLORIDA CROCODILE.
"We're not making out at all, and we're all going down and out. Even the baby 'gators are being jack-lighted at night."

spent a month in a jungle on Indian River, then rich in wild life.

In March, 1926, my good friend Frank Seaman gave me an automobile tour from Charleston, S. C., to Jacksonville, Tampa, Winter Park, Okeechobee, Palm Beach, Miami, and up the east coast to St. Augustine. Our tour was chiefly by daylight; and we watched for birds of all kinds, throughout all the daylight hours.

The absence of bird life of all kinds was ghastly, and appalling. While we did not expect to see a great amount, we did expect to see *some;* but with the exception of about 75 mudhens and a few little ducks on Lake Okeechobee, there was practically *nothing!* The statement that I made to the lonesome and discouraged crocodile represents Florida as I have seen it during the past fifteen years, very nearly all around it.

As a once-teeming paradise of wild life, I now regard Florida as done-for, excepting the fishes that are at present beyond the power of man to exterminate.

A HEART-TO-HEART TALK WITH A SKUNK

GOING or coming, a live skunk is a hazardous risk. Except when his fur overcoat is "prime," he is to be regarded as a liability rather than an asset. For something like fifty years we puzzled over the question, "Why is a skunk?" And at times it hurt our head. This was not due to our lack of knowledge of the brain and personality of that little beast, but rather because of too much of it. Even as with people who persistently offend, the more you see them the more you can't account for them.

Ever since my earliest recollections of skunks, I never loved them, and had no use for them in my sphere of influence. This was partly due to instinctive prejudice; because thus far no skunk ever has put anything over on me. In these later years, I learned that in polite society the fur of the skunk lifts you up financially, but the name of the animal drags them down socially. It is safer to mention a rope in the family of a man who was hanged than to say "skunk," suddenly or loudly, in a company of fur-bearing women.

My first interview with a skunk was in the month of wild roses, on a virgin Iowa prairie as cleanly shaven as a lawn. I was an assistant pioneer, and for once in love with that job. Out in the open, where the meadow larks were sweetly warbling, and all Nature was smiling and glad, a big, bad skunk suddenly rose out of the landscape, and confronted me. He was a perfect whale of a skunk. He was heavily armed, and I was not. He carried a deadly revolver. Most truculently that big and insulting tail of his went straight up in the air, and became fixed, like a black flag of piracy.

He faced me. His beady, black eyes glared. He made a series of short runs at me,—snarling, showing his teeth, and stamping on the ground with his black, front feet, most defiantly. Few and short were the words we said.

He said: "Run, you little skeezicks! Run, or it will be the worse for you."

I said: "You get off this prairie. You are too fresh."

"I dare you to try to put me off," said he. "If you dast to try it, I'll make you bury your clothes for four weeks." (And—he—meant—it!)

If he had not run such a mean whizzer on me, thataway, that skunk might have gone on living. As it was, I whistled shrilly, three times; and soon my big brother came a-running, with his new shotgun in his hand, and fire in his eye. He lost not a moment in deciding that as a candidate for membership in our pioneer club, that animal must be black-balled.

But the flight of time brings changes galore. Even the social status of skunks is affected by it. Many years after that first offence, I went out of my way to make the personal acquaintance of the pet skunk of a quondam friend. I should say that any friend who has pet skunks is quondam. The animal, however, had been disarmed at an early age, and the horrors of war had been somewhat mitigated.

THE NORTHERN SKUNK.

"He said: 'Run, you little skeezicks, or it will be the worse for you.'
"I said: 'You get off this prairie. You're too fresh!'"

"I see that you don't like us," was Meph's cool remark after he had given me the once over. Confound my tell-tale countenance, anyway! He reminded me of the way a Nice Lady once rapped out at me most suddenly, "I see that you don't like my necklace!"

"On the contrary," said I to Meph, "I have entirely recovered from it. Just put it down to my lack of prevision. Now, I have come to congratulate you."

"On what, for example?"

"On the high rank that your tribe has attained in this fickle world. Fifty years ago every skunk was an Ishmaelite, an outcast, pariah, and so on. And now look at you! Above the line of the tropics the world is groveling at your ugly little black feet. Your company,—properly dressed and dyed,—is sought for by the fashionable women of all nations, from Judy O'Grady to the Colonel's Lady, from cotton pickers to queens, and——"

"Ye-es!" burst in Meph with a savage snarl, "and what good does it do us?"

"Why, look at the notoriety, old chap. Thousands of animals would give their heart's blood to figure in The Papers as you fellows do. You are famous, now! Don't you know that?"

"Yes, I do know it." (He snarled, peevishly.) "And we are dying by hundreds of thousands to pay for it. What is the good of being mentioned in the despatches when your pelt has been taken off as the price of it. *I* don't want any bloody "fame." None of us do. Why, even that poor, little striped hydrophobia skunk is no longer safe."

"Now," said I severely, feeling that I had him at a disadvantage, "Do tell me, why is the Striped Skunk, anyway? You know very well that it does sometimes spread hydrophobia, and blood-poisoning, which is almost as bad; and a fur coat composed of its skins is an atrocity."

For one tense moment that beady-eyed, black-and-white skunk eyed me as if intending to devour me. Then he spoke in withering tones.

"You are, by the ignorant, regarded as a naturalist. You ought to know that the great aim and end of the striped skunk of the South is not to grow nightmare garments for giddy girls to wear, but to destroy the millions of rats, mice, weasels, centipedes, scorpions, snakes, toads, lizards, bad insects and other things that otherwise would completely overrun the South, and drive all the Best People out of it. Is it possible that you never have heard of such a thing as preserving the balance of Nature? Are you a total stranger to the divine law of compensation?"

He paused for breath, but I kept silent. Presently he turned around, and continued in a milder tone,

"But, of course you must know the rudiments of elementary science." (Pretty hot, that was!) "If you do, you must know that all this systematic slaughter of skunks, weasels, wolves, mountain lions and other flesh eaters for their fur,—the most of which is wastefully and wickedly worn as dress and coat trimmings, not for warmth,—is going to react in the form of vast increases in the pests that do damage to man's trees and crops of all kinds, and to man himself. The world will yet pay dearly for having so wickedly and foolishly upset the balance of Nature by killing off us fur-bearers. You are already down to rabbits, and soon you will be down to wearing the skins of rats and mice. Think it over, you alleged naturalist."

"I have thought it over. You fellows eat up ten times more ground birds than you protect by killing weasels, and the bulk of your claim for compensations is disallowed. Moreover, in this zone people have got to wear fur to keep warm."

"Fully one-half of that idea is nonsense, and the other half is untrue. The Eskimo and the Indian of the Far North do need the skins and fur of caribou, bear, wolf, fox, and seal; but not you. Here in this country,—aye, and up in the coldest regions of the air, men and women can keep warmer in woolen garments than they can in fur, and the woolen garments are far better than fur in nearly every way. But your pampered women, and your hothouse men, want to ornament themselves with fine fur that they hardly have strength enough to carry around, because it shows the world how Rich they are, and makes other people envious. Now, Fashion has ordered that every woman shall wear *some* fur! Be it ever so humble, there's no going on without *some*."

"Well, what is the use of having hordes of fur-bearing savage beasts, mostly living upon other beasts, if they don't give up some fur? The fur-bearing animals are not good for pets, they all hide away from the sight of everybody, and it takes a good trapper to catch one."

"There you are again, with your boomerang logic. Speaking of traps, they are mostly cruel, torturesome things. A dead-fall is not so bad; for it kills pronto; but all steel-traps are savagely cruel; and all men and women know it; but nobody stops them. The sufferings of steel-trapped animals are incredible. (I knew of an Alaskan lynx living for thirty-seven awful days with his foot in a steel trap!) Why don't you invent a steel trap that don't torture animals, and kills them at once?"

"It can't be done!" I cried, hotly. "The S. P. C. A. tried it, and offered $10,000 for a model of one that would do, but they got nothing good out of the ninety-five submitted."

"Well, that shows that you men are not as smart as you are advertised to be. You can't invent a decent steel trap! The idea! Don't talk to me about any man-made 'dominion over all the beasts of the field and fowls of the air.' You make me sick."

Being quite jolted by this embarrassing tirade,—and from an impudent *skunk,* of all created animals,—I hastily withdrew.

BORNEO'S NEVER-SEEN NOSE-MONKEY

IN the golden days of my youth I set my heart upon visiting the great East Indian Island of Borneo, on the equator, and if I could not have gone there pronto, I think it might have stunted my growth.

Just think of it! That "Garden of the Sun" is the home of the amazing Dyaks; of the big red-haired orang-utan; of the swinging gibbon; of the rarely seen Nose-Monkey; of the rhinoceros and banting; of the argus pheasant, the rhinoceros hornbill, the python and the man-eating crocodile. Body o' me! Even today, that magic word "Borneo" thrills me!

In the rank and dank, silent and awesome forest of the level zone nearest the sea, where we found lots of brick-red orang-utans hanging out over the flood waters that covered the forest floor, we also found troop after troop of big Nose-Monkeys. Nearly always we discovered the latter sitting at luxurious ease, in high, open-work tree-tops, sunning themselves.

Occasionally a big, old he-one would exclaim to his troop, "Kee-honk," in the deeply resonant tone of a bass viol. It meant in his language "all's well"; and it never once has been heard in America; because that great monkey we never see alive outside of Borneo. They either cannot live in captivity, or they will not!

That astonishing animal is a perpetual challenge to the animal dealers and zoo men of the world. For a century he has defied them. Even with my field glasses I

BORNEO'S NEVER-SEEN NOSE-MONKEY

could see that that nose was not an ordinary monkey nose. It was a zoological Foundation and like nothing else under the sun! This made me wildly impatient to possess alive, even if only for a few days, a big one of those unparalleled monks.

It was the Dyaks who finally managed it. Wise animal men rarely undertake to tell native hunters how to catch their home animals. The thing to do in such difficult cases as that one is to harangue the natives, hang up a good cash prize, and then let Nature take her course. We believed that the Nose-Monkey famine in America and Europe was not due to the inability of the Dyaks to catch the beggars; for they can catch almost any wild thing, provided the clouds of Doubt have a silver lining.

And sure enough, the Dyaks of our river soon caught a big "blanda," by chopping down his tree, rudely rushing him with forked sticks, and pinioning him down to the earth without ever giving him a chance to bite any of his captors. They gently but firmly hog-tied him, slung him under a pole, paddled home to our longhouse, and proudly delivered him.

With almost human foresight I had made ready a very comfortable bamboo cage, with a small log for the nose-bearer to sit upon, but the captive was so peeved by that Dyak mastery that at first he registered nothing but disgust. His face was cinnamon brown, his thick head and body hair was reddish-brown and white, and his big and clumsy tail was snow white, with a lion-like tuft at the end. And then that Nose!

There is nothing else like it in the wild-animal world.

In length, breadth and thickness it is enormous. There is a shallow valley down the middle of it, the septum partition is too short for the two sides, and therefore the organ terminates in two rather neat points that hang well down below the chin.

The first thing that I did was to make a careful sketch of that rare monkey and its astounding nose,—which I will wager put the latter on record, as it really is, for the first time. The reader will see a copy of it herewith. The Amazing Monk watched me with evident interest and curiosity; and two or three times he muttered, "Kee-honk."

"I say, old chap," said I at the finish, "What will you have to eat? I want to feed you fairly."

"Give me durians," said he, as plain as print.

"I'm sorry; but I can't. You know dinged well that this is not the durian season! You'll just have to guess again."

"Well, then, given me a rasso, or some kapayangs."

"There are none. You couldn't find any yourself if you were ever so loose. I'll just give you a banana, and you can take it or leave it."

He took it; but do you think that perverse monk would eat it? No, sir. No more would he eat a nice, golden-yellow canned peach from California, that was worth a silver trade dollar to me, right there. As the Texas cowboys say, I just "couldn't sort-of" make him eat.

"Nosey," I said, despairingly, "your cussed perversity about eating will put you out of business, and break

THE NOSE–MONKEY.

"Are you afraid of big snakes?"
"Yes, indeed we are. We are always watching for them."

my heart. If you play the game that way you simply can not carry on, and you never will live to see the inside of a zoo."

"Kee-honk," said he dismally, just like an old Mohammedan fatalist who gives up, and says, "Kismet! It is the will of Allah!"

The Dyaks looked on sympathetically, but with academic interest only. They were sure that I could not make the beggar live. I changed the subject.

"How do you get on with the "mias" orang-utans of these woods?"

"Oh, very jolly, Tuan. We never fight; but they fight each other, umbrageous. We like their leafy nests to sleep in, but we can't make nests like them! With our weak hands we can't break off big branches as those rude mias do. But say! When they are asleep we sometimes warn them of danger, by shouting to them. Did you ever see a big snake go after a sleeping mias?"

"Never; and I hate to think of it. But does a python ever dare to tackle a mias besar?"

"No, Tuan! They look them over, and let the big ones alone. Even a big snake knows what fear is. But the little ones are different, that is, if there are no old he-ones around. One evening about sunset we heard a young mias screaming for help. Do you know how horribly they can scream? [It is just like a human-girl scream.] It was near by, and we rushed over to see what was the matter. A big python had seized a little-girl mias on her nest, and he was trying to squeeze her in his terrible coil, so that he could swallow her."

"Next thing, we heard a perfectly awful roar, close by; and here came an old-man mias, a-rushing through the tree-tops like a typhoon. You ought to have seen him swing, two yards at a time. When he got there, he just flung himself all over that python, grabbed him with his own big teeth, and all four of his huge hands, and *down* they went, smashing through the tree-branches clear to the ground, and fell in a fighting mix-up that was awful."

"Heavens, what a fight that was!" said I, admiringly. "And how did it end?"

"End?" cried Nosey, swelling with pride and animation. "That old mias besar polished off that snake something proper. He broke its back, and its head was bitten almost off. We went down to see it the morning after; and the big jungle-hogs were eating it. The little-girl mias was badly hurt; but she got away. You know the bite of a python is not poisonous. It is the crush of those powerful coils that we all look out for. If one is flung around you, you never can get loose alive, unless some one kills the snake, and mighty quickly, too."

"Are you afraid of those big snakes?"

"Yes, indeed we are. We are always watching for them, and whenever we see one we shout out quickly, and tell all the jungle people to 'look out.' We've got to stand together, all that we can; because we have so many enemies."

"Why are you monks hanging out over this flooded forest down below?"

"Oh, that means nothing to us. We never feed or sleep on the ground, and we were here first. That flood is a mere incident," said Kee-Honk, loftily, with a perfectly plain attempt to turn up his nose at the whole matter. But his nose was not made for scorn, and the effort was a failure.

THE ALMOST-GONE WHOOPING CRANE

IF you can envision the wide geography and local color that surrounds every Whooping Crane now left alive on this old murderous sphere, you will be thrilled.

In the first place, old Whooper is a vanishing bird, and the sole-surviving two hundred head (or less!) are standing upon the brink of the precipice of Life, at the foot of which lies Oblivion. In other words, there are only about two hundred cranes of that fine species alive today, and it is safe to wager that they are being killed faster than they are breeding.

The great white Whooping Crane is the largest American crane, and a stately bird at that, standing four feet three inches in his stockings. As he stands before you with wings closed, his plumage is wholly white, and his jet black primaries are unsuspected, but the top of his head is bare. You may recognize him at once by his whiteness, and the jaunty plume that is made by the saucy uplift of his upper-tail-covert feathers. He has a fine voice for singing, and when he walks his stride equals that of a drum major for aplomb.

Going or coming I love his joy call, "qua-KEE-oo!" because it is so trumpet-like, so musical, and so strong that it easily carries half a mile.

Once in the days of my boyhood on an Iowa prairie, I suddenly saw in my father's pasture a whole flock of six whaling big and beautiful white birds, shining in the sun; and being all alone, the thrill of it nearly upset me. It was not until I got hold of Audubon's "Birds of America" that I found out truly and correctly that they were Whooping Cranes.

Now, here is a curious little circumstance. The geographical centre of these sometimes United States is in the devoted state of Kansas, and it is a positive fact that more Whooping Cranes on migration have landed in Kansas than have appeared in any other state. I have been personally acquainted with at least six birds that so landed, were caught alive by amazed and excited farmers, and sold to zoological parks, or other persons of less renown. I have a story of one other that a fool hunter shot to death just because he didn't know what it was, for which he was fined $25 for breaking the state migratory bird law.

For a dozen years or more, we have had in our zoological park a fine old Whooper who is one of my most prized friends. A thousand times I have passed the time o' day with him, and once I got a real story out of him.

"I was born on the Kenai Peninsula, if you know where that is," said he.

"Were you, really? That is in Alaska,—south side of Cook Inlet, with grand mountains, big forests, lots of lakes, and good fishing."

"That's it," cried Whooper, "There is scenery to burn, and no end of good food for young cranes. My home was in a marsh at the head of a lake in the heart of that wilderness, where no man lived, and few ever came. The moose were thick, and *big!* I can't tell you how big they were, and what awful horns they had."

"Did the big bulls ever fight?" I hurriedly cut in.

"Oh, yes! In the fall, just before we were due to start south, they used to fight umbrageous. Once I saw two big bulls fight, and spring their horns together so tightly that they couldn't pos-sib-ly get loose again!"

"And then what happened?"

"Why, they struggled, and struggled; and finally one of them fell down and couldn't get up any more. Very soon he died; and at last the other one died; and there they were, piled up together. It was awful!"

"*Three years afterward we got their horns!*" I fairly shouted.

"*Did* you, really?" Whooper jumped up in the air, and flapped his great wings in amazement at the coincidence.

"Are there many of you fellows in the Kenai Peninsula now?"

"No," said Whooper, calming down. "Seven flocks only; that's all. But I know that just a few more nest in Alberta."

"How do you travel to and from Alaska?"

"Well," said Whooper, pausing a spell in the act of thinking hard, "we come down for a long ways between the Coast Mountains and the Rockies, and then where that big river runs off to the east we follow it through the Rockies, to the edge of the Big Plains. Then we follow the edge of the plains down a long ways. We sometimes fly right over those nesting birds at the edge of the plains in Alberta, and we stop and visit with them."

"And where do you winter?"

"Oh, down south, in southeastern Texas, or Louisiana; but we always stop in that Kansas Garden Spot; and it was there that I was caught, just as others of us have been, too."

"Why do you do it?"

"Well, in that state everything is so be-u-tiful, and it seems so much like home, with lots and lots of frogs and other food, that we just can't resist it! But I had an accident there, and that was how I was caught."

"Good land! Tell me all about it," I exclaimed.

"No, it wasn't a good land for me. You see" (apologetically), "we got lost in a fog, and couldn't see the earth; and we had to land without getting any bearings. Well, sir, I'm a crow if we didn't land in a farm yard, close to a man that was milking a cow! Up he jumped, threw his arms around the bird that was nearest to him, and held on. I was It! . . . And here I am."

"Yes," I said, "and you seem to have made a final landing in the lap of rank luxury. Now see that you make the most of it. You are in distinguished company. This assembly of cranes is made of delegates representing many different lands. Have you become acquainted with any of them?"

"Yes; I've spoken to that nice little Young-Lady Crane over there."

"Oh! I might have known it. The Demoiselle Crane! You have a good eye for beauty, and those slow-moving fellows from India will find that you are a dangerous rival."

"Rival?" barked the Whooper. "Rival me no rivals.

THE WHOOPING CRANE.

"Up he jumped and threw his arms around the bird that was nearest.
I was It; and here I am."

In this case there will be none! But is she not an exquisite little creature, so petite, so gentle, so ladylike, so———"

"Oh, the dear little Demoiselle is all that. She is charming to live with, but she comes from lower Egypt where crane-food is scarce, and she is so small that you will just have to do all her fighting for her."

"I will fight for her, all right," said Whooper sharply, ruffling his plumes, and snapping his bill, warningly. "But won't you tell me who the others are?"

"Oh, yes, I will point them out before you are formally presented. Now, this one in the next park to yours is the beautiful and strange Paradise Crane, from Central Africa. You can recognize him as far as you can see him by his delicate blue color, his graceful tail plumes that sweep right-down to the ground, and his very thick head, set on a slender and delicate neck. He is a very refined bird, and his nerves often are jarred by the rude conduct of that rough pair from Central India."

"And who and which are they?"

"They are over yonder in the farthest park,—the tall husky ones, pale slaty blue, with a red cap on the head. They are Saras Cranes, from the country below Delhi, India, and when they feel mean they are bad fighters. Be on your guard when near them, and don't let either of them get the drop on you. I will say for them, however, that they are mighty good dancers; in fact, the best in the Crane Family. It is wonderful. And then their voices! When they feel joyous, and pipe up strongly, they can be heard a mile."

"Fine," said Whooper. "I will be pleased to meet the Sarases. And now about the others."

"Well, the one on the right yonder, who looks so much like you, is an Asiatic White Crane, now seldom seen. The pair next to him, lead-colored, with a patch of white on the neck and back, is the rare Japanese White-Neck. That big, staring chap is the Manchurian Crane, of Eastern Asia, and beloved by the Japanese makers of bronze cranes. That smallish slate-blue chap is your own countryman, the Sandhill; and this one off here on the left, all alone, is the exquisite Crowned Crane of Africa, and the dandy of them all,—present company excepted."

"Thank you very much. But I can't be presented this week. I must defer it until I can look my best. You see, my plumes are some mussed up, and I must get a permanent wave before I can come out."

A GIANT TORTOISE RECALLS THE PAST

TRULY, the most amusing thing ever seen in our Zoological Park is our oldest and biggest Giant Tortoise, "Buster," solemnly marching at "slow speed" over the lawn in front of the Reptile House, head and neck outstretched, eagerly trying to overtake a tempting apple that is held a foot beyond his jaws, on the end of a stick operated by a small boy, who is comfortably riding on Buster's own back. Old Buster has a single-track mind, and he feels sure that he can overtake that apple if he only pursues it long enough. So he ponderously marches here and there, guided by the apple, and the crowd laughs.

There is no doubt about it. The giant tortoises of the Galapagos Islands, in the Pacific, 500 miles off shore from Ecuador, and those of the Sychelles, in the Indian ocean, do take all the first prizes for size and for long life on this earth, in this period.

Possibly it was all of 150 years ago that Buster was hatched out of an egg lying in a sun-kist and super-heated canyon, under the influence and spines of the biggest flat-leafed prickly-pear tree that we ever heard of. No, we cannot tell his age by looking at his teeth. He hasn't any; but the edges of those horny jaws are sharp enough to cut your finger off, even as the teeth of a small boy nip off the end of a stick of candy. Buster's former post-office address was Albemarle Island, Galapagos Islands—probably the most rugged and terrible

THE GIANT TORTOISE.

Old Buster has a single-track mind, and he is perfectly sure that he can overtake that apple if he only pursues it long enough.

lava-and-cactus islands of Godforsaken sterility and heat to be found on this whole earth. But thousands of tortoises actually flourished in that inferno—until predatory men came.

Buster I, our very largest Giant Tortoise, came to us in 1901, accompanied by three others. He weighed 310 pounds. The length of his shell on its curve was 4 feet and 3 inches, its width was 4 feet 7 inches, and its height was 20 inches. The largest one captured at that time, for Lord Walter Rothschild, weighed nearly 500 pounds, and it required twelve men to carry it over the last six miles of its journey out of the rugged heart of its native isle.

Buster II (now 220 pounds), was so pleased at being out of Albemarle Island, and safe in a good boarding house, that he became a regular chatter-box. Thousands of people have talked to him, and questioned him, but even yet it has not made him nervous. In the twenty-six years that he has been in our midst, and steadily playing his part in our educational scheme, he has become much more than a tortoise. He is now a small institution; and I have no doubt that he will be "as is" a hundred years from now, and millions of people now unborn will then know him personally, as we do now.

The virtues of our flock—or herd, whichever it is—of Giant Tortoises are almost too numerous to mention. Of course those giants have been furnished sunny and hot indoor apartments for the winter solstice, excellent sand-covered yards and a bathing pool out of doors for summer, plenty of food, and plenty of society, such as it is. They eat all the kinds of vegetables and fruit that they can crush up and swallow, save those that are too expensive. They have a high opinion of the vitamines that dwell in ripe tomatoes, and always want more. When herded on a lawn they industriously crop the blue-grass and white clover. Apples are a luxury that are always wanted but seldom enjoyed, because of the price of good ones.

Those tortoises never fight, never get angry, nor try to break out, and glory be! They never criticise their food. This last fact shows how far removed they are from the humans of today.

When our acquaintance with the flock had become well established, my opportunity arrived. One fine morning, before the opening hour for visitors, I repaired all alone to the low wire fence, and gave Buster the grand hailing signal. He rose from the sand, dignifiedly marched over to me, and inquired the object of the meeting.

"Buster," said I, "I want you to tell me the story of your life on Albemarle Island, and all that you saw and heard."

"Well, the first thing I knew I was living in a thorny jungle, on terribly rough lava, at the bottom of a gulley, up near the summit of the central mountain. A thousand feet down below me was a big crater like the inside of a huge wash-basin. I remember thorny brush and prickly pear trees ten feet high, with leaves on them as big as your two hands. Down at the very bottom of the big basin there was a pond of water. That was where all the tortoises of that crater drank and bathed."

"Were there many of you?"

"Yes, hundreds and hundreds at first. But all that has changed. There is not one big tortoise there now."

"Really? How did that come about?"

"By men, of course. At first all those islands had tortoises upon them—hundreds of them. Many of them lived near the seashore, but my folks and I lived miles away. The men on the whaling ships sailing up and down the west coast of the Americas always were hungry for fresh meat. Many years ago they discovered two fatal things. They found out that our meat was good, and also that a tortoise could live in the hold of a ship for days and weeks without food or water, and when finally killed would even then be good to eat.

"The whalers began to come after us, and each year they took away many hundreds. Many a ship took 150 of us on board at one time, and in those days the whaleships were many. Every whaleship meant death to a lot of our people."

"But they didn't get you, Buster!"

"No, I was too many hot and rugged miles away from the shore for the sailors to carry me. I belonged to the last colony on Albemarle. At last we began to feel that we were safe; but it was not true. Ten miles from the shore, high up on the mountain, a man from Guayaquil settled down to kill wild cattle for their hides. On his ranch there still were many tortoises. My family and I lived in a little valley ten miles beyond the ranch, nearly at the mountain's top, where there was plenty of water and food. It took eight men to carry me down to the shore.

"Even thirty years ago there were hundreds of us

A GIANT TORTOISE RECALLS THE PAST

high up on Albemarle, but the wild dogs killed many of the young ones, and ate them, and then came those awful men, to slaughter us for our oil. Yes, oil! Can you imagine such a thing as getting oil from a tortoise like me! But they did their work. They slaughtered all of us that they could find. They intended to leave none of us alive, and they left acres and acres of ground strewn with our dead and empty shells."

"Yes, Buster, and now the tortoises of the Galapagos Islands have been so nearly exterminated by 'civilized man' that the Zoological Society has gone to the trouble of sending a ship down there, collecting all that could be found, and placing them in United States homes, where they will be safe from quick extinction."

"Outside of this place, it would seem that life on this earth is not all that it is cracked up to be," said Buster, gloomily. And I could not dispute him.

AFRICA'S MOST WONDERFUL BIRD ARRIVES

QUITE recently a long and tiresome effort culminated, and a thrilling experience was mine. I was the first interviewer to welcome the first Whale-Headed Stork that ever set foot on the Western Hemisphere! Throughout fifty years of zoo-making in America, not one Ba-len-i-ceps *rex* ever had accomplished the long and perilous journey from the wild heart of Central Africa to this side of the world! And as you know, the "first" specimen of a wonderful and highly-prized species never "arrives" but *just once!*

Draw as well as you can a square of reasonable size at the geographical Centre of Africa, and you will have the home of this vastly-prized bird.

The efforts that fruited last week, as gently implied above, began three long years ago. Turn by turn they engaged a somewhat shop-worn zoo director, a sporty and daring dealer in wild animals, an enterprising Egyptian traveller, a courageous English missionary, a fine United States Minister to Egypt, and finally a "perfectly-splendid" British High Commissioner. That was a rather capable array of talent, was it not? And yet, had any one of those personages failed to function, that Distinguished Arrival of last Friday never would have taken place.

Even when the zoo man in the case heard that the bird was "still alive," and "on board for New York," he dared not hope that it would live to make a successful landing. When a wire told him that it was actually in port, he repressed his joy, and sadly muttered, "There's many a slip!"

The next day he flew down to the zoological storm centre, to be told the worst. As he broke through the cordon of gatemen at the entrance, they said: "No, we don't know. But truly, it has not arrived here." Five minutes later when he rounded the starboard quarter of the Aquatic Bird House,—there, upon an elevated bank of grass, standing absolutely free in the glorious sunshine, and calmly posing for Mr. Sanborn's best camera, was the Great Bird. Had there been no ribald rabble near, it is very likely that the Chief Worrier in the case would have thrown his arms around that outlandish bird and kissed him!

But not on that illimitable void of a mouth! Oh, no! Any stranger would respectfully pause at the sight of that enormous beak, like a round-bottomed row-boat turned keel upward, with a throat attachment of a calibre sufficient to take in a four-pound trout.

"Welcome, thrice welcome, Whale-Head of Storks," cried the transported interviewer.

"Just forget that whale-head appellation, and call me Rex for short," hoarsely croaked the bird from his throat cavern.

"Right, Rex! Quite right. And I am delighted to hear you converse in such choice English. How in the world did you acquire it, and in Egypt of all unlikely places?"

"I was brought up in a highly respectable English-missionary family," said the Whale-Head, proudly arching his neck some. "I heard of you from Dr. Olson, but for two years and nine months I never really expected to see you."

"And you surely never would have done so had not United States Minister Howell at Cairo gone to Lord Allenby, the British High Commissioner, with your celebrated case; which swiftly led the High Commissioner to send a telegraphic order to Kartoum that opened the road out from that mysterious Lake No, where you were born, and gave you a passport to fame in New York. Personally, I think you are a mighty lucky bird. I see that you are looking fine, old boy. Were you comfortable on the long, long trail?"

"Not on your life. Just have a look at my travelling cage, over there by the Bird House."

I looked, and saw a queer wedge-shaped crate, heavy in slats but small in size, standing on its base with its point up in the air. Never have I elsewhere seen mortal cage like that; and it looked as if it had come through a hurricane.

"Gee whiz, Rex! That is a mighty bad one! I think you must be as tough as a pine knot, or you never, never could have survived four thousand miles of travel in that atrocity."

"I just *refused* to die!" said Rex with pride and dignity. "But that trip out of the wild heart of Africa,— by black-boy carriers, ox cart, boat and rail nearly broke my heart, I admit. The trip down the Nile was not so bad, except that it was awfully long, awfully hot, my food went bad, and I was pestered every day to open my bill and say something. On the big sea-boat I grew seasick, and had awful headaches; but you see I stuck it out." (He looked about.) "Now, I'm glad that I did. It looks rather good here, even though it is a goodish bit from the Nile. Have you plenty of fresh fish?"

"We have, Rex; fresh fish galore, summer and winter. Order whatever you like best."

I was about to say more; but just at that point Rex carelessly opened up all his beak in a perfectly enormous *yawn!* The audience saw that the roof of that amazing mouth cavity was bright red, and that the cavern beyond it had capacity to hold a quart of smelts without any strain. Rex's beak seems to be about twice the size of his skull; and at its tip it has a quite powerful hook, for use in tearing up food. The eye of the bird is small, and straw-yellow in color; and his plumage just now is dull blue. At the back of his head he has a queer tuft of half a dozen long feathers, like a scalp-lock; evidently meant to be jaunty and chic, but decidedly droll.

The height of the bird at present is forty-two inches; but it is due to grow much taller than that.

"Tell me all about your home, Rex. Where were you born?"

"Well, sir," said the Noble Bird, beginning to look back into the past. "I was born at the north end of Lake No, in the head of the loveliest papyrus swamp I ever saw, in a nest that overhung nice, clean water that was warm, and full of fish and frogs. That swamp was the home of some big hippos, many crocodiles (some of them mighty big ones), and very many beautiful pink and white flamingoes."

"But everybody had to look out for those crocodiles. Those ugly old reptiles just lived by the mistakes of other wild people. If a young bird fell into the water,—zip! It was seized and swallowed in a minute. The wild buffaloes, elands, waterbucks, hartebeests and oryx antelopes came there to drink, but believe me! they were mighty careful to post sentinels to watch for those crocks, and give the alarm whenever a big one tried to swim up, slowly, within grabbing distance."

"But even with all that, those crocks lived mostly at the expense of those animals, with some fish for variety. The wisest animals cannot always escape. Even when they know their danger, they grow careless of it."

"Men also are like that, Rex," said I. "And it will always be so, as long as men are men."

"I miss all those interesting wild people," said Rex thoughtfully.

"Well here you will be surrounded by wild people until you grow weary of looking at them. It is easy to get fed up on just people. Are there many of your people where you were born?"

"Oh, no," said Rex promptly. "There are only just a very few. Once there were more; but now there are hardly any of us left."

"No; I imagine there are not enough, even if all of you were caught, to supply one-half of the zoos of the world. It is no wonder that you are closely guarded."

Rex kindly explained to me, as I took his right foot to say good-bye, that his name Ba-len'-i-ceps is Latin for whale-head, or something like that; and of course "rex" stands for "king"!

THE WHALE-HEADED STORK.

"Well, sir, I was born at the north end of Lake No, Central Africa, in a swamp."

While I still lingered, gaping in rapture at Baleniceps, and mentally exulting in an excess of joy at the sight of him, alive, well and actually in our possession, Keeper Atkin calmly and dispassionately thrust his friendly right arm under that priceless body, and lifted the rarest bird in all America in his arms, saying pleasantly:

"Come on Rex, old boy. It's time for you to go to your royal apartment in the Aquatic Bird House. You have posed enough for one day."

Like the wise bird and good sport that he is, Rex submitted with the grace and affection of a prince; which led people to exclaim:

"Well, I declare! And him only just come wild from the heart of Africa!"

Do I believe that "Pursuit is better than Possession?"

Most assuredly, with birds like Rex, I—do—NOT! Give me safe and sound possession, every time.

THOSE GIANT LIZARDS OF KOMODO

A COUNTRY, an island, a lake, a wild animal, bird or reptile is not really "discovered" until it has been reasonably described, more or less appropriately named, and put on the map of the reading and thinking world. After that all the public writers and printers can exploit it for the benefit of the millions who read.

Away out yonder in the great maze of land and water called the Malay Archipelago, 380 miles due south of Macassar, Celebes, and between the Islands of Flores and Sumbawa, is a lusty little tropic isle called Komodo. For centuries it seems to have bloomed and fruited without the knowledge or consent of the great powers who make books. Today it rides into the eye of the world on the back of the biggest lizard species now alive, propelled by a truculent monster with the grace of a tortoise and the table manners of a hyena.

Now, going or coming the Island of Komodo is a hard nut to crack. It is reeking with poisonous serpents, bad bugs, disreputable wild hogs, nondescript "buffaloes," and big, waddling lizards that give one the creeps to behold. The plains are no good, the mountains are worse, and nothing looks natural. The only human inhabitants are found in one small colony of sick and dying convicts, who are dragging out their wretched and hopeless lives in the best imitation of hell that I have heard of this side of the Styx. Truly, that island is no place for men.

And such is the favorite habitat of the world's biggest lizards. They have been credited, somewhat overgenerously, with a maximum length of twenty feet, with tiger-like ferocity and flesh-eating habits of the blackest dye; but their alleged length is about seven feet too much.

Into that welter of lizards and blood-curdling lizard stories there plunged in 1926 Mr. and Mrs. William Douglas Burden, of the New York Zoological Society. They took with them ropes and cameras, to drag big lizards from their lairs, photograph them, and if possible to bring some of them alive to New York. They went, saw, and conquered on all counts. Their fine moving pictures and living specimens fixed Komodo Island in the restless and fickle public eye for at least seven days.

The pictures show a tropic isle becomingly diversified and adorned for human interest. Its shores are palm-fringed, its coastal plains are mostly treeless prairies covered with lush grass two feet high, and its forest assets are open to suspicion. The lofty, jagged, crocodile-toothed interior mountains are so high and so towering that it is difficult to believe them. They are said to be volcanic masses that once filled the interiors of active volcanoes, hardened in situ, and finally the outside of each volcano weathered away and left nothing but those sharp-pointed lava casts of those interiors. Tough story; but many others are charged up to the geologists, with long rows of ciphers after them.

When word came that Mr. and Mrs. Burden were bringing us two real, living giant lizards from Komodo, we felt that the news was too good to be true. When the ship docked, and the reptiles were reported discouraged but alive, it was incredible; but we made haste to believe it.

Swiftly and soon the distinguished arrivals were convoyed to the Zoological Park, and turned loose in a sandy yard with high sides, and a vaulted roof of wire netting.

The strangers were heavy of body and limb, powerful of jaw, and densely covered with a protective armor of fine gray scales. The whole reptile looks as if solidly covered with glass beads. Most ground lizards have enormously long and whip-like tails, but these have rather shortish tails; and their burly bodies are built for strength rather than for grace and speed.

The most striking features in the excellent moving pictures made by Mr. Burden were the great number of lizards on Komodo, their ferocity, their dauntless courage in searching for prey, and their strength in tearing to pieces and devouring their prey when found. I cannot at all understand how they can bite their way through the tough hides of wild cattle, and swallow wild hogs, as they do.

I lost no time in calling upon those two wonderful lizards at the Reptile House, but it took minutes to engage the attention of the old he-one. He was busily engaged in walking to and fro, and round and round his wire-covered yard, seeking either what he might devour, or else how he might break out and escape.

As he passed me on his third round, I hailed him thus: "Hi, there! Big-One! I wish to speak to you."

Slowly he turned his scaly head and basilisk eyes in my direction, grunted "Meat!" and then briskly moved on.

As quickly as possible my keeper-guide procured a big chunk of raw beef from the cook-house, and carefully selecting a chance, we lashed it tightly to the inside of the wire fence, a foot from the floor, and awaited results.

We were out not a moment too soon. The Big One saw it, rushed for it, fastened his greedy jaws into it, then braced back and began to tear loose a mouthful.

I hate to use a commonplace word in literature as polite as this,—but oh, man! How he yanked! He snatched, he jerked, he tugged, and he worried that mouthful of meat as if it were a living thing. In fact, I never knew how plain yanking could be raised to the horsepower standard until we saw that fearsome tug-of-war.

The meat was quite firm in its resistance, but very soon it gave way. It had to. And then that glutton stretched open his throat, gulped greedily a few times, and swallowed it whole! And that, children, is the way those largest and most savage of all flesh-eating lizards tear dead animals to pieces in the wilds of Komodo. If you have any yanking that you want done, just give the job to a big old Va-ran'us Lizard of Komodo.

"Say, Big One. How long are you?" said I.

"Eight feet or more, and heavy at that."

"How long is the biggest one of your kind on Komodo?"

THE GIANT LIZARD.

I never knew how plain yanking could be raised to the horse-power standard until I saw that fearsome tug-of-war.

"Ten feet. We can grow up to thirteen feet; but never to twenty."

"Are there many of you over there?"

"Plenty. There are hundreds. But most of them are small and trivial."

"Do you fellows ever voluntarily attack men?"

"Naw!" (scornfully). "We know better."

"But you could fight men in self-defense?"

"Oh, yes, of course; and we know how to give some mighty nasty bites, too; but only when we are attacked."

"How were you caught?"

"In a miserable box cage of wire, with a low-lived dropping door, loaded inside with a hind-quarter of banting-buffalo meat. But any one would fall for a dishonest trick like that. It's mean to deceive a poor old Va-ran'-us that way. Don't you think so?"

"That depends, old chap," said I with diplomatic reserve. "Circumstances cover a multitude of sins. But for that cage you would not be here, alive and well; now would you? You should be thankful that you are out of that awful island."

"I prefer the grassy meadows and green shoals of my home island,—if it's all the same to you."

"But the road to the Hall of Fame for big lizards runs right through this zoo, and this is the Life for you."

"This life looks to me rather trivial. What relatives will I find in these Americas of yours?"

"Well, as lizards go, you will find some very good families. The Iguana family contains some of the best reptile blood of Pan-America. The first that comes to my mind is the big Rhinoceros Iguana, of Hayti and

San Domingo. You can recognize them anywhere by the little imitations of rhinoceros horns that they carry on their snouts.

"On Narborough Island, in the Galapagos Archipelago, away down yonder in the Pacific Ocean 500 miles west of Ecuador, Rollo J. Beck found in 1902 three acres of bare rock at the edge of the sea, completely covered with Marine Iguanas, quietly lying there, wideawake, and calmly waiting for something to turn up. But they couldn't last. In 1925 when William Beebe went there, he found only a dozen or so. The great herd had been destroyed, or driven away."

"How I wish I could have known those people!"

"Yes. It was a wonderful assemblage, but too big to last. Well, down in Central and South America there lives the Common Green Iguana, from four to five feet long over all. It has a jaunty crest of spines along the middle of its back, its tail is very, very long and whip-like, and its color is mostly green. Its flesh is good to eat,—if you are really hungry."

"Were you ever hungry enough to eat it?"

The question implied a doubt.

"Yes; once upon a time, in the hungriest reaches of the Orinoco River, I was just that hungry. I ate minced Iguana, and it nicely filled a long-felt want. South America is one of the hungriest countries that I ever found, and down there I collected several new experiences with alleged food products."

CORDIAL RELATIONS WITH A KUDU

> Yes, a wonderful beast is the Kudu.
> His horns spiral upward as few do.
>   No doubt you suppose
>   They can puncture his foes,
> And that is just what they are *to* do.

WHENEVER a well-armed wild animal, standing free out of doors, accepts food from your hand without chewing your hand off, or striking you, or thrusting six inches of sharp horn into your vitals, you may say that you have established with him an "ontont cordyal." The French write it *entente cordiale*, but it is not our fault that the French language never spells a word as it is pronounced.

To our mind, the Greater Kudu carries the most beautiful antelope horns of all Africa; and that is a large order. Each horn is a high, open spiral from three to four feet long; and the pair of them are set on the top of the head in stately and jaunty fashion. Each horn is beautifully modeled, and finished as if turned out on a lathe, with the surface smoothed and polished by machinery. In my favorite room one of the last lone horn tokens of my ups and downs with wild animals is a pair of Kudu horns; and it rests my eye to look upon it.

Even on its native veldt, the stately Greater Kudu always has been a scarce animal, excessively prized, difficult to find, and usually difficult to stalk and shoot. He who finds and kills a big one will earn it. Although this is one of the big antelopes, and in our opinion one of the very handsomest, it has more "protective coloration" per capita than any other large antelope known to me.

Be it known at once that when Nature elects to clothe any living creature with fur, feathers or scales of such colors and patterns that they naturally blend in with their surroundings, and at times render the creature inconspicuous, or even invisible, that is called "protective coloration." Much has been admiringly said and printed about it, but Mother Nature rarely is taken to task for the mistakes she makes in putting white animals into dark stage-settings, and thus leading straight up to their betrayal to their enemies.

But this animal of ours is a notable example on the right side of the story. Mr. E. Blaney Percival says that once when he stood within thirty yards of a large Kudu that was standing motionless under a tree, the animal was actually invisible to him until it moved its ear! The adult animal is slaty-gray in color, with six or eight widely separated perpendicular body stripes of white, and the modeling of the form is exquisite. It is a fine-grained and blue-blooded aristocrat. A big bull carrying huge horns is a grand and beautiful animal.

A hundred years ago the Greater Kudu, which is the species of this story, thinly inhabited the brush and forest country from Cape Colony northward to the border of Abyssinia, and northwestwardly up to Angola. To-day it exists, in a small number of small and widely separated island-like localities, from Rhodesia to northern Kenia Province. They live in little bands of from five to twenty individuals, usually in brush or forest country, and it is impossible for them to live in waterless deserts.

Living specimens of the Greater Kudu seldom reach the hands of animal dealers, and always they are difficult to obtain. They are always young, they are "delicate," and they die much too easily. If they would be just a little indelicate, and live longer, we would love them even more than we do. At New York's Zoological Park we waited long for our first one, and when it did finally arrive we greeted it with near-royal honors. I have heard that less deserving visitors have been presented with keys to New York City, and have gone away with them.

I was among those present at the Antelope House when our First One arrived, and was uncrated. Without any loss of time, it signified its approval of the raising of its rear door by quickly backing out into the yard, looking about, and taking a stretch. He was a trifle thin in flesh, and by no means more than half grown; but he was sane and sound, and bound to grow. He was as calm and self-possessed as if he had always owned the whole place.

"Well done, Kudu," said we. "You show much intelligence and a sanguine temperament; and you will acquire merit."

"Will you give me something to eat?" quietly observed the distinguished stranger.

"We certainly will. Here are some bits of bread, and some slices of raw sweet potato that are fit for a king." I held out a handful. To my delight, Kudu walked up to

CORDIAL RELATIONS WITH A KUDU

me as if we had been pals for a year, and with most perfect manners began to eat.

"How did you leave things in Kenia Province, Kudu?"

"Mixed. My people are seldom found and molested. For us, life was growing rather dull. There was very little work to be done, which is bad for wild beasts. It makes them soft, lazy and self-centered, and it invites disease and early death."

"Truly, Kudu, you are wise for your age. I must tell you that here workless men and women are also beset by the same line of dangers that you describe."

"Well," said the stranger, "believe me, the other big animals in Kenia Province have to step lively,—all except the giraffe and buffalo, which are so well protected that they are increasing. But the zebras are too fresh, and they are getting on the nerves of the farmers who are trying to make a go of farming."

"I must ask some of our new zebras about that," said I. "I will do so at once. But tell me, Kudu, what is your private opinion of lions?" The answer came promptly.

"I'm afraid I don't hate them half as much as I ought to. They pester us some, and occasionally kill a Kudu for food; but dear me! They are not wasteful, like the safari sportsmen. The lion is not wholly a bad fellow,—but a great many people will try to make you think that he is. He *never* kills more animals than he can eat. Of zebras, and elands, and roan antelope, and Kudu, and sable, and hartebeest, he kills only about two each week. In the old days before the white men came, this just served to limit the wild animal population. You know, where there is no killing of the big, grass-eating game animals, some kinds become too numerous. Then look out for disease! In 1896, a scourge of rinderpest contracted from domestic cattle came along, and just slaughtered the settlers' favorite animals, and an awful lot of game, also. It slaughtered the buffalo herds, as well as domestic cattle! It so nearly exterminated us that it was ten years before we really began to recover from it."

"But, tell me," continued the Kudu, "do you not think that a lot of sensible animals from my country could be brought over here, and let loose in big tracts of country, to live on their own hook, and stock the country? I see that you have a large lot of them here already, in this house."

"Alas; no, Kudu," I said, regretfully. "In a dozen different ways this is a terrible country for imported big game. First, there are the fiendish hunters who poach,—which means killing game against the law. Then there is the strange animals' ignorance of our plants; and the poisonous weeds and other plants, that either make animals crazy, or kill them. After that there is scarce water, and bad water; too much rain in some places and too little in others, too much cold, and too much heat. No; I am not advising any of my wild-animals friends to try it and take all those risks. Life is too short, and good animals are too few."

"I hope I can always stay here," said the distinguished arrival, with an anxious look in its big and handsome eyes.

"I wish to heaven you could, *and would*," said I fer-

THE GREATER KUDU.

"Believe me, the other big animals of Kenia Province have to step lively—
all except the giraffes and buffaloes."

vently. "But alas! Wild animals are no more immortal than tame men are. Meanwhile, do not over-eat, nor stay out late at night in New York. It's bad for strangers."

"Oh, I say," said the Kudu, a bit hurriedly. "Are there any of those infernal Cape hunting dogs over here,—those savage devils who hunt you in relays?"

"Oh, no! None whatever, except in cages; and in view of our sacred sheep industry it's a good thing that there are none. Nor are there any lions or leopards who can get at you, to eat you up."

"Gosh!" exclaimed the Kudu. "This is a regular wild-animal paradise."

"Now look at that," said I, rather irritably. "Here are you, less than two days in America, and already using American slang. And I just hate slang!"

"I fail to comprehend you," said the Kudu with slightly ruffled dignity. And before I could smooth down the ruffle, the offended animal turned and marched away from me, just as a British Deputy Commissioner does when you speak to him without an introduction.

PLAIN TALK TO A FOOL-HEN

AS a rule, I have found it difficult to interview birds in the wilds. The majority are afraid to take any man on trust; and few men, savage or gentle, can furnish collateral offhand. But even to the rule of man-shyness in birds there are some exceptions.

I have noticed that the birds who know most about men are the very ones who are most fearsomely afraid of them. Can you wonder why? It is because the killers of wild things have given all other men mighty bad reputations throughout the wild-animal world.

I am now going to lay before the reader the sad story of the Franklin Grouse of the Rocky Mountains. The bird is fatally lacking in inherited knowledge of savage man, and in ability to transmit warning messages of his murderous ways. This is the story of an interview with a fool-hen in the Canadian Rockies, where white goats and grizzly bears and mountain sheep and elk and moose all live together in peace and harmony.

One bright day when our pack train was pegging along up the valley of Elk River it chanced that while riding ahead of the outfit I entered a stretch of green jack-pine timber.

Half a dozen dark gray birds one by one quietly flew up from beside the trail, went about thirty yards apiece, and lighted on the lower branches of the pines in fearfully exposed positions. When tall pine trees grow thickly together, the lower branches die and drop off, and the few that do remain are just mere skeletons. Well, on those skeleton limbs, not more than eight or ten or twelve feet from the ground, those birds quietly perched, and looked wonderingly at me.

I never before had met those birds, and I knew that they didn't know me, but they were absolutely unsuspicious and unafraid. They were fool-hens. The men of the Rocky Mountains call them that because those birds do not know how merciless and deadly men are, and therefore do not at once fly from man's baneful presence. If you pretend that you are harmless and friendly, sometimes you can slowly walk up to a fool-hen, near enough to kill it with a stick.

Without any stick or other evilmindedness I slowly walked toward the nearest Franklin grouse—a handsome male bird in his fine, new, fall plumage. Without a flutter of wings he sat there and actually permitted me to come within seven feet of him. And he sat on a limb not an inch more than six feet from the needle-covered, sweet-smelling forest floor.

"Well, simp," said I affably, "what in the world are you thinking of that you don't make a good get-away?"

"Why should I? I don't fly half a mile from every bear and skunk that comes near me, so why should I fly clear away from my feeding grounds just for you? You have no big teeth nor long claws."

"But has no one ever told you that two-legged man is the deadliest animal there is toward all birds that permit him to come close to them?"

"No," said he calmly. "No one ever mentioned it to

THE FOOL-HEN.

"What are you thinking of, that you don't make a good get-away?"
"Why should I do so for you? You have no big teeth nor long claws."

me. What does man do to birds like me? I'm not a wild animal with horns, or a furry hide."

"Well," I said, "he kills you with shot-guns, rifles and revolvers; and many a foolish grouse is knocked to death by a stone or a stick."

"I want to know!" exclaimed Simp slowly.

"You fool-hens," I continued, "are victims of misplaced confidence. All of your mountain relations are so dull and stupid about man that they actually seem demented. Even after a man begins to shoot or to throw stones at one of you, you'll just sit there as if glued to the branch until at last a bullet or a stone gets you. You fellows don't know enough to grasp a new idea until you are in the frying pan."

"I guess it's because we don't understand why we ought to feel scared, and why we should fly away. But honestly, sir, I never dreamed that you could be more deadly than a skunk or grizzly bear, or that you could be mean enough to keep on attacking a poor foolish bird after it had shown its confidence in your sense of right and wrong, and your goodness of heart."

"Goodness of fiddlesticks!" I exclaimed, peevishly. "Out in the wilds there ain't no goodness of heart in men toward the wild birds and beasts and fishes." (That was a little too strong; but I was some wrought up.)

"That may be true of you men," said the grouse, "but not of the wild creatures. We give one another a square deal. It's our rule to live and let live. But apparently we do need to turn over a new leaf about men. Now, what would you, as a friend of the fool-hens, advise us to do?"

PLAIN TALK TO A FOOL-HEN

"Well," said I, "first off, quickly pass the word around that man is the most dangerous animal that roams the earth; that every man, boy and baby-in-arms must be ticketed 'dangerous,' and that every grouse, big and little, must fly whenever he appears. And you must be quick about it, too. Learn from the ruffed grouse of the East. He knows men. When he suddenly meets a loaded man on a trail he don't hop up to a lower limb, in plain sight, and sit there as an easy mark to be murdered in cold blood. No, sir!"

"What does he do?" queried the fool-hen, with interest.

"He leaps high up, explodes in the air like a bomb, scares the man out of his wits, and with a roaring burr and whirr he goes rocketing off through the timber at sixty miles an hour. Just why he doesn't knock his brains out against half a dozen trees at once, I never could make out. And nine times out of ten he saves his bacon."

"There's risk in that plan," said Simp, "but it's better to take it than to leave it and be killed. Really, I must at once get busy and tell all my people what you say, and start a reform. Our grouse mothers must teach the wisdom of the ruffed grouse to all their children, and bring them up right."

"Now you are on the right track!" I said. "This 'fool-hen' business has gone far enough."

"Well, here is one that is going to turn over a new leaf today. And now, if I am not too inquisitive, may I inquire who you are, and where you are going, and what for?"

At first the answers seemed easy; but soon I saw that they were not as easy as they looked.

"I am the Man From the East," I began ponderously.

"Are you a tenderfoot?" cut in the Fool-Hen.

"No; not exactly. I have plenty of sage-brush and alkali in my blood, but as yet no jack-pine tar. I'm out here to get that last."

"Where are you going?"

"Up to the summits of these Elk River Mountains."

"Then I'll bet you are going up there to kill billy-goats!" exclaimed the F. H. in a hard tone of voice, accusingly as it were. "You have a rifle; there are no bad Indians here; you will not shoot guides and sportsmen as your eastern hunters do in the Adirondacks, and so you must be intending to kill wild animals. Some of your ideas on not killing birds are not so bad, but, good gee! I do *not* see how you can go about murdering poor old innocent billy-goats, and sheep who never once have done anything against you. . . . Well, what makes your face turn red?"

He must have caught me in the act of blushing; for I surely felt some embarrassed by that call-down.

"Why, F. H.," said I pulling myself together. "You see, all the wild animals, and many of the birds, were made to be killed and eaten by man."

"Pardon me, but I don't 'see' anything of the kind! You are not starving for wild meat. Goat meat is not good food for men, and you have plenty of tame food."

"Well, most people believe that where game is very plentiful, and a very few old he-ones never would be missed, it is right for men to kill a few, if they make good use of them. There are reasons that you can't be expected to understand. Now, we think that the right kind of hunting is good for men, and it is called sport."

"I've heard that last word before, and it stumps me. It means the same as 'fun,' does it not? It means that you think it is 'fun' to kill wild animals, and I do not agree with you at all. I must add that you and your kind have a mighty savage idea of 'fun.'"

"But F. H.," I protested, "I want to study those goats up on the summits, and find out what they look like, how they live, what they eat, and what they think about. There is a lot that no one can find out without killing a few, to examine them. I have waited twenty years for a chance like this, and in all that time I found out mighty little about goats. I tell you, F. H., I really must know more about them, and you shouldn't call me down for taking two or three."

"Two or three? Is that all you want?"

"Sure. Why any more? I'm no hog."

"Oh, well, if *that's* all," said the bird in a tone of mollification, "go ahead and take them. I was afraid you would want from six to a dozen of each kind."

"I pledge you, my dear Fool-Hen," said I, "that none of us will abuse our privileges. In the matter of numbers, our hunting permits are entirely too liberal, and——"

"What's that you say?" cried the bird, with a show of emotion.

"I said 'too liberal'! And we are going to protest to the government against a hunting-license privilege of

6 goats, 3 sheep, and no limit on grizzly bear. It is not right to——"

But I never finished the sentence.

The bird's head fell forward limply upon its breast. Its wings sagged, its eyes closed, and in another clock-tick it fell off its perch—dead!

It was heart disease!

It was the surprise, and shock, of my last statement that did it.

THE HOME LIFE OF THE YOUNG LADY TIGER, AND THE END OF IT

WHEN it comes to falling in love with them, I do not wear my heart upon my sleeve for every wild animal to peck at. As a rule, wild animals do not dig into people's affections as fine dogs, horses and cats so easily do. It rarely happens that a wild animal, equipped with sharp teeth, claws or horns, is entirely free from freshness and the spirit of offense. For several years I have been warning my friends against "pet" bear cubs, and encouraging my enemies to acquire them.

Once, however, and practically at first sight, I did fall in love with a Wild One. She was a queenly young tigress, a stately and superb creature, much more beautiful than any picture tiger, and in color a brilliant harmony in gold, black and white. Her form was a model fit for sculptors; and the poise and grace of her "action," as they call it, was exquisite.

But, while keenly appreciative of Princess Sherni's beauty and grace, it was not that alone that enthralled me. Her crowning glory was her amiable and sweet disposition. As in girls or women, that was her most fetching charm; but there were times when I felt that she was a little too forward and demonstrative toward other men.

The Princess manifested her regard for me by promptly skipping down to the bars whenever (by her keeper's permission) I appeared quite near. On coming to a close-up, she would rub her velvety black and white cheek against my hand, and joyously exclaim: "Ah! Ha-ha!"; which was half laugh and half purr. (No. A tiger cannot purr, really.) After I had foolishly risked a ten-thousand-dollar hand in stroking her cheek and her neck through the bars, she would gracefully warp her body forward and bring her whole velvety side into the contact.

Never before nor since that tigress have I risked valuable hands and arms in tiger or lion cages as I did for that striped Siren; and I warn you never to do it! For other persons than an animal-man, a transaction like that is a hazardous risk, and never should be indulged in, unless the human in the case has an arm or hand that he or she is willing to dispose of cheaply, and see no more. Remember, when around dangerous carnivores, that *the paw is quicker than the human eye!*

"Princess," I said one day, "you were jungle-born, of course."

She archly smiled assent, and said, "Ah-ha!"

"I see that you came from southern India. Were you not born on the Nilgiri Hills, or the Animallais?"

"I was born in thick bamboo jungle, on the eastern edge of Animallais." (I was sure from her bright colors and finely athletic form that she was not a plains tigress.) "There were three of us; a boy and two girls. My father and mother were honest hunters of big game, and both of them were grand people. I wish you had known my father." ("Heavens!" thought I. "It may have been her great-grandfather whom I *did* know on

THE TIGRESS.

"My father and mother were honest hunters of big game, and both of them were grand people."

those very Hills,—to his undoing!" But I was afraid to say it.)

"My parents were high-caste game-killers. Never once while I knew them," pursued the Princess, "did they kill a bullock or a man; and truly, they had chances a-many. Perhaps you think it was a pity for the game to be killed."

"Oh, no. Not under the circumstances," I hastily offered. "It is Nature's own plan that the surplus of big game, and the undesirable generally, may be killed as food for primitive man. It was in accordance with the basic law of Nature that the flesh-eating wild beasts were created, to keep down the surplus, and preserve the balance of wild life."

"Thank you," said the Princess. "That is real science language; and of course I couldn't frame it up all alone."

"And what kinds of animals did your folks kill, mostly? Gaur, for example?"

"No; not so many gaur. They are rather bad subjects for tigers. The big ones are too big and too powerful for convenience, their skins are too tough, and they fight too hard. My folks preferred wild hogs first, and axis and sambar deer next. They are of reasonable size, and one is quite enough for two persons. And then how exciting it is to hunt them through that most beautiful bamboo and teakwood forest!" And there we broke in:

"I call it a hunter's paradise! I never saw its equal anywhere else, save in the Canadian Rockies where the Elk River Mountains are. But pray do go on."

"At a very early age my parents permitted me to occasionally trail along after them when they went hunting, and see how they did it."

"Tell me, Princess!" I again broke in. "*Is* it true, as many books say, that tigers kill big gaurs and buffaloes by leaping upon them, and wrenching their necks until they break them?"

"There's but little in that," cried the Princess. "The big gaur and buffaloes are too big, too strong and too tough to be killed that way, but of course the smallest ones can be, by the big tigers. As for the small and helpless bullocks in the yoke, or tied fast, yes."

"But don't all large wild animals fight when you attack them?"

"Fight?" echoed the Princess, "I should say so! Once I saw my mother and a big sambar-deer buck have a terrible fight in tall grass nearly as high as an elephant's back. The grass over a space three times the size of my apartment was trampled quite flat. With his long and sharp horns, the buck tried to kill my mother! Yes, I did help,—what little I could; but that made no difference. Oh, yes; my mother conquered; but she was badly hurt. It laid her by in our lair for several days."

"Once more, Princess,—if I do not tire you too much,—what was the very worst fight that your parents ever got into with a big-game animal?"

"Oh, dear! It was that perfectly awful fight they had with a young tusker elephant! That was in the Government Reserved Forest."

"Ah! That is what I wish to hear about. A great many people have asked me whether tigers ever attack elephants. Up to now I have always said, 'No.'"

"Well, that young elephant grew too smart, and ran away from his home to lead his own life. He thought that by leaving the herd and the slow-going Old Folks he could have more fun, better things to eat, and less work to do. If he had stayed with his folks, my parents never would have thought of touching him. But he undertook to bluff my father! That was an awfully rash thing for him to do,—alone, as he was."

"And then what happened?" said I, eager to hear.

"Well, father roared and sprang at him, and seized him by the fore leg, high up. Then mother she roared horribly, and seized him by the hind leg on the other side, to help pull him down. He trumpeted and fought, and they had a perfectly—awful—fight! I don't like to talk about it. It scared me horribly. But if that young fellow hadn't tried to scare father, it *never* would have happened,—never. And of course father and mother won the fight. They *had* to!"

"Well, that is important news, Princess; and now if you are quite willing, I would like to know how you were caught and brought here, and what you think of us all."

But just then a loud "bang" and "rumble" was heard.

"There! That's our feed-car!" cried the Princess, excitedly. "I will just have to see you later about that."

Springing up, she began to leap and race to and fro, and while the car slowly rumbled up the rails, she gave us a moving-picture act that was perfectly fascinating.

But at that point that interview abruptly halted for a more convenient occasion.

THE YOUNG LADY TIGER

"However did I get here?"

The Tiger Princess echoed my question, a bit teasingly, as if in doubt about answering. Sphinx-like, she reclined at ease on the clean and polished floor of her royal apartment, head fully erect and turned a trifle to the left, as if posing for a stunning close-up. She had recently dined, and felt at peace with all the world.

"Yes, Your Highness," I said respectfully. "Your views of life are quite different from those of most tigers I have known, and I am fair bursting with curiosity to learn the details of your tale. You know, some tigers seem to think that it is their duty to the profession to hate everybody, and raise Cain as long as they live."

"Different here, partner," said Sherni glibly; (and I wondered where and how she picked up that Montana-cowboy expression). "Ah-ha-ha'! Since you are interested, I will tell you all I know, and more. But, are you ready to listen?" she asked a little sharply.

"Yes, yes! Of course. But why on earth do you ask that queer question?"

"Because I have noticed that among the visitors who come to see me, very few persons care to listen to what other people are struggling, or even fighting, to tell them." (How keen and quick she was in sizing up New York crowds!) "Well then, attend closely to what I say; and mind that you exaggerate nothing.

"As I told you yesterday, there were three of us tiger children, and we lived in the thorniest and densest bamboo thicket that mother ever found. A low tunnel ran in to our lair; but no man, brown or white, ever had nerve enough to crawl through it to see where we lived, and whether we were at home.

"My sister was a good little thing, though not very pretty; and my brother was a rough and strong young devil, always getting up disturbances. We all followed our mother until we were a year old,—and then I was taken away, suddenly. I suppose my sister and brother followed mother until they were almost grown up. Tiger children usually do."

"And who was smart enough to catch you, Princess?"

"Well, it was a bright young shikari who was always trying to read the thoughts of wild animals. He thought out a new plan.

"One fine day when my brother, Bagh, and I were starting out for a stroll through the forest near our home, we noticed a leafy hole in a thicket, and at the same time we smelled fresh meat. There was no man about, and no bullocks. We carefully investigated. We found some small bits of fresh meat near that leafy lair. 'That's funny!' said my brother; but there being no man-smell anywhere about, we ate them, and looked for more.

"At the farther end of that leafy lair, there was something lying hidden under a green branch. "What can it be? Meat?' said Bagh. 'Maybe,' said I. 'Let's see,' said Bagh. 'Go slowly,' said I. 'Fraid cat!' said he. 'You can stay back if you want to.' That vexed me a lot; and when he went into that green hole, I just trod on his heels, going after him.

"He clawed off that green branch, and found half a goat, freshly killed. With a greedy growl he seized it, and then, 'Bang,' went a trap-door dropping close behind me,—and we were caught! Yes, sir! Caught! That smart shikari had made a big box trap, of heavy wire in frames; he had lined it and covered it with fresh green branches, and taken great care to keep man-smell away from it. Four men had carried it and gently shoved it into the green tangle at the edge of that thicket, raised the trap door, put the log upon it, fixed the bait,—and caught us so *easily* it was just *awfully* mortifying!"

"My brother began to roar, and charge about; and at that men came a-running. When Bagh saw them, he became furiously angry, and he attacked *me!* The wretch really tried to do me mischief; and at that the men roared out something,—I know not what."

"I know!" said I. "I can guess precisely what they said. They shouted: 'Take that little devil out before he kills her!'"

"Yes. Probably that was it. Well, they worked frantically with a little rope, made a noose, got it around my brother's neck,—and in another minute he was out, but fighting like a little demon; and I was at peace."

"Good work!" I cried, in genuine admiration. "And then how did you get on? Did you fight the cage, refuse food, injure your mouth, and all that?"

"I certainly *did not!* But my madcap brother did all those things. How did you know? . . . Well, I was interested in seeing those men, and in watching them do things. They treated me well, oh, ever so well! Chickens, little pigs, fresh goat meat, milk, clean water to drink, —*and* a nice grass bed to lie on. They carried me, they hauled me in a bullock cart, they put me in a big box on iron wheels, and finally they fixed me up on a fine, big boat.

"Oh, it was wonderful! I was so *interested* that I just spent all my time in looking, and in eating. Everybody was nice to me; and many said, "Why, how *gentle* she is!""

"Righto!" said I. "You were intelligent, you saw things, and you used your brain to think with. That is logic, and *reason!* Straight thinking and sound logic promote peace, prosperity and long life, for wild animals and tame men, alike. Now, do not wild tigers have their rules of conduct, their rules and regulations, so to speak?"

"In-deed they have," was the brisk assurance. "Why, we never could live without rules."

"Now, Princess, think hard, and try to tell me what they are."

"Well—" said Sherni, poising her head gracefully as most girls do when in the act of thinking. "In the first place, there is to be no fighting in the Stripes Family. The big ones must not bite nor scratch the small ones, nor drive them away from the family kill. The youngest ones must have first chance at the kill."

"And then," she went one, "the big ones must defend and fight for the young ones, and see to its that the children do not get killed. If it is a man fight, the biggest and strongest old one must make the stand, to give the weaker ones a chance to get away."

"Fine!" I cried. "Some men do that, too. But pray do go on."

"Well, the young ones and the children must obey their parents, and the old ones that are responsible for the family."

"But, *do* they obey?" I demanded, doubtfully.

"Oh, my! Yes indeed. If they do not, then they are almost sure to be hurt, or even killed. You know those jungles are just full of dangers. Even the children are compelled to do their duty, and obey all the rules."

"It's fair wonderful," I said. "I've seen it in elephants, and deer, and mountain goats and sheep; but I couldn't be so sure about tigers, for I never saw enough of them running wild. Well, now I would like to know what you think of your new life, and everything."

"Oh, I've seen so *much,* and so many people, that I can't tell you the half of it. And now that I have this beautiful suite of apartments all for my own, and I'm so comfortable,—I just wish my mother and sister were here to live with me. Just why that big old stripes in the next room growls and roars as he does, *I* can't understand. Can you?"

"It's the point of view. He's sore because he can't do his own killing, have a fight every week or so,—and now and then maul a keeper. He's just naturally mean, as some men are; and you are just naturally wise and good, and appreciative,—if you know what that means. You know when you are well off. Many humans do not; some animals do not. And there you are."

And I went away feeling thankful that that big houseful of lions, tigers, leopards, jaguars, cheetahs and pumas were safe from the rifles of sportsmen, and living

"Free from all care, from sorrow free,
   Krimbamboli, krimbamboli!"

MARY GIRAFFE AND HER BABY

WITH captive or controlled animals anywhere, the crowning glory of possession is breeding and birth. There are many, many species of rare and beautiful wild beasts and birds that simply will *not* breed in captivity, and you never can tell what a species without a record will do until you have a pair. The best course is to expect nothing, and secretly hope for the unexpected.

One of the great compensations for worrying with living wild animals is the securing of "never-before" rarities from the ends of the earth. Second only to the old he-one himself is human interest in the never-before baby; and the mind that fails to respond to one is fit for treason, and so forth. Lion cubs, buffalo calves, young elk and wolf pups we receive with entire calmness; for they are the regular thing; and they only mildly stir our emotions.

But there are other babies who impart electric shocks, and send thrills of life along our keel. A mountain goat kid, a musk-ox calf, a chimpanzee baby or a preposterous pygmy-hippo rolypoly is, each one, enough to shake the biggest zoo in the world from stem to stern, and shiver its timbers with excitement.

Be it known to all who aspire to own and control, or guide and direct wild-animal pets, and preferably babies first, that full-grown giraffes are about as difficult animals to handle safely in a cold climate as erratic Nature ever turned loose upon this dull world. The chief trouble is that they can break their own long necks and legs easily, quickly, and without the slightest excuse. If you must have a giraffe baby "for the children to play with," take only one that has been successfully weaned, and is able to go ahead under its own steam.

Incidentally, quite a number of widely scattered giraffe babies have been born in captivity, but there are uncountable human millions who never yet have seen one.

The storks who work for us at the Zoological Park on piece work occasionally bring in a world-beater baby. Then there are thrills on the domestic wires, and much scurrying to get an early private view. It may be the most beautiful of this or that class, the most uncanny, the most vigorous, or the most something else.

When several storks joined forces, and one morning delivered to Mary Giraffe her third baby, and the keepers of the Antelope House phoned the news that "it is the finest one," we lost no time in registering appreciation. And the case was worth it. Mary is a wise and handsome mother, and her third one really was (and is today) a record-breaker.

Mary's husband was 16 feet 5 inches high, and all well enough as far as giraffe fathers go at such times; but that was all. In his behalf I now enter a claim for an honorable mention, for his "horse sense" and steady nerves.

I found Mary standing, like Melba, in the center of the stage, with her most gorgeous baby standing beside her, receiving the plaudits of the multitude. She was fondly beaming down, and it was joyously beaming up.

"Well, baby," said I. "I'm glad you have come. Welcome to our family circle."

The illustrious kid craned its neck into a hazardous curve, looked down at me and artlessly replied in a thin, squeaky little voice:

"I slept all the way!" At which the crowd laughed; and Mother Mary blushed, and looked almost annoyed.

"Mary," some one cried out, "it's a world-beater!"

"I think so myself," modestly admitted Mary. "But I must ask you not to mention it to my boy Lado."

Really, that giraffe kid was the most beautiful ever,—that is, if any baby with a four-foot neck can be called that. The poise and aplomb of that little beggar, not yet half a day old, was fit for a sculptor. Its lines were much more graceful and artistic than those of an adult giraffe; because some of them are mighty angular, and some,—if I must say it,—are unlovely in profile. But for the matter of that, where is the rough-necked and swashbuckling full-grown cave-man who does not look like a bull buffalo in comparison with the cupid curves of his own baby?

The colors of Mary's baby were brighter and more intense than the colors of Mother Mary herself,—and right while that thought was struggling to take shape in my dull brain, here came hurrying a Lady Artist, with paint-box, canvas, stool, and surpassing enterprise,—to oil-paint that long-necked, long-shanked little beggar on its first day. We all respectfully made way for her, and in less than five minutes she was behind the guard rail, her studio and sitter were all in order, and she was busily at work!

The Artist beat our Early-Bird reporter by seven minutes. Breathless he came, scrawled down on some pieces of waste paper a few ragged pot-hooks, gave the beasts, baby, men and women the once over, and was about to duck out when this happened:

Mary Giraffe and her husband, Long John, touched their noses together over the top of the high partition wall, and were whispering soft nothings, lip to lip, when a lovely girl visitor of seventeen summers saw it, and joyously cried out:

"Oh, Mama! Look! Look! *They're kissing each other!* Isn't it lovely!"

At that the abashed reporter rushed away to hide his confusion; but the common people laughed aloud in glee.

"Mary," said I, "how do you think this kid of yours would come out in a beauty contest with a small zebra colt? They are beauties, you know."

"Oh, yes," said Mary judicially, "those little colts are all well enough,—in a way; but their necks are far, far too short, and their color scheme is too monotonous. It is a rather pretty form, but it has far too many stripes. And you know, stripes have gone out this season. They're not wearing them."

The sublime coolness of this criticism was charming. Now, as a matter of fact, a mountain zebra colt,—but here let us pause. That is quite another story; and why spoil it here?

"I'd like to go back," said Mary, "under the Ringling's big top once more,—just for half a season,—to show my baby to the people. Do you think you can manage it for me?"

"Mary, you're a regular female; always looking for something else. No, you vain thing. Big tops are not for you any more. You have graduated; and you are too big to get into any animal wagon that could travel safely on any American railroad. How would you like to send Baby out alone?"

"Oh!" snorted Mary, and glared at me with her great, big brown eyes. "The I-*de*-a! Nottobethoughtof! Impossible! The poor thing cannot live without Me! Do you not know that!"

"That surely is true just now, Mary. If you should run away tonight, all the king's horses and all the king's men couldn't rear this baby, without you again. It's queer about these blasted wild-animal babies. Only a buffalo calf, that is as tough as any pine knot, can assimilate a milk-bottle and strange milk. All the rest of 'em seem to prefer to die."

"Well, old man," said Mary—rather familiarly,— "You just watch me bring up this baby! If it don't get whooping cough, or croup, or throat-ail, I'll soon show you the finest little-girl giraffe this side of the Blue Nile, where her grandparents live."

"Mind your step, Mary, whenever baby is lying down, or you may tread upon her with awful results. More than one baby like yours has been snuffed out that way, and whenever it happens it breaks people's hearts."

"Will you put our pictures into the next new Guide Book?"

THE GIRAFFES.

"Those little zebra colts are all right,—in a way. But their necks are far too short, and their color scheme is monotonous."

"We will most joyously do so. But you must help Mr. Sanborn to get a surpassing picture, that will do you both justice."

"I'll tell you what I'll do," said Mary very impressively. "I'll have baby put that wonderful double curve in her neck, which is so very fetching in a giraffe kid."

"It's a bargain," I said. "Do your best, Mary, to keep up the reputation of the Antelope House."

And she did.

THOSE RIVAL WILD BABIES,—ZEBRA AND GIRAFFE

FOR a dozen years or more, that Zebra and Wild Horse Collection in the New York Park has been to all its promoters a source of pride and satisfaction; but we have refrained from calling it "the best in the world." Such comparisons in big zoos are not according to Hoyle. If your visitors think that you are making good, that should be sufficient.

But when it comes to stripes, local color and geographical background, our collection is something to gloat over, with many gloats. Just stop and think of the wild countries represented. They are Cape Colony, Rhodesia, British East Africa, Abyssinia, the Sudan, Beluchistan, Tibet, and the Gobi Desert of Central Asia. The ground colors are white, ecru, and buff, and the stripes vary all the way from only one (on the back of the Gobi Desert wild horse) to about a hundred and fifty in the big Grevy Zebra from "British East."

And these motley and ring-streaked beggars have lots of "character," too. They have all kinds of tempers and temperaments, just as people have. They love and they hate, they are true and they are treacherous, they are wise and foolish, turn by turn. As for their fighting qualities, beware! When provoked they become wild with rage, and fight man or beast with fury. The English have a queer term for the biting of a horse. They call it "savaging."

I think that amateur wild-baby beauty contest was due to the doings of two rival flocks of storks. That zebra colt arrived so soon after the landing of the giraffe baby that it looked very much like a put-up job. Some storks are mighty long-headed and secretive in what they do. Perhaps there are times when they have to be.

The very next morning after Mary Giraffe's lovely little girl baby arrived with a bang and shook the whole park with the noise of it, the administration had another jolt. It was the arrival of a little-boy zebra; of the Mountain species, from South-West Africa. Of course the storks made their landing in the Zebra Field, right out in the open, with no secret about it; and at once people flocked to see it.

Now, people may talk all they please about the beauty of South African diamonds; but where is the Kimberly or Lichtenberg gem that for all-around beauty, and grace of form can surpass that scrumptious little zebra colt? Honestly, that was a wild-animal baby that I wickedly desired to steal and take away with me for better or for worse, until death us did part. When I tried to analyze the fascination of that dainty little beggar, it was a medley of ideas jumbled up like this:

"Color pattern and brush execution, without a flaw; curve system, the most graceful ever; broad hind-quarter stripes, bold and presuming; head and face, like a striped heavenly cherub."

After I had absorbed the whole personality of that little beast into my system I felt that I must talk to some one.

THOSE RIVAL WILD BABIES 255

"Well, you scrumptious little cuss," I exclaimed at him. "I wish you were small enough to be carried in my pocket."

"I beg pardon," said a calm voice, with a shade of menace in it, "but what was it that you called my baby?" It was Mountain Maid speaking.

"Why," I said, quite startled. "I just called it scrumptious; and that means superfine, you know."

"But you also called him a 'cuss,' " said the mother.

"Well, Maid, that is now a common term of endearment. For instance, if you call a man a 'versatile cuss,' he will be your friend for life."

"Do you not think he is the most beautiful baby you ever saw?" demanded the anxious mother, quite seriously.

"That is a very large order, Mountain Maid. I've seen many a prize baby in my time."

"Well, then, is he not the handsomest baby in this Park?"

I was hurriedly framing in my mind a diplomatic reply, to avoid hurting the feelings of the various mothers then in our midst with baby entries, when a strident voice rather near me rudely broke in. It came from an insolent looking man who seemed to be looking for trouble.

"Naw! It is not. It ain't nearly so handsome as that giraffe kid!"

Mountain Maid suddenly laid back her ears, shot some sparks from her eyes, and with jaws thrust forward and teeth bared by an angry snarl, she rushed straight down toward the disturber. "Bang!" She went into the wire fence, breast on; and for a hundred feet the fence quivered like a thing of life.

"There!" rebukingly cried the lovely lady who was with the fat man. "She understood every word that you said! Look out, Max, or she will be jumping out to get you."

"The ugly brute," said the scared and flushed disturber. "She needs a good hosswhip to make some more stripes onto her."

Now, this will be believed by but few persons. At once that usually docile zebra female reared high up on her hind feet, until her head towered far above the top of the fence. She hooked her front feet over the top wire, and then threw her weight upon the fence to bear it down, so that she could scramble over it. (Only a few big animals know that trick; but bad buffaloes know it only too well.)

"Maid! You Maid!" savagely yelled the Zebra's keeper. "Behave yourself! Get off that wire,—quick now,—and settle down!"

The zebra mother hesitated; and finally obeyed.

"Now just see what you've done,—blaggyardin' of her like that,—and all for nothing. Whatd'ye mean by it, anyhow?"

McBride was the maddest I ever saw him.

"Aw, go on! She didn't understand me," said the disturber of the peace.

"Understand ye, is it? Of course she understood ye, when ye blaggyarded her. Most big animals do. If she was a dog she'd bite ye."

THE ZEBRAS.

"Her baby *is* the prettiest one in the Park!" was the challenge flung out by a sturdy boy visitor.

"Her baby *is* the prettiest one in the Park!" was the challenge flung out by a sturdy boy visitor.

"I don't think so," piped up a blonde girl visitor. "I have seen Mary Giraffe's baby, and *I* say *it's* the prettiest! Now, what do you all think?"

There arose from the crowd a rattling fire of answers, impossible to record by hand. Some said "Zebra," and some said "Giraffe," until finally there arose a storm of "giraffe—zebra" shouts and cries that wrecked the dignified silence of the Park. And it ended thus:

"Keep still a minute," cried the strong-voiced boy. "Keep still now, and let's settle this thing right." There was a hush. "Now, Mister," (to me) "won't *you* decide which is the handsomest of these two rival babies,—giraffe or zebra?"

"Thanks for your confidence," said I, grandly. "My answer is all thought up. Here is the frozen truth: *The color pattern of the giraffe baby is the most beautiful, and the form of the zebra baby has the most graceful lines.* In other words,—the contest is a draw."

The visitors laughed, but Mountain Maid eyed me very doubtfully.

As I turned to go away, that handsome, bright-eyed boy addressed me once more and said:

"Mister. Won't you tell us more than the label says about the Mountain Zebra? I'd like to know a lot more about it."

"Indeed I will. In the first place, this zebra is the one that lives farthest south in Africa, away down in Cape Colony, where there are so many white people to kill game that only a few remnants of the wild big game are left. But for the interest of some wise and public-spirited Boer farmers, every Mountain Zebra would have been killed, years and years ago,—just as the quaggas were. But the farmers saved the last wild herds of that zebra, and stopped all shooting of them."

"Twenty years ago, it was said that there were only about 400 head remaining; but now the total is put at 500. These zebras live in wild and rocky mountains that are not good for farming. None are molested save the very few that are caught for the very few big zoos that can find the money to buy them."

"And how do they catch them?" queried the boy.

"By assembling a lot of men on good horses, then carefully cutting out one or two colts, and riding them down. They keep after them until the zebras are so exhausted that they can be roped; and many a good horse is badly hurt, or killed, in that rough riding. The director of the South African National Zoo, at Pretoria, once complained that even they could not obtain a pair of those Mountain zebras without paying a heavy price for it."

"And here you are, getting a new one for nothing!" cried the boy with a sympathetic grin.

"Well," said I. "let us hope that it will not be the last one that our storks will bring to us."

And it wasn't.

CLARENCE, THE WART-HOG

CLARENCE came to New York from Kenya Province,—"British East,"—as the only living prisoner of war at the chariot wheels of three young sportsmen who had killed enough African big game to load a boat. Considering the number of replicas of him that have been exhibited to the masses during the last fifty years, I nominate him as the representative of the most unappreciated of all of Africa's herds and hordes of land-going animals. However, that fact dampens his ardor not at all; and as for looks,—he that is homely, not wanting absent beauty, tell him not of it, and he is not peeved at all.

Judged by the artistic ideals of the present day, Clarence has sufficient beauty to carry on with; but measured by the moth-balled standards of the Victorian Age, certainly he is some plain-looking. He has a head like a hippopotamus, but two very swell tusks of solid ivory. His face is smooth-shaven, and ornamented with tall buttes of bone and tanned leather, called "warts." Except for a mantle of long, long hair growing southward along his spine, his body is covered with bare, sunbaked rawhide.

The tail-piece of an angry wart-hog is the funniest thing in Africa,—the Land of No Laughs. For size it is like a surgeon's probe. On dress parade it is held stiffly erect, not far from perpendicular, and at its tooth-pick end it has a tiny flag of dark hair as a fixed signal of defiance.

But it is not the beauty of Clarence that endears him to his keeper and the rest of us. It is his sweet and sunny disposition. Girls, learn from Clarence the basic fact that in the race of life a sunny disposition often beats beauty under the wire.

In cold weather, when its animals are all indoors and glad of it, New York's Kangaroo House is one of the most comfortable and interesting hotels that I know. Then, its flood of light and warmth makes its kangaroos, wild swine, anteaters and other queer animals feel just like living, and showing off. If a certain popular swine apartment is empty, Keeper Riley will yank on a certain chain, and as a door back-stage rolls back he calls out musically,

"Come on in, Clarence! Come in!"

In three seconds, a lively conglomeration of hide and hog nimbly ambles in at the open door, and trips up to the footlights to take its curtain call.

"Clarence, old man," said I on a promising day, "how on earth do you fellows manage to live and carry on in African country that is just running over with lions and leopards, and wild dogs and hyenas? Why are not all your little pigs eaten as soon as they are born, and the mothers killed, also?"

"All the swine of Africa," replied Clarence in excellent jungle diction, "who were unable to take care of themselves, were killed and eaten long ago. We, and the bush-pig, the river-hog and the giant forest-hog represent the invincibles."

"I have heard that you wart-hogs are terrible fighters,—when you are really interested."

Clarence's vast face blushed with pride and pleasure. I really didn't think he could do it.

"Yes, I imagine that some of the hardest jungle battles ever put up in Africa are between my people and the leopards. Many a Spotted Terror has taken second money in fights with us. But of course they punish us a lot."

"So I have heard: and I am glad that you can fight when you are attacked. But when it's a lion,—you don't stop to fight him, do you? Or a pack of those awful and terrible hunting dogs?"

"No, indeed," said Clarence, vigorously shaking all of his head at once. "We run for all we are worth, and more;—for an earth-pig's burrow if there is one, than which there is no better 'ole in Africa."

"I know! I know!" I cried. "They go into the basements and sub-cellars of big anthills; and some of the big ones are two feet in diameter."

"Yes, sir!" cried Clarence. "And the best ones go down deep,—more deep than you can believe."

"But hold on! Surely you can't turn around in one, can you? How do you get out again when you dive in head first, with a tight fit at that?"

Clarence grinned pleasantly from wart to wart, and said:

"Really, I must hand you one for your ability to reason. No, we don't go in head first. We daren't! We always go down *backwards!*"

"Well, you fellows *are* cute! You can think some, if you are homely. Now, I think that nearly all other animals go into holes head first. Even the aard-vark,—that you call the earth pig, does so,—does it not?"

"Oh, yes. And the way he can *dig*,—say! When he is in a hurry, he sure is a world-beater. Why, even when a lion overtakes an earth pig and grabs him by the tail,—if the digging is good that king of diggers can make a hole for himself before the lion's teeth can land in the middle of his back."

"That's some digging, Clarence."

"It is, baas. But I have seen holes that prove it."

"I say, Clarence. Why did Nature give you such a—well, such a remarkable head,—more queer than a hippo's for instance? Doesn't your face ache sometimes?"

"Well, it was this way: I was cast to play a part in the open jungles and grass lands of that nice and hot African plains country. The bush pigs and red river-hogs got all the beauty there was, and so Nature said, 'I'll just compensate this fellow, who will be exposed in the open country, by making his face so horrid and awful that his enemies will be afraid of him, and will let him alone occasionally. And honestly, it was a good idea, and it has saved me a lot of trouble. But you know, when you are living among rogues and fools, familiarity breeds contempt, and contempt is always the mother of Trouble!"

"Clarence, your unbelievable head contains,—somewhere in its awful anatomy,—a lot of real wisdom. For one thing, you have shown me that brains and personality can illuminate and glorify even the broadest and flattest face ever made. I wish I had met you when I was a young man, and needed a lot of ready-made wisdom. There's no inferiority complex about you. I never knew how you wart-hogs could fight until I read what A. B. Percival says about you in his "Note-Book."

"Well," said Clarence suspiciously, "what *does* he say?"

"He says that you are as plucky as you are plain-looking, you never know when you are beaten, and you fight to the last gasp. He says his admiration for you and your kind centres on your splendid fighting qualities."

"I want to know!" exclaimed Clarence.

"Yes: and Mr. Percival tells what fighters old male wart-hogs are when they are pursued by gentlemen pig-stickers on horseback, with spears. He says to the hunters, 'Look out! As often as not the hog does not wait for the spear. He rushes right at it, backs off afterward and takes a look at the pigsticker that says: 'Well, if you are ready I am!' "

"Fine!" said Clarence, with an 18-inch smile. "That man is a gentleman of discernment. I'd like to meet him, —at lunch, of course, not fighting."

"Yes. And he said he knew a female wart-hog that charged the spears seven times, and finally had to be finished by men on foot. Another time five horsemen attacked an old boar and he cut up their horses and whaled everybody so badly that the whole outfit had to walk home. Can anybody beat that for points?"

"Well, well, well!" exclaimed the hog, fairly dazed by

THE WART-HOG.

"He says that you are as plucky as you are plain-looking; you never know when you are beaten, and you fight to the last gasp."

the tale of his people's exploits. "It seems strange to hear all that over here. However,——"

"Yes, however you look at it, it's highly flattering to you; and honestly, I'm sorry that the sporting world doesn't know the amount and quality of the red blood of courage that courses through your tough system."

"Can't you broadcast this just a little?" said Clarence diffidently.

"Well, to get the ear of the masses is a tough job for any truthteller; but I'll see what can be done about it. You certainly deserve to be registered as a game fighter."

THE YAK FROM THE WORLD'S ROOF

IF I had to choose one wild animal out of the great Cattle Family to be my life companion in a frozen land, I would instantly call for the yak, of Tibet and Turkestan. He is big and hardy, handsome, sensible and kind. If the snow is so deep that you cannot wallow through it, he will take you upon his ample back and do your wallowing for you.

After much experience with this odd animal Col. Theodore Roosevelt thus testifies regarding its qualities, in "East of the Sun and West of the Moon." (Scribner.)

"A yak is not an uncomfortable animal to ride, but patience is necessary. He goes very slowly, his gait is reasonably smooth, and he always gets there. Also, he goes over the most impassable country imaginable about as fast as he goes over level ground. He plods unconcernedly through snow up to his belly, or up a boulder-strewn slope of forty-five degrees. He moves over obstacles with the same deliberate unconcern with which I have seen a tank in the war negotiate a shell-hole.

"He is guided by a rope through his nostrils, and steers like a dray. He blows like a porpoise, keeps his mouth open a large part of the time, and lolls a long anteater-like tongue from side to side. I have seen a small icicle form from the saliva on the tip of his tongue, but could not see that it inconvenienced him in the least.

They carry from 160 to 180 pounds apiece, and work up to elevations of 16,000 feet."

When we were ready to start a yak herd in our Zoo, we scorned the hornless and piebald domestic offerings of the dealers, and waited nearly five long years for a big, shaggy, black and broad-horned pair that was fit to found new herds. And truly, that royal pair has well repaid us for waiting. Its children are scattered all the way from Boston to Melbourne.

Judging by the members of our herd, I am ready to declare that Yaks are about the most sensible and efficient range cattle in the world. They love peace and prosperity. The big ones do not bully and oppress the weak ones; they treat their keepers right, and they scorn sickness and death. Their inky-black and heavy fur coats, trimmed underneath with waving black hair-fringe a foot long, defy the cold and ornament the landscape.

For an animal that lives at a mean elevation,—yes, and a very mean one, too,—of 14,000 feet, the fur suit of the yak is none too much. And glory be! The fur-hounds of that heartless huzzy, Fashion, have not yet attacked our shaggy friends of Eastern Turkestan and the Russian Pamirs for their "fur."

Eastern Turkestan! Can you turn to the map of Asia, and at once put your finger upon it? Can you tell where it is without looking? I opine that very few gentle readers can do so; and no wonder. There's a long, long road awinding from that country to the wild-animal column of our favorite newspaper. West of Bombay I fancy that the Central Asian Roof of the World

THE YAK.

He is guided by a rope through his nostrils, and steers like a dray.
He carries from a 160 to 180 pound load, up to
elevations of 16,000 feet.

is about as much known as the Canals of Mars. That majestic display of sky-piercing peaks and gigantic ranges exhibits the highest peaks and plateaus on this globe. On some of those plateaus horses cannot negotiate the snows, and then the yak is the only beast of burden that can navigate those howling wastes. And just fancy living upon a level country as high up as the top of Mount Rainier!

When the two founders of our yak herd arrived, they were duly installed in the excellent house of rustic stone that we had provided for them. Soon after they had presented us with their first calf, the lusty young bull surveyed the yak house critically, grunted affably, and thus expressed himself:

"Huh! It looks good. It makes me feel at home. It looks some like the stone yourt where I lived before I came here."

"Tell me its post-office address, please," said I.

"Ugh! Call it Kashgar. That's near enough."

"The name thrills me," I said.

"And why does it do so? Huh?" grunted the yak,—just like a man.

"For a matter of twenty years I wished to go to Gilgit and Kashgar. And here you are from both of them, just as easy as breathing."

"Steady there," grunted the bull. "In order to rise in the world I had to qualify as a mountain climber, and also as an expert snow-wallower with a man on my back. You really ought to see me climb," was his modest boast.

"Then tell me all about it, and I will see it."

"Well, it's like this: In that country you can't walk five miles without climbing over something steep and high. If ever you are born again, and live out there as a yak, you will have to climb through snow, straight up bare and rocky slopes as steep as a house roof. Ugh! It will make your tongue hang out, and swing from side to side. And grunt! My goodness how you will have to grunt in order to get on."

"There now!" I broke in. "That grunting you mention must be the reason why your Latin name means Grunting Ox. You grunt when you climb, do you not?"

"Uh-huh! That's it. We are great burden carriers, up to 200 pounds. Nearly every sahib hunter of the big sheep you call Ovis Poli rides a yak from the plain up a thousand feet or more to the bare rounded summits where the sheep live. I hunted sheep twice myself, and I carried Douglas Sahib both up and down."

"Did he get his sheep?" I hastened to inquire.

"Uh-huh! He was most determined; and he got one pukka big one. If he had not,—huh! We might be hunting there yet! As it turned out, I carried a load of his stuff down to Gilgit."

"And how did you ever get out of Turkestan?"

"You never could guess. . . . I carried two living ibex kids in shipping crates from Kashgar southward over the great pass when it was deep in snow. Clear down to the Vale of Kashmir we went; and there, to my great surprise, I found that my young wife and I were booked to New York;—and here we are."

"How did you like the traveling?"

"At first we thought that the close confinement, the

awful heat and the thick, heavy air would surely kill us. Going up the Red Sea in that awfully hot weather we would have died but for the water they threw upon us with a hose. I never, never wish to see anything else like that."

"It was a long journey, too. When you came out of your crate, you were so stiff you could scarcely walk."

"Yes; it was an awful journey. Had we not been of tough stock, we could not have lived through it. Your heat here," said the Yak, with a little hesitation, "is sometimes very bad, but it don't last very long."

"How do you like these ranges?" I modestly threw out.

"Fine. A great deal of animal intelligence has been shown in making them. We are now delighted with the change, and we will live here a long time,—in fact, just as long as you wish us to."

"What a very queer idea!" I said, with a jump of the nerves. "And how I do wish that all the Park visitors could know your life and your story, and see the local color that surrounds you two strangers from The Great Roof. The ibex cannot live here for any length of time, so you and the Himalayan wild goat that we call the tahr are the only live animals here from that all-highest country. Your country is built on so big a scale that its gigantic mountains make ours seem like nothing but hills."

"Once I heard a man call it the cradle of the human race; the birthplace of the first sheep,—and speaking of young stock, just look at that calf!"

THE YAK FROM THE WORLD'S ROOF

Sure enough! That first yak calf, a funny little tyke built like a mechanical toy, and as black as any limb of Satan, was racing up and down like a mad calf, showing off, and bent upon getting its name in the papers.

"Let it run," said I tolerantly. "Three years from now it will run for $500, bring it home, and then take a pleasure trip at the expense of some other zoo."

It is a noteworthy event to meet the only member of the whole great Cattle Family that seems to have been specially created to live on the inhospitable high plateau of south-central Asia, to climb steep mountains, wallow through deep snow, and carry men and other things upon his back. It is only by long and close observation that the wisdom and cunning of Nature, in fitting strange animals for life and service in strange places, can be discovered,—and appreciated.

Remember this, gentle Reader, the next time you see a yak; for physically, mentally and temperamentally he is "fearfully and wonderfully made." Without him, life in the highest parts of Turkestan and the Russian Pamirs would be even worse than it is with him; and this is saying much.

And really, does not the bold and hardy yak, unterrified by wintry storms, cold, hunger and hard labor, make our American and European domestic cattle seem almost as trivial as sheep? Why, on the western cattle plains, even in the days of 1886 which I knew, the range cattle of Montana and Wyoming were such poor rustlers, and so incompetent about finding shelter from the whizzing cold winds of the northwest, that sometimes they froze to death in herds, standing up in the snow, even on ranges where deep coulees and bad lands were plentiful and cheap.

In the days when Charles Goodnight, Buffalo Jones and other western stockmen were doing their level best to breed a strain of hardy buffalo blood into the range cattle of the west, to carry them through the "bad" winters, and not succeeding at all well, I used to wonder why under the sun western stockmen did not test out the possibilities of the yak as a hardy cross.

THE ARRESTED DEVELOPMENT OF THE SLOTH

HE who would study and interview the Three-Toed Sloth of South America must have the wisdom of Solomon and the patience of Job. Mr. Dick Swiveller would call him an unmitigated staggerer. His physique is unaccountable, his temperament is a compound paradox, and his mind is a Chinese puzzle. In judging him, all existing rules and regulations are off.

Because of a dozen reasons, the two sloths of South America (Three-Toed and Two-Toed) to about 110 millions of United States people are almost as little known and comprehended as if they had only yesterday climbed down from Mars. This is all wrong, because those animals are amazingly odd, unthinkable and uncanny. They display only two of the long list of things that every fully-equipped four-footed animal should have and do.

In their own jungles they are tough and enduring. They swim amazingly well, considering; but on the ground they just wallow and flounder along, worse than a man crawling on his hands and knees. On a good open lawn a sloth might travel a mile in a day, but on the floor of a forest his limit would be perhaps half a mile.

At very rare intervals a Two-Toed Sloth is seen in a big zoological park; because it is possible by extremely careful work to keep that kind alive for a year or so. The Three-Toed species just cannot endure life in a northern zoo, and the majority of them pass out in about two months. That is why there is no good sale for them.

Of those two sloths, it happens that I am best acquainted with the poorest liver. In the delta of the mighty Essequibo river of British Guiana, I broke into the ancestral home of the Three-Toed Sloth. In my first day of exploration by dug-out canoe, we saw eight of them, all in the tree-tops, and by cutting down a tree we essayed to secure one alive.

The top of the tree fell into the river, and with much concern I saw my sloth disappear beneath the waves.

But not forever. Presently a living something was seen most slowly and mechanically swimming up toward daylight. It looked like a strange mechanical toy covered with coarse gray tow instead of hair. Finally it reached the surface; and I wish that you might have seen the look of disgust and contempt on its stuffed-up face as it finally sighted us. Presently, to our amazement, it slowly swam to our boat, as the nearest solid object, and as plainly as print those dull eyes and wooden mouth said these two words:

"Mean. . . .Unfair."

Down to that moment I never had believed that a sloth could swim a stroke. But they can swim; and quite well! A sloth can swim a mile; and in that quiet delta I think that many of them do so. The mechanical toy arms do all the work, and that tow-covered body seems right buoyant.

We saw that the blinking eyes of the animal saw

ARRESTED DEVELOPMENT OF THE SLOTH

things very poorly; just like a person three-quarters blind. It made no attempt to bite us, and it looked as if it were unable to bite anything, even in self-defense. All the time it moved just like the movie animals we see in slow-motion pictures. Those queer stubs, where good, serviceable hands and feet should have been, are no good for standing, walking, running or fighting. They need ages of further development.

"For goodness sake, Sloth, what are your feet good for, anyway?" Slowly and haltingly came the answer:

"With these claw hooks . . . I hang . . . underneath . . . branches . . . I can fight . . . my sister . . . and tear her skin . . . I can . . . pinch flesh!"

"Well, Sloth, for the love of mercy, tell me who protects you from the harpy eagles, the vultures, the ocelots, margay cats and anacondas? And who saves you from being exterminated?"

With a dismal squeak through its shapeless nose, the Sloth gave up one word: "Nobody."

"Then how do you manage to escape being killed and eaten every day of your life?"

"Color protection," came the short answer, delayed in transmission.

"Oh! I see! That coarse and chaotic hair of yours, growing wildly in every direction, is the color of rough bark. By keeping yourself always at parade rest, you attract no hostile attention."

"Yeah. . . . That's it," said this chatterbox of the tree-tops.

"But, say! You said something in your first lucid interval about fighting your sister. Why do you do that, Slothie? What is your grouch about?"

"She is . . . a female . . . and I hate . . . all other females."

"How primitive!" I exclaimed. "I wonder if that was the slant of the female mind generally at the beginning of the age of mammals."

The female sloth slowly turned her head, just as I have seen taxidermists turn the heads of half-stuffed sloths into "artistic" positions, and silently blinked at me.

"I have seen seven other sloths to-day," said I, "each one alone, never even two together. Why is that? Do sloths always live alone?"

"Uh-huh! . . . We hate to be . . . crowded."

"Well, then, tell me what you eat when you're alone?"

"Leaves."

"Oh, you chatterbox! Do you want to know what I think of you? 'Yeah.' Well, listen." (I waited three minutes for that New York idea to penetrate.) "I think you are just one remove from a stuffed sloth in a museum case. I think that your family tree is a dead one, and you are just a hanger-on to a dead branch, and ready to drop into Oblivion. With your claw-hook feet and hands you must date back thirty thousand years at least; and just as you were then you are now. You're Arrested Evolution. You are 300 centuries behind the times.

"I think, friend Sloth," I continued, "that of all created land animals, you are the slow-motion champion. Your birth, life and death are regulated by just about

THE THREE–TOED SLOTH.

"With these claw hooks I hang underneath branches. I can fight my sister and tear her skin."

twenty-five thoughts, that could be expressed in about fifty words. It is no wonder the harpy eagles and ocelots don't pick you off every time you pick a leaf. They thing you are made of wood!

"But cheer up, Slothie. We will take you back to a good zoo, associate you with giant tortoises, and see if they will not give your nerves some stimuli. For ages you have been running in low gear. It is time for you to speed up."

We took that sloth up north, we placed her in a perfectly good zoo, and everybody tried to put vitamines and new thought into her. But it was no use. She shrank from the new regimen, she blinked at Life until she could blink no more, and at the end of the customary two months she died of nervous shock.

The tortoises wore her out by their restless activity.

With the above we were about to wind up this veracious but odd-come-short interview, when we found that it wouldn't close. Some of the relatives of the Sloth, past and present, wirelessed me a protest that their only chance to be shown upon the screen should not be lost and far be it from me to refuse even a fossil animal its place in the Sun.

And truly, the garrulous Sloths, from whom I have with vast difficulty extracted, as with dental forceps, an irreducible minimum of words and ideas, have as queer a bunch of relatives as any animal ever owned. Take, for example, the one I have known the longest and lifted the hardest.

At Ward's Museum, in 1874, I became intimately acquainted with the plaster-of-paris skeleton of a huge

ARRESTED DEVELOPMENT OF THE SLOTH

back-breaking beast of the past that was known to us as the Meg-a-the′ri-um, of South America. We called him "Meg" for short. When alive and kicking, he had been as large as an African rhinoceros. After years of blundering about his pedigree, the best zoologists of the past finally boiled him down to his lowest terms, and found that he was a great ground *sloth*, who lived by eating the tops of low palm trees and other things. His ancestral home was in Buenos Aires and he lived about a million years ago, more or less.

As ancestors come and go, the Two-and-Three-Toed Sloths of today may well be proud of their Great-Grandfather Meg.

The sometimes miscalled "sloth" of India is not a sloth at all. It is a slow lemur.

The nearest living relatives of the sloths are the anteaters of South America. The great anteater is the long-snouted black-and-white one with the enormous tail; and the tamandua is the middle-sized one. The smallest one is the exquisite little silky anteater, the size of a chipmunk, with hair like real silk, and a constitution as frail as a China teacup. But glory be! the sloths and the anteaters are scattered through so many millions of miles of impossible tropic jungles that none of them are likely to be exterminated in our day.

THE CONFESSION OF THE SPOTTED TERROR

SPEAKING of cold-blooded cruelties, and killings by bandits and other savages, by man-eating lions and tigers and others, I think that none of them equal in ferocity and cunning the methods of the African Leopard. Mr. E. Blaney Percival, for years a daring and keen game ranger of British East Africa has, in his "Note-Book," given the world a very jarring new conception of that most savage of Africa's dangerous beasts. The fierce and cunning Leopard of the African big-game country seems to be the four-footed prototype of the modern American bandit, who certainly is a man of nerve.

Even when the acts of a criminal are generally known, whenever a bad one elects to tell all of his own crime story, his confession is quickly given a clear wire. There is no history of crime like the story of a killer about himself.

Not long ago I had a rare opportunity to take down a four-footed killer's confession. On being "bawled out" by a newly arrived African Leopard, I provoked him to the point of bragging outrageously about his exploits. He "charged" me, as far down as his front bars, using very provocative language. Then, with fierce coughs and snarls he said:

"Curse you, I'd like to get at you once!"

"What's the matter with me?" I shot back.

"You are a cruel fraud. You pretend to be kind, and you don't give us half enough to eat."

"You glutton, do you wish to become as fat as a hog?"

"Yes! I want enough! And I'd like to eat some of these young and tender visitors,—but not you. You're too old and tough! I've eaten better men than you already."

"I think you are a liar!" I observed pleasantly.

And then what a rage consumed him! He became a perfect cyclone of black, tawny and white hair, and cruel teeth and claws.

"Liar am I? Come on! I'll just tell you about it. I was a man-eater once——"

"Mighty few men did you ever eat," said I, as offensively as possible. "I know your kind. You lived on patas monkeys, young baboons, foolish little nanny-goats and mangy dogs. You're a professional dog-stealer——"

"You bet I am. Once I grabbed a dog on a veranda from between its master's feet; and I got away with it, too. I raided a farmer through his own kitchen window, bit him, and jumped out again with his dog in my mouth. I can climb any tree that a monkey can climb, and any baboon rocks that ever were made. If I had been lazy, I could have lived on women and children; but they were too easy. I like to go against men, and beat them at their own game. Do you know that beside me lions are stupid animals?"

"The lion is the king of beasts, and a gentleman," said I, with a show of dignity.

"King of big stuffs!" rudely snorted the leopard. "I could teach the lions of Africa the elementary principles of cunning in hunting. They make me tired. You ought to see me in action."

"Well, old blow-hard, what do you do that is so wonderful?"

"First, when I climb a tree up twenty or thirty feet, and lie out on a limb to take the air and see the scenery and watch for game, there is always good cover below me. I see the hunters first, and down I drop and slink away before they can get near enough to shoot. I live in thick and thorny brush, or in holes in the rocks, where no man, dog or wild beast can get me first. And when I raid men's houses and villages, my dash and getaway are wonderful. I love most of all to attack a hunter in his own tent, with his guns all around him, and maul him, or kill him, before he can get black help. I've accounted for more than one mighty hunter. But I had a bad accident once. I sneaked into a farmer's house at night. He saw me; he grabbed a terribly big rhinoceros-hide whip, and he whipped me so ferociously that I couldn't do a thing but run, and jump out of the window where I came in. It took me two weeks to get over it."

"How many women and children have you killed?"

"More than I can remember. And as to dogs, why I have killed probably as many as you ever saw."

"But you can be caught in a trap," said I, spitefully, "or else you wouldn't be here."

"I admit it. All leopards are dumb about traps. The trouble is, we are too brave and impulsive. That is be-

THE LEOPARD.

"When I climb a tree and lie out on a limb to take the air and watch for game, there is always good cover below me."

cause we hold men in contempt, and are afraid of nothing of flesh and blood. Why, man, there is not a beast of prey in all Africa that can escape after a killing as we leopards can. You don't begin to realize how smart we are. I'll escape from this Lion House yet," he concluded with a wicked look.

"Well, when you do I hope I'll be around somewhere. But in any case you won't last long."

"Won't I? You just wait and see. You white men of America have a mighty lot to learn about African leopards."

"Yes, and when a bunch of good animal-keepers get after you, you will soon wish you were back in that cage. But you'll never get there."

"And what do you think will happen to me?"

"You will be killed by a high-power rifle, because you are a merciless and dangerous beast, just as one hundred thousand spotted terrors like you ought to be killed in Africa tomorrow for the public good.

"I would not have believed you could be so vindictive," said the leopard, thoughtfully.

"As a bandit and murderer, you are in a class by yourself. This earth is no place for you, save as you now are."

And that was the last word.

But, after all we must give the leopard devil his due, and fail not to set forth whatever virtues we can find. Some leopards that are reared in captivity from kittenhood, and well treated, become friendly and sociable, and are not at all dreadful until they become fully grown. Then,—it is best to look out, and take no chances.

Mature leopards nearly always hate the stage performance in which they are called upon to act. Most of the trained-leopard exhibitions I have seen were to me painful, because usually the leopard has so fiercely hated the trainer, and thirsted so much for his or her blood, that I always have dreaded an arena tragedy. In one clinic that I attended, the lady operator wore spangled tights and a wicked, nickel-plated, two-tined steel pitchfork with which she always presented arms to the snarling and coughing leopards.

I must set it down to the credit of the leopard that ordinarily it is not a wanton wholesale killer, like the wolf, skunk, weasel and sheep-killing dog, but as a rule seems to kill strictly for food. And of course the leopard does not know that it is any more wicked to kill women and children than it is to slay goats and sheep. The unarmed natives of India have it not in their power to shoot up the leopards in season and out, and teach the leopards that it is wisest to let the human animal severely alone. On account of this lack of education and this background of firearms, the leopards take heavy toll of human life in the districts they inhabit.

Once upon a time, I had reason to be particularly interested in the statistics of 1878 touching the wild-animal population of India and its doings. At that time India contained about 300,000,000 people, and was also saturated with leopards. In that year the leopards killed precisely 300 people who were heard of, but 3,237 leopards were killed in punishment for those crimes. The Province of Bengal headed the list, with a loss of 149 persons, offset by 1,033 slain leopards.

In North America we have no animal species in any way comparable in death-dealing ferocity with the leopard of Africa and the East Indies; and we may be thankful that we have not. Our bears, wolves and mountain lions are, as man-hunters and killers, nothing but rank amateurs beside the death-dealing leopard. The twenty million outdoors people of the United States go everywhere, and camp out everywhere, with no fear of harm from any wild animals larger than skunks. Beside the leopard, even the Canada lynx is a joke, and the mountain lion is only a scared cat. Our native animals are very interesting, but for fangs and claws only the Alaskan brown bears and the grizzlies are to be genuinely feared by man. It is only on rare occasions that the jaguar and the gray wolf elect to attack man, but they are mighty destructive to his domestic animals.

THE GRAY WOLF REFUSES TO BE CROSS-EXAMINED

"I REFUSE to be cross-examined. I hate you!"

Big and savage Gray Wolf snapped this defiance at me through the bar-work of a perfectly good cage; and it almost wrecked my poise.

"What's the matter with me?"

"You're no friend of mine."

"How do you happen to know all that?"

"I can see it in your left eye. I've been told some of the mean things you have printed about me. You blame me for killing my food, and put big bounties on my head, and yet you are a killer yourself. All the men who blame me are worse killers than I am, and you can't deny it. I *never* kill just for fun!"

"Did I ever print anything about you that is not true?"

"You never printed anything on my side."

"Do you never kill more than you can eat,—just for the joy of killing?"

"I refuse to answer. I stand on my lawful rights as a witness. And besides, real friends don't go about advertising each other's faults."

"Well, Lobo, you can suit yourself about answering questions," I snapped back, "I just thought that in view of your off-color reputation, and the hundreds of thousands of dollars that Congress appropriates every year to kill you off on the cattle ranges, you might like a chance to make a statement for publication. I'm not your attorney, but I offer you the opportunity; and you can just take it or leave it."

It is quite true, as charged, that I am not in love with Gray Wolf. His angry defi, and that old crook's court plea about refusing to answer for fear of self-conviction, riled me up some.

Glowering, Gray Wolf started to walk away from me; but suddenly he whirled about and rushed back to the front bars, with contracted brows, snarling lips and an angry gleam in his slit-like eyes.

"You *never* gave me a square deal!" he snapped.

I was glad there were bars between us! After a pause I said, sarcastically:

"Well, go on and put your cards on the table,—if you have any."

"You never have admitted that I do some good in the world, as an offset to—to some other things."

"Now, just calm down a bit, and give me a bill of particulars. An angry witness is always a bad witness. To prevent people from overlooking any more bets about your moral character, just tell me about your virtues, and I'll write it down."

To encourage him, I got out my notebook and made ready to take down his testimony. This seemed to mollify him some.

"Well, you know perfectly well that I kill and eat hundreds of the prairie-dogs that spoil the cattle ranges, and thousands of those gray ground-squirrels that eat up the farmers' crops umbrageous."

"There's something in that," I admitted. "It saves some government poison."

"And I help the cattle-men in getting rid of starved and frozen cattle that otherwise would poison the air. You know that if there had been any of my people in that elk range that you visited last year, you never would have found that dead elk by scenting it on the breeze, now would you?"

"However did you find out all that?" I exploded. "Your private information certainly gives me my time. I never printed anything about that visit."

Gray Wolf licked his lips in a conceited way, as if well pleased with himself; and his eyes lost a little of their fire.

"Never mind about that," he evaded, "I see it's true. In all these years your humane society never gave us any credit whatever for putting out of their misery the maimed, the halt and the blind among the herds of buffalo, elk, antelope and deer. We have saved an awful lot of helpless animals from dying lingering and painful deaths, have we not? Well, why has no one ever *said* anything about it, and given us a little credit?"

In choosing my words for a reply, I was silent for so long that Gray Wolf drove on.

"You know the skunk tribe, don't you?" he demanded truculently.

"I do pass the time-o'-day with some of them," I grudgingly conceded; "but the ones you are thinking of are not down in the Social Register."

"Well," he flung back, "now look here. *You* know that all skunks are bad citizens. You know that in good society it's not polite to say 'skunk' to a lady. You know that the pesky little striped skunk of the southwest sometimes gets rabies, and kills sheep-herders and prospectors, by biting them while they lie asleep beside their own camp-fires."

This touched me on a tender spot. Once in a black night a skunk made so brazen free as to come into my tent. It was a most unwarranted intrusion, but we dared not resent it by firing at him. He was too well armed.

"Well," pursued the Wolf, "in bad times my people and I sometimes have to eat skunks to keep from starving."

"That is in mighty bad taste," I jabbed with the spur of the moment.

Then I remembered that once while hunting in Mexico I found the tail and jaws of a little striped skunk who on the day before had been killed *and eaten* by a wolf. That made me loathe wolves more than ever.

"They do taste bad, for a fact," said the interviewed one, mistaking my meaning. "We are entitled to some credit for ridding the country of a lot of those beasts, but we never get it.

"And now look at this greatest service of all. Who is it, I ask you," pursued Wolf, "who puts pep, stamina, and the savvey of the trail into the pampered domestic dogs of the North, and produces the best, the bravest and finest sled dogs in the world? Northern wolves, sir, and nobody else! Who takes the yellow curs of the Alaskan frontier camps, and produces gray-coated heroes, sir? The Gray Wolves of that cruel country. Whose blood was it that pulled those sleds through seven hun-

THE GRAY WOLF.

"Your humane societies never gave us any credit for putting out of their misery the maimed, the halt and the blind among the herds of buffalo, elk, and deer."

dred miles of snow, from Anchorage to Nome, and carried that serum to those dying people? Was it domestic-cur blood that did it! No, sir!" roared the captive. "Not —on—your—life! It was the strong Gray-Wolf blood in those huskies that did it. You know that! And all the world ought to know it! Woo'-o-o-o-o-oh!"

"Lobo, perhaps you are partly right about that,—for once in your life: but I don't back your play entirely. At all events, I will do my share toward printing your testimony, but after that you must fight it out with the huskies yourself."

"And now, Wolf," I went on, "I have listened to your testimony in your own behalf, and I am going to show you the seamy side of yourself. In the first place, you are the most savage and most cruel game and stock killer of all North America. Your taste is so finicky that usually you scorn to eat any meat that you have not killed yourself; but you have been known to murder sixty-five sheep in one night. Slaughterings like that prove that you are a black-hearted murderer and criminal, because you love to kill so much that you enjoy killing more than you can possibly eat."

"Why," he snarled, "I learned that from the sportsmen! More than half of them kill all they can, don't they?"

"Never mind about that. I'm talking now about what you do. You are too brave. You travel about too much. You have been known to travel from fifty to sixty miles in one night,—for your own devilish purposes, of course. You are not content with killing colts and calves that you can eat up, but you kill big, fine steers and heifers, ready for the market. You sneak up behind them, hamstring them just about the hock joint, down them, and then sometimes you eat them alive!"

"How did you learn all that?" yelled Gray Wolf. "You never saw me do it."

"Never mind about that. I know wolf trappers who are just as smart as you are. They know that the best time to hunt wolves is in hot weather, and the best places are in the canyons, where you go to get out of the heat. In cool weather you travel high, so that you can see the hunter first."

"You think you are mighty smart, don't you," snarled Lobo, sarcastically.

"Lobo, I think that you are the meanest and the cruelest animal of all North America, and if I could do it I would exterminate all of you but one pair. You and your mates and litters, and your scouts and packs, are much too expensive for people who sometimes consume beef and mutton. And speaking of 'services,' and 'credit,' Lobo, I think you have boundless nerve."

At that Lobo stared at me in stupefied surprise, glared a few glares, then turned, and slowly marched off back stage in unspeakable disgust.

THE GOLDEN BIRD–OF–PARADISE

WHEN I was a boy the bare thought of the dark green jungles and red-haired orangs of Borneo always made my heart beat faster. Even the thought of some day going to New Guinea, to the home of the scarlet and black and golden birds of paradise, gave me thrills and goose-pimples. The romance wrapped up in the thought worked upon my imagination like hard cider. I just wonder if any boys feel that way now.

I never have felt satisfied about the name of this so-called Greater Bird of Paradise. (If you wish to speak scornfully of any bird that you do not like, refer to it as "so-called"; and if it is a man, say "*One* Jones." These formulas are sarcastic, but genteel.) The beautiful bunches of soft plumes that spring from the side of this bird, curve upward, and then droop outward and downward in a golden-yellow spray should have suggested to Mr. Linnæus the name I have rebelliously set forth above.

I could, if granted time, tell a good story of my appeal in 1913 to the people of Holland for a royal edict to stop the killing of birds-of-paradise in the Dutch East Indies for their plumes, and the surprising result thereof; but that would be no wild-bird interview. Anyhow, the Royal Zoological Society of Amsterdam at once rose to the occasion, and secured some fine practical results in 1915; which was in marvellously quick time.

THE GOLDEN BIRD-OF-PARADISE

For fifteen years I have been in touch with beautiful living specimens of the golden bird-of-paradise, and many is the time that we have given each other silent treatment. The largest and most brilliant male bird I call Aru, in honor of the little group of islands off the northwestern point of New Guinea, where his kind even yet abound.

Aru's body plumage, of chocolate brown, emerald green and lemon yellow, is beautiful, when it is all there, and his plumes are not savagely moulted out. Regarding his voice, well, the less said about it the better. It is odd and sad that a bird so beautiful should have for a singing voice a raucous, ear-piercing squawk like that of an infirm automobile horn. But Aru's talking voice was different.

"Are you from the Aru Islands, Goldie?"

"No," he said. "No Aru Islands for me. I was born in New Guinea, well back from the coast, in a forest as wild and romantic as any you ever saw. It was just full of birds, and wild hogs and tree kangaroos, snakes and big bugs, and everything. That Raggy-anna Red bird-of-paradise in the next cage, and the Blue and the King, all came from there. But I can't see," said Aru reflectively, "just why you-all make such an awful fuss and to do over that old Blue bird-of-paradise. Even if he does display while hanging head downward, his display is nowhere near as graceful and recherché as mine,—now, is it?"

"Well, Aru, your display is mighty fine. I will not discount it for any other."

"Thank you. I thought I could rely upon you. But

oh, man! If only you could see one treeful of my kind in the mating season, fifty or more together, and sometimes a score of them displaying and carrying on all at once, it would give you an eyeful. It's the most gorgeous sight in birds *I* ever saw. And now tell me, man, what is your honest opinion of me, and my kind? I would like to know."

"Well, Aru," I said. "I'll pull my wits together and try to tell you. Let's go right back to the beginning. In the first place, while the great Linnæus who named you was a real prince of discernment, in naming you he certainly nodded, and skipped a cog. The first skin that came into the hands of a man wise enough to classify birds, and bestow names upon them, Linnæus, had been prepared by a savage Aru islander, who cut off the feet, legs and wings, because he knew no better.

"Instead of being thrilled with admiration of your gorgeous side plumes, and the rest of the plumage, Linnaeus was so peeved by the absence of those legs that for the moment he lost his sense of the eternal fitness of things. Instead of giving you a Latin name that meant magnificent, or gorgeous, or golden, what did he do? He called you *a-po'da,* which in English means "without feet."

"That was a raw deal," observed Aru, judicially.

"It was all that," said I. "Now, taking the Birds-of-Paradise all in all, judging plumes, wires, colors and sizes, it is my opinion that you get the highest mark, and take first place. Why, those side plumes of yours, sometimes eighteen inches in length, are like sprays of liquid gold with brown tips,—exquisite in filmy texture as well

GOLDEN BIRD OF PARADISE.

"I was born in New Guinea, well back from the coast, in a forest as wild and romantic as any you ever saw."

as in color, and they beat all the other display plumage of the Birds-of-Paradise. And then, the rich mahogany brown of your wings and tail, the purple-brown and blackish-violet of your breast, your straw-yellow head and neck, and the brilliant emerald green of your throat and forehead,—all combine to give you the gold medal when displaying—as the most gorgeously colored perching bird in the world. I understand that it was when you male birds used to get together and hold display contests that those naked, brown-skinned Papuans with their long blowguns and nasty little arrows, got after you and shot you up so terribly for the millinery trade. How about that?"

"Once that was true," said Aru, sadly and reflectively, "But that has changed a lot. First there was less of it, and finally it stopped, almost wholly; but I don't know why. Do you?"

"Yes. First it is because of the new Regulations of the Netherlands Government. Secondly, the bottom has fallen out of the ornamental-feather market. America, Canada, and England now are closed as tight as three drums against millinery plumage, and now it is unfashionable for a Real Lady to wear any more wild-bird feathers."

"You astonish me. But isn't that wonderful for us! Well, now the worst thing for us will be the call for live birds for the zoos. That bothers us some; but at present there is so little of it that it doesn't hurt much. But don't you know all about New Guinea?"

"Goodness, no! Nobody does. The place is too big, and too bad and difficult. Nobody seems to get to the heart of New Guinea,—and get out again to tell of it. But I know a lot about that green and wonderful country above Port Moresby."

"I have never been there. What is it like?"

"Good people live there. They never kill white men, only just each other. They build houses away up in trees, fifty or sixty feet high, run rattan ladders up to them, and carry up tons of stones and scores of spears to throw down at the bad fellows who come to attack them. I wonder that none of your golden people ever got down there."

"Too far from home," said Aru with a lofty expression. "But what real birds do you find there?"

"Why, the red bird-of-paradise, and the little king, and rhinoceros hornbills,——"

"Cheap! Too cheap, by far," squawked Aru.

"Well then," said I, a little nettled, "this Blue bird-of-paradise is from up that way, a little toward Mount Owen Stanley; and he is the top sawyer of all paradise birds for value."

"I know he is for price," said Aru with a sulky look. "You threw away $1,000 on the very ordinary-looking pair in that cage over there; and what did you give for me? Only a measly $250!"

That was our good luck, Aru. Now, I love you much more than Blue, and I am sure that you are going to outlive him."

"You bet I will. If I'm not stolen by a Bird-House burglar, like that one who stole my friend Oro, I'll be here when that old Blue stuck-up one turns up his toes, and goes stuffed into a glass case in the museum."

"I'll be much obliged to you if you will," said I.

"All right. Here goes for the world's record for longevity."

THE AMAZING PLATYPUS THAT CAME TO US

I HAVE held in my hands, all dripping and squirming, a real living Duckbilled Platypus; and I do not believe that more than four other living Americans can say that. That was America's first one, and the chances are that it will be long ere another one comes alive to New York. The cost is great, the obstacles are many and serious, and the risks are appalling.

And yet, in its Australian home-land, this strangest of all animals is not so frightfully rare. It thinly inhabits at least a dozen of the small rivers of Australia, and because the stock is so widely scattered it is not likely that the species will quickly be exterminated. You may look for it, if you have a license, in at least 21 different rivers of Australia, east, south and west, the names of which are duly recorded in Mr. Burrell's "Platypus" book.

It was just 125 years ago that the Platypus was put upon the zoological map of the world. And yet, in all this intervening time not one single living individual ever has gone away from Australia and landed on foreign soil,—until ours came to New York, in 1925. The well-nigh insurmountable barrier to Platypus travel is its abominable food and water habits, and the number and variety of good things that the perverse little beggar will *not* eat. No wonder that all collectors and dealers, save one, have shied at taking on a little glutton that can eat a third of its own weight every day, and demands nothing but angle worms, grubs and small shrimps, costing from $4 to $5 per day. If you assume a live Platypus liability, prepare yourself to dig angleworms for it until you are quite ready to collapse with fatigue. However, it is natural for a fourteen-hundred-dollar "duckbill" to expect high living.

I invite you to know that the Platypus is as large in the body as a woodchuck, its head terminates in a widely flattened beak of horn, its front feet are fully webbed for swimming, and each hind leg is armed with a formidable spur of horn, nearly an inch long. Beware of that spur, for it is poisonous. It has thick brown hair on its body, a broad tail that is haired on top,—*and*—*it*—*lays*—EGGS!

Just think of it! Here is a living "connecting link" between the birds and the mammals,—that ought to have become extinct a million years ago, and to have been buried under a mile of solid rock,—living today, in our midst, and carrying on in twenty or twenty-five Australian rivers just as if the Pliocene times never had passed away!

Really, it makes my head spin around to think of it.

At home this utterly unbelievable little beast demands for its home place a natural park with a rich meadow, with frontage on a nice, clean river of steady habits, in whose waters the Platypus can spend about one-half its time. Through the moist earth banks it digs a burrow, anything from 20 to 50 feet long, back into the hinterland. Finally, when the terminal facilities seem quite acceptable, the mother Platypus builds a

THE PLATYPUS.

Through the moist banks it digs a burrow, from twenty to fifty feet long,
to a good nesting-place in which to lay its two eggs.

comfortable round nest, of gum leaves and grass stems. Therein she lays her eggs, and in due time hatches them.

The length of the hatching period is not definitely known, but Mr. Burrell thinks it is about fourteen days.

After hatching out her young, in a round nest of leaves, at the extreme farther end of her burrow, the mother suckles her young after a mean and stingy fashion, by which the young one earns twice over the little milk that it gets.

The mother's milk is forcibly drawn through tiny holes in the skin of the breast; and could any nursing arrangement be more primitive than that! It is a tough infant that can be nourished and reared on milk procured by that very laborious process,—the worst on record!

The eggs of this amazing quadruped—which has no right to lay eggs at all,—of course stagger the imagination. They may be one, two, or three; but two is the usual number. Each egg is about three-quarters of an inch long, by two-thirds of an inch in diameter. When first laid in the nest, they are covered with a sticky coating like fish glue; and as they settle down side by side, *they stick together*, and remain so until they hatch. The shell is horny, and slightly flexible. During the hatching period, which is conducted by the female only, she folds her tail against her stomach, and within it holds the eggs, to obtain the warmth of her body.

A really big old he Platypus may be 20 inches long; but that size is quite unusual. The average adult male measures about 18 inches in total length, and females 17 inches.

THE AMAZING PLATYPUS

For years and years, people had said: "It is *impossible* to take a Platypus to Europe or America, and land it alive." That was because Mr. Harry Burrell, of Australia, had not yet made his determined and successful researches and experiments on the housing and food habits of the animal, and Mr. Ellis S. Joseph had not tackled the task of transportation. It was due to the genuine scientific spirit, and the indomitable perseverance of those two men that ways were found to house and feed a Platypus in captivity, and to transport it ten thousand miles alive. Mr. Burrell invented the amazing contraption in which our specimen traveled and lived, and Mr. Joseph did the rest. And now, Mr. Burrell's wonderful new book, "The Platypus," tells most perfectly and delightfully all that is known about that astounding animal. Its publishers are Angus & Robertson, of Sydney, Australia, its price is twenty-five shillings and sixpence, and I can do no less than to help the reader to this desirable information.

It was on July 14, 1922, that Mr. Joseph landed our Platypus at our door, alive and well. Its palace car was shrewdly designed to afford dry parking space, a dry burrow, and deep water in which to find refuge and exercise. There are not enough words in the English language by which to make my reader see in his mind's eye that amazing contraption, which was invented by Mr. Burrell.

Mr. Joseph unlocked the wire-netting cover, and threw it back. Rolling up his sleeve he reached down into the water, carefully took hold of something elusive, and gently lifted out a squirming, wriggling, reeking-wet, brown-haired creature that looked like no other animal under the sun.

"There she is!" cried the collector, triumphantly. "Take a living Platypus into your own hands!"

Gingerly and fearsomely I did so; but I was horribly afraid that I might break it!

"Oh, Platypus!" said I. "Welcome, distinguished stranger! We long have awaited you, and feared that you never would come. All New York is yours. But are you really a connecting link between the birds and the mammals of this topsy-turvy world?"

"Yes; I suppose I am. But that is not half so important just now as a pound of big white grubs."

"A whole pound?" I gasped. "For you? And for only one day?"

"Goodness, yes," said Platty, almost annoyed. "I can eat one-third of my weight every day, if I try."

"You shall be well fed. But tell me quickly, Platypus. How long can you endure to have a moving line of people violently looking at you,—provided they don't ask any foolish questions?"

"Just one hour a day, and no more. I'm nervous; and too much people make me sick."

"While you are here will you please lay just *one* little egg for us,—to prove to the proletariat that you *can* do it?"

"No, of course not. How trivial that would be! But tell me, man. Is this the country of the head-hunters?"

"Just what do you mean?" said I, rather puzzled.

"I mean the people who wish to have all Platypuses killed and skinned for the fur market."

"No, indeed! Americans don't do it. We can prove an alibi. Only a hardened thief would kill a Platypus for its contemptible little skin. And besides, our fur-hunters never had the chance."

"Well, then I will be glad to live here. But you must hustle to get me quarts of fat angle-worms, pounds of big white grubs that cost ten cents a piece, and many shrimps of tender age."

We pledged to make good; and then the welcoming ceremonies had to be abruptly terminated.

We installed the platypus contraption and its habitant in our best tortoise yard, and opened two narrow gates for just sixty minutes per day, and no more. We admitted a well-behaved single file of visitors to see the stranger, but all were solemnly forbidden to talk to her, or to offer to shake hands.

That arrangement suited our star-spangled Platypus quite well. For forty-nine days it did well by us. And we solemnly recommend that exhibition method for application to overworked Presidents of the United States when they really must be placed on display before gaping crowds of wild visitors fresh from the jungles of America.

Our Platypus was far more energetic and active than we had anticipated in a species so ancient. In its tank it swam round and round in lively fashion, paddling rapidly and independently with each outspread foot. The front feet are generously webbed. The naked and leathery membrane extends far beyond the ends of the claws, and on its outspread semicircular front outer margin it measures five and one-half inches!

To keep the restless little animal from acquiring momentum that would carry it violently against the wall of its tank, to the injury of its duck-like bill, Mr. Burrell erected in the centre of the tank a smooth, cylindrical, sheet-metal conning tower, with a flat top. Round and round in this circular moat the animal swam, while feeding or exercising, and when tired of the water it would scramble out and perch on the top of the metal tower, to view the landscape.

When tired of gormandizing and showing off, Platypus would scramble up the water tunnel to its imitation river bank, wriggle one by one through a series of big holes, scraping off some surplus water on a rubber gasket each time it went through a hole. Finally, on reaching its nesting place, in the ultimate corner, it would curl up in its bed of fine, dry hay and go to sleep.

MAY 9 2002